The Ben-Hur Murders

INSIDE THE 1925 'HOLLYWOOD GAMES'

A NOVEL

John W. Harding

Editor: Bob McLain
Layout: Artisanal Text

ISBN 978-1-68390-243-0
Printed in the United States of America

Pulp Hero Press | www.PulpHeroPress.com
Address queries to bob@pulpheropress.com

Contents

The Fugitive and the Cyclops Queen

People are always saying our lives are in the hands of fate, but how many of them can tell you the day they saw its knuckles?

For me that was one sunny Monday morning in the fall of 1925. It was an Indian summer's day, which even the Indians in Southern California back then probably looked on as nothing special. Ask some historian what big event occurred that bright October day and he will stare at you blankly. But to me it was the day everything changed, and it began with a fat set of dirty knuckles clamped around the iron bars of a small window up at the top of the old Los Angeles city jail.

There was no telling whose knuckles they were. His face was hidden in the shadows. But those fingers looked as thick as radiator pipes to me, and they fired my imagination. Maybe he had dug canals through a malaria-infested swamp, or driven longhorns across some tumbling mountain range. What great wrong had he done, I wondered, to be locked away so far from the course of history?

Whenever I stopped to wipe my brow and take a dipper of water I stole another look up. At some point even the old shovel jockey next to me stopped jabbering to himself and caught my eye, speaking just loud enough for me to hear.

"You see him, don't ya?"

All the men went out of their way not to be drawn into a conversation with this old coot. His name might have been Jimmy. Anyway, I always pitied him at his age, lowering himself into the earth a shovel at a time. I decided I'd answer.

"Sure I do."

"Why's he watching you?" returned Jimmy with a grunt, pulling up another bite of dirt.

"That's why they call it *jail time*," I said. "Goes a whole lot slower than free time."

Jimmy stopped and his two eyes fastened on me like compass needles. He must have been wondering if I really spoke or if he was just hearing a new set of voices. I stomped hard on the rear of my shovel, wishing I could take back my words.

"Sounds like you know something 'bout that," he said finally, then cackled privately.

"Look at me," I wanted to say. "Do I look like someone who knows anything about anything?" ... something short and rude to put an end to his chitchat. But I bit my tongue and kept on digging, cursing myself all the while for starting something that could not be unstarted.

Next day, those knuckles were nowhere to be seen. Then an hour before lunch I heard the field boss calling out, "Link! Grover Link!," and I knew it was over for me. I raised my shovel over my head like a flag of surrender.

This particular crew chief, I remember, favored a straw hat with a ragged brim. Aside from that, there was nothing setting him apart from all the other county bosses I had worked for. They would show up at the start of a new day looking more or less like the rest of us. But then at quitting time they still smelled sweet.

Straw Hat Man seemed friendlier than most and I could tell from his walk that he wasn't too happy about the job he was coming to do. "You from out in Missouri, Link?"

"Yes, sir."

" 'Round Everton?"

"That's right."

"Grover Link," he repeated. Under the cover of that brim I knew his shaded eyes were mapping out every rise and furrow of my face. "Had you some trouble back there in Everton?"

The entire world seemed to be eavesdropping on us now. It was like someone fired off a pistol and even the birds in the trees stopped chirping to see what would come falling out of the sky. I just held tight to my shovel. "Nothing much," I said back.

His lips puckered but he didn't say a thing as he reached into his shirt and pulled out a folded brown paper that looked like a government cable. "With the *law*."

Well, I had run my mouth enough, I figured. Anyone who didn't want to fruit-pick in the valley at a penny a sack and lucked into a good county job should have known better than to spout off about "jail time" and such to folks with relations and war-hero neighbors all desperate for work.

"This wire I got here from Everton ... says some judge put a warrant out for one Grover Link."

Field bosses didn't get paid to let things like that drop. He had the cards and he was turning them over one after the other.

"Nothing in your papers about a run-in with the law."

Another load of dirt went over the bank.

"You're a hard worker, Link. You been good on my crew. You square yourself with the judge, you come back and ask for me, hear?"

Now maybe Mr. Straw Hat Man knew a lawyer who took up charity cases, but I didn't feel it was the time or place to ask. There was exactly eighteen bucks in my wallet, with another week of board-inghouse rent coming due. Old Mrs. Addison was a sympathetic soul in every regard except when it came to her livelihood.

So that's how it began for me, and why I still recall that particular Monday, the day I spotted the knuckles. Tell me it wasn't the hands of fate that sent me slapping my soles back towards Silver Lake on that perfect blue-sky afternoon.

Mrs. Addison was more than a landlady, it turned out. She once worked in the movies, sewing costumes and such for the various studios around town. She told me about one that was looking to hire what were known as "extras," and she pointed me to an advertisement in one of her magazines.

"How much they pay?"

"Buck-fifty a day," she said, "plus lunch, of course. This one might pay more. It's got itself a huge budget. There's New York money behind this one. ... *Jewish* money," she added with a knowing wink.

"I can ride a horse," I said.

Her white-fringed head bobbed up and down. "Well, there ya go. Wranglers and cowboys get double the pay the extras do. Of course, they got their own stunt folks for that. But I'd mention it if I was you."

Tom Mix happened to be my favorite movie actor at the time. In fact, Tom Mix was the only one I cared to watch. But Mrs. Addison said he wouldn't be working in this one because he was under contract at Paramount, one of the biggest studios in town. The movie this ad was talking about was being made by a brand new company formed out of the old Metro Company and the Goldwyn Studio. They had taken on an independent producer named Louis B. Mayer and were now known as Metro-Goldwyn-Mayer.

Mrs. Addison could see my disappointment over Tom Mix. "But they got their own stars," she said, "some big ones too. Lon Chaney, Norma Shearer—oh, and Mr. Francis X. Bushman. He's got a part in this one. I used to think he was such a dream!" She heaved a sigh and her gray eyes went all girlie a moment before snapping to. "Hey, here's a deal for you. You can have my bicycle to get to that cattle call. But you got to take my autograph book along too. If you do run into Mr. Bushman or any of them stars, you got to have them put their names down in it. Is it a deal?"

I had been living in Los Angeles for most of a year but the movie business was the farthest thing from my mind. Even so, I knew something about this picture they were making, because it was based on a thick book my mother had read one long, snowy winter back home in Missouri.

It was called "Ben-Hur: A Tale of the Christ," and she said it was the finest book ever written, besides the Bible, of course. The author was an old Civil War general named Lew Wallace, who set off on a pilgrimage to the Holy Land once the war was over. He was looking to make amends for all the bloodshed, I think, so he dreamed up this story set back in the time of Jesus. It told about this young Jewish prince named Judah Ben-Hur who gets sold into slavery by the Romans. He and Jesus cross paths a couple of times as prisoners, and when he gets free again he finds his family is all gone. So he sets out to have revenge on the Roman officer who stole his life from him. Their big showdown comes at a chariot race in the ancient city of Antioch near Syria, where Rome had its second largest coliseum.

Mrs. Addison told me the rights to that book cost a bundle, which was why the studio was forced to take on some partners and reorganize. They started filming it in Italy, but labor strikes and storms slowed things considerably. Finally old Louis Mayer pulled the plug and ordered everyone back to the states to start over. That cost them another fortune. Now they were all set to shoot that chariot race again in Culver City, and that's why they ran an ad looking for as many extras as they could find.

"This race has got to be exciting," said Mrs. Addison. "It'll either make or break the whole picture. And if the picture doesn't make back what it cost, that fancy new studio will be sawed up for firewood and all the big chiefs will be back on their reservations, making gloves and peddling scrap metal."

At the bottom of the ad was a quotation from some columnist saying that "Ben-Hur" was going to be "the picture every Christian had to see." I asked Mrs. Addison why a bunch of Jewish businessmen would risk everything on telling a Christian story?

Mrs. Addison lapsed into some serious cigarette hacking before smiling and fixing me in her watery gaze. "Why, that's easy," she said. "A Jew wins the race!"

The way I saw it, I had nothing to lose. Making movies had to be a lot easier than digging ditches. If it staked me to a few more meals, at least my ribs wouldn't be showing through when I was left to live on the streets. Without watching what I was doing I traipsed after Mrs. Addison as she returned to her kitchen.

As she grabbed a ragged oven mitt from the stove I told her I'd take her up on that loan of a bike.

"And the autograph book," she stressed.

"Yeah, okay."

Then she turned around and shook her mitt at me like some tribal shaman warding off evil spirits. "You jes' watch your fanny out there, Mr. Link," she said with an arch to her brow. "Them folks have smelled failure, and failure smells a whole lot worse to the rich than it does to you and me. This picture has been cursed from the start. So keep your eyes wide and watch your step, hear me?"

That morning before dawn as I went pedaling off towards the flatlands and the walled iron gates of Metro-Goldwyn-Mayer I didn't know the difference between the costliest production in the history of silent film and some back lot two-reeler starring Ben Turpin or Charley Chase. Hollywood film people held no special magic for me. I didn't daydream about hobnobbing with stars or think of running off with some sexy screen vamp. The thought of sitting down for a chat with a fancy-suited businessman like Irving Thalberg would have made me scream with laughter.

But all of that would happen to me that day and something more I didn't count on. I would witness Hollywood's first industry scandal and get myself mixed up in murder. Over the years, it's that last thing that has bothered me most because of the part I played in covering it up.

There has been lots of whispering and lies about what happened on that day in Culver City, that October the 17th of 1925. Some say dozens of horses were injured in the race and had to be destroyed. That's not exactly true. Others claim they heard of stunt drivers being crippled or killed in accidents on the track. Well, I'm here to say there were deaths, all right, though not all of them were accidents.

It's time for me to set the record straight before I shuffle off with all the rest.

While I'm separating truth from hearsay let me add this right up front. It's a thing I never breathed to a living soul before now. Concerning the winner of the "Ben-Hur" chariot race: With due respect to Mrs. Addison, it wasn't a Jew at all. It was me, yours truly, Grover Link.

***

What was the hallmark of a successful marriage? The Cyclops Queen rolled her good eye and wondered. Was it all-consuming love—the burning ardor of the romance novelist? Or was it mutual dependency—a vulnerable but determined vine that scratched its way up from the sod and risked everything for its moment in the sun?

Perhaps it was some of both. There was no telling what to look for beforehand. It was all quite unsettled and unknowable.

Yet here was her heart racing with hope at the arrival of another engraved envelope, stiffened with a bit of cardboard and tissue paper. It would be another breathless announcement of a union between the daughter of Mr. and Mrs. So and So J. Somebody to the son of Mr. and Mrs. B. L. Whatsit of the Far Schenectady Whatsits.

But this time it was no wedding invitation. No, there wasn't any tissue paper, and the return envelope was crude, with an address printed directly on it in some ordinary business font. It was addressed to a building at the studio! It was *from him*. And looking again below the canceled stamp, it was addressed to her ... in typewriting! Her name and postal information had been typed there by some office secretary. No doubt she had been working off a list of hundreds of other names and addresses.

So, that was all she was to him, just another entry—one of the many colleagues and business leaders included on an approved roster of invitees.

She could almost hear him instructing his assistant: "Make it in gold—you know, with the fancy type? Calligraphy!" That's what he would have told her, but he would have given her no directions about the proper paper to use or the printing of the labels. The poor secretary wouldn't have the moxie to go back and question his orders. So there she would sit behind her stacks of plain white cards embossed in gold, and she would begin to type directly on the envelopes from the names on her list. The envelopes would all go out on time to the untold hundreds, making who-knows-what sort of initial impressions? Couldn't he see that? Did he not care?

Well, of course. That latter part—that *was* the question, wasn't it?

It was all so predictably male. And she had just begun to let herself dream she might be more to him than that.

She slapped old Dr. Bates' eye charts back in their box and put his sheet of patented eye-muscle exercises on top before closing the lid. That would have to do for today. She couldn't concentrate any longer.

She had another look at the engraved words on the card she knew could have only been dictated by *him.*

It was a company event. It was a filming! Oh, the beastly man! How disappointing. *On a Saturday morning?* As if she didn't get enough of it during the week! There was a scrawled note on the back: "You must come, Norma, it will be like a party!" it said. *A party!* Out in a muddy field, miles from the studio, with the crews working and moving lights around and stringing cables and—the *press!* The horrid press! They were sure to get their invitations as well.

A spout of temper shot to her fingertips. Taking the card in both hands she ripped it in two.

That's what one did with such things—with such slights—one placed them in the bin where they belonged and went on with one's life. There were scripts to be read, parts to learn. ... *But wait.*

What if he noticed she wasn't there? What if he went roaming around asking "Where's Norma? Did she come with you? ... She's *not?* ... Oh, no, not that, exactly. I just hoped she'd take a bit more interest. It's her studio now, after all. And this is only the biggest damned thing we ever ordered up."

That's how he would probably put it, too. *Ordered up.* Was she just another of the things he had ordered up?

More likely, he would hardly notice her absence at all. There would be so many other people hanging around, trying to get in a word with him here and there, wanting to introduce a friend or some relative or a dear friend of some relative. If no one else, there would be *that other woman*. She was almost certain to come. Perhaps she had gotten her own special invitation. Maybe even in person.

And here *she* was, just one small entry on an impersonal list of invitees. Like she was another L.A. councilman or corporate attorney or Indian chief, for Lord's sake.

It was all abundantly clear now, thank you. She had been fooling herself to think the social dates and business lunches ever meant something more.

So she used her will power to force the matter from her mind again and went to find her script. It was a good part, and after it there would be other good parts, if fortune was kind. And it would be years before she would be out grazing with the other well-groomed cows, batting at pesky flies with fans instead of tails—still, *cows* all the same.

How could she leave it all up for fate to decide, anyway?

As the days passed, her thoughts returned to that card, to that impostor and fraud of a personal invitation. She heard from this or that actor that so-and-so was planning to attend. And then Ramón called to plead with her to come because it was going to be such an important day for him. She always enjoyed Ramón, even at the start, but he would be far too busy to notice if she was there or not. Maybe it would be the same story with her *IT boy*, Irving Thalberg, the single most eligible bachelor in all the kingdom.

So more time went by and then, only days before the big shoot, she phoned the studio and told them she had misplaced her invitation and would they see that her name was added to the list of Mr. Thalberg's special guests?

She didn't think to ask the person's name. That showed how little she really cared about the matter. But she did thank the person on that other end, ever so warmly and politely. Just like a true star.

PART ONE

CHAPTER ONE

Molly from Raleigh

On a quiet Saturday morning before dawn, when a Pacific fog has rolled into the basin and there's an eerie orange smear seeping up through the gauze, Los Angeles can look like the victim of a car wreck, all neatly bandaged and awaiting the ambulance.

That should have been warning enough for any young man such as myself. But I never did put faith in omens, and I was tired of running.

So I sat on the open-sided tram as it turned its headlights toward the center of that orange smear. We rattled down from the foothills until the road grew flat and ran out of asphalt. Tall weeds whipped past the tires and an oasis of parked trucks popped up in a field, part of the land staked off for a city just eight years before by developer Harry H. Culver.

The answer to the mystery of the orange smear was something of a letdown. It was only a glow from the studio bonfires lit to keep the briny night air from gumming up the camera gears. We circled for a place to park and I could see the naked limbs of men and women gathered by the flames, tugging off work trousers and unbuttoning blouses to put on togas and robes packed in parcels tied with string.

Some fellow passengers hopped down from the runners before we rolled to a stop and I watched as they vanished in the black canyons between equipment trucks. Our headlamps blinked off as the engine gave its final spits and then darkness settled close with the heady stench of seaweed and tar.

There was just the faintest hint of sweet paddock hay on the breeze. I figured I would go find the horses and look for my team. But out of the night came a milky blur of boney elbows and bare legs wrapped with a ribbon. It was skinny little Molly from Raleigh, dashing at me with her bed sheets flying.

"Hey, good lookin'!" she called out, as happy as if she had just been made queen of the ball. I looked closer to be sure it was really her under all that mascara and face powder. She was talking a mile-a-minute, saying how she had been keeping an eye out for me and how she was sure that I would be on one of the studio buses. She only paused long enough then to make a small circle with her head. "D'ya ever see the like in your life?"

Behind her was the dark outline of a grand old fort. High on its walls swayed saw-toothed fronds that appeared downright lively compared to two stone-still eagles perched over an archway. My interest in ruins at the moment was limited as my eyes kept jumping back to the half-naked sprite before me.

Molly was nothing more than a stranger herself, of course. We only met that once at the cattle call, and she hadn't made too strong an impression. She was pretty in her own way, but standing next to the other girls in line she appeared underfed and scrawny. She noticed me right off, I guess, and her interest perked up more when one of the studio men pulled me aside to ask me questions. He called to an assistant with a clipboard and said to put me on a team.

Molly told me about herself after that, how she had come from North Carolina to stay with her brother and his family and was hoping to make a name for herself in the movies. "My only stroke of luck so far was getting to play an Indian girl dancing at a campfire for *Mr. Lionel Barrymore,*" she said, emphasizing the last part like it was of particular importance.

Her rapid way of talking didn't sit well with her Southern drawl. When I asked what part of North Carolina she was from she said Raleigh, so I told her from then on she would be known as Molly from Raleigh. Her black eyes crinkled and she broke into a grin like someone's gawky sister at her first school social.

She was meant to be an Egyptian slave girl, she said, but it must have been a heap warmer back in Egyptian days because her outfit didn't help at all to keep her shivers in check. There was a thin copper snake coiled around her left arm, its snout buried in the black swirls of hair. Up below her shoulder hole was a darkened patch that I imagined was a smudge from her messy mascara.

What Molly lacked in chest size was more than made up for by two rock-hard nipples apparently raring to get out. Somehow she was no one's kid sister anymore. Maybe she read the look in my eyes because she reached out playfully all at once as if to yell "Tag!" and blurted out instead, "Come on!"

She turned and made a beeline for the columns of that old fort entrance, grabbing a horse blanket off the side of a trailer as she ran. It came flying back at me over her head and I caught it as we went ducking under a rope and continued on in a crouch. Our footsteps slowed as they became a crunching in the sand and we found ourselves standing on a deserted racetrack staring off into eternity.

"This is where it happens," whispered Molly in awe. "Antioch."

I opened my mouth to answer but she placed a finger on my lips. The walls around us rose a story or so above our heads, and all I could see were benches and steps leading up to cordoned-off sections of canopies and gold-fringed rugs.

Molly gave me a naughty smile and took off again, this time heading for a long central island made of marble and stone. Huge urns and potted trees sat on staged plateaus next to wading pools and banners on poles. The Italians called this midway island a *spina*, Molly said. Then she reached for my hand and pulled me toward an open passage in the side. I felt like Adam following Eve into the Garden of Eden. But inside the air was calm and smelled of cut wood and wet dirt, like a pine box funeral right after a rain.

There was no doubt we had the place to ourselves, and it didn't take a second to spread out the blanket and start to get cozy. I felt around for Molly and slid closer to give her a squeeze. "Man, oh, man," I said without thinking, "how'd you get so skinny?"

"Oh, that's because I like to sleep in, most of the time," she said. "Mama always said I didn't want to get born at all, and I wouldn't come out when the doctor was ready. She said everyone was getting hungry because a whole day went by without anyone cooking and they couldn't tell for the life of them why I wanted to put up such a fuss. Everyone always said I'd rather sleep than eat, and I guess they were right. You think I'm too skinny to be in pictures?"

"Too dark in here to tell."

"Hold on," she said. I heard her scratching around for something, then it got quiet again and she must have had a box of matches stashed on her somewhere because there was a spark and a wooden shaft crackled and burst into fire.

Behold! There she sat. It was Mount Molly, looming before me like a passing glacier. One arm held the folds of her slave dress at her belly, and her thin shoulders and small breasts stood undraped and defenseless in the flickering flame. The vision stole my breath away,

I must admit, and just before she shook out the match I glimpsed that dark circle on her arm again and a matching one at her neckline.

We sat a moment in darkness and did not talk.

"This photographer fella," she said at last, "he wanted me to pose for him. Undressed, you know. I half thought I should. Here in Hollywood, a girl has to do something to get herself noticed, don't you think? I told him—this photographer—that I had my mind set on being in the movies. You know what he told me?"

"No, ma'am."

"He said all the young actresses get their start these days doing figure modeling. You believe that's so?"

"I don't know. I never saw any pictures—quite like that."

"You think I have a nice body?"

"Yes, I do."

She seemed to take comfort in that and I moved in close for a kiss. Say what you will about skinny girls, but I used to find they were the world's best kissers. Chubby girls tend to take the wheel, if you get my drift. But with skinny girls it's more like saddling up a stallion and making sure to hold on. Molly's body felt about as weightless as a sack of goose feathers. Even with calluses on both my hands from months of shoveling I could feel her skin and how smooth it was. She arched her back to return my kiss and hooked a bare foot over my boot so I couldn't get away.

"You're a sweet boy, aren't you," she purred and I nibbled her ear and began to unbuckle my belt. Then I whispered a bit more, and said something about being bad, and she whispered something back that I couldn't be sure of but sounded like she was saying "Mr. Eason."

"Huh?"

"I said I'd be truly grateful if you'd introduce us, that's all."

"To who now?"

"Why, Mr. Eason."

"Who?"

"Reeves Eason. ... You know—*Breezy*."

I decided to ignore her and pulled her toward me harder.

"Well, don't that beat—" She broke off and pushed me away. "B. Reeves Eason, the second unit A.D. on this picture? ... The assistant director?"

She wasn't likely to let me get back to business until I answered her. "I don't know him."

"You *talked* to him. I watched him pull you out and take you to the casting director."

A small light dawned. That odd little fellow at the cattle call. I thought he might have Indian blood because his cowboy hat was extra large for his head. I could still see his pitch-black hair and skin the color of wet sand at low tide. If anyone had told me his name, though, I sure didn't recall hearing it.

"He knew you all right," Molly was saying. "That's how come they put you with a team."

"You think so?"

"Don't you deny it. Things like that do not happen in this town. Not without pull."

I could hear her scooting away to the edge of the blanket. "I don't believe it," she muttered to herself.

"What's wrong?"

"You honestly mean you didn't know him? He just picked you out of the crowd and put you on a team with a bunch of regulars because he liked your looks or something?"

"I guess so. Maybe because ... because I been outdoors a lot?" That could have been it. After working so long in the sun without a shirt my skin was nearly as dark as his.

I reached toward the sound of Molly's breathing but she yanked away again.

"Don't you try it. Who said you could make love to me, anyway?"

"Well, for cryin' out—. Why'd you bring me here?"

"Does that mean a person is inviting someone to take liberties with her body? What makes men think that way? I swear, if my brother was here you'd sure mind your manners."

She fell silent, and for a while I just sat and listened to her breathe.

"When I think of all these girls—young ones, too—run off and leave their mamas with nowhere to turn, bawling their eyes out 'cause they find out that all men want is a good time!" It was like she was spooked now and her thoughts were ready to stampede. "You can't just party forever. Mornings come, and then who is left to care if you can act? Who was there for poor Virginia Rappe? ... I refuse to end up like her, with all those nasty newspapers printing their lies and not a soul around to say a friendly word at the funeral!"

The newspapers had been full of stories for a time about this actress named Virginia Rappe who had died at a party in Frisco with Fatty Arbuckle. I thought maybe that was what she was talking about, but I still wasn't sure. I felt on the blanket for her box of matches and fished one out and scratched the end across the rough spot.

Molly sat hunched over, looking like she had been attacked. Her eyelashes were wet and sharp, bristling with anger.

"What is it, Miss Molly? Molly from Raleigh? What'd I do, honey?"

"What do you even know about me? You ever bother to ask? How old you think I am?"

"Don't know."

"Seventeen."

"No, you aren't. ... *Seventeen?*"

"Come March. You know how ancient that is in this business? Mary Pickford started in movies at sixteen. Norma Talmadge was barely in her teens at all. Miss Lillian was fifteen, and sister Dorothy—she was just thirteen years old!"

The match burned to my fingertip and I gave out a yelp and everything went dark again. Through it all Molly from Raleigh went on and on about how she wasn't going to give in and wind up like "poor Ginny," and how this wasn't just another job to her. Today was going to be her break. It was the biggest thing to ever happen in this town, and she was going to make the most of it. Mr. Louis B. Mayer might be up there in the stands, and the same with Mr. Irving Thalberg and everyone else in Hollywood with the power to lift a girl out of obscurity and change her life into something elegant and important.

She was going to make all those bright young producers and casting directors sit up and pay attention. No one was going to stop her from doing that.

Well, I got the point. Molly sure wasn't going to get down to any serious lovemaking now. For a second I thought how easy it would be just to grab her and squeeze and kiss her until she begged for me not to stop.

I heard horses off in the stables growing restless. It was dawn now and the tenders were coming to get them up and fed. For me it was too late to start anything. Time to get going.

A wedge of light filtered in through the entryway and I could make out shapes in the darkness for the first time. Frames of timber were propping up crossbeams, and here and there was a tarp slung across a stack of paint cans. Sawhorses and wood chips were scattered around, and off to one side sat a pile of buckets spattered with plaster.

Why was all this construction junk stored off inside a marble spina? And quick as lightning it hit me: This wasn't an ancient ruin. I wasn't inside some old stone museum attraction. I had been the world's biggest sap. It was Hollywood, after all! Everything was phony. Molly and me were just sitting on a blanket surrounded by wooden girders and beams covered in nothing more than canvas and plaster.

Molly rustled when she heard me snort, and she must have looked at me like I was going crazy. I roared and roared over my own damn denseness.

"What in thunder is so darn humorous?" she asked.

Before I could answer we heard a male voice call out "Molly!" Through the entryway I glimpsed a man coming across the track. He wore dark pants and a work jacket, and there was just a bit of a limp to his stride.

"Holy hell!" breathed Molly. "You better run."

"Who is it? Your brother?"

"He'll kill ya. I'm not joking!"

That was enough for me. I could handle myself in a fight but I'd seen enough of these studio roustabouts to know they weren't anyone you wanted to tangle with. Some wore holsters and side arms, or packed ugly hunting blades in leather carved from the carcasses of God-knows-what animals. By their number of missing fingers and teeth, you could tell they had been wandering in the wilderness for most of their lives, prospecting for a future that turned out to be nothing but sore backs and bad dreams. Hollywood was no golden gate to fame or fortune to any of them. It was sure no jumping-off point to something grand and elegant. This was the final stop for most—and it might be for me, too, if they caught me looking at them with the pity of it.

I was already up on my feet and cinching my buckle. "Your bro— brother. He the over-protective type, is that it?"

Molly shook her head but she was no longer the wronged lover. She was that naughty little girl again. "He's my husband," she said.

"Your hus—"

And with that I was off, loping like a crazy fool over buckets and boards towards a gap in the far wall. I saw Molly blow me a sad little kiss and I turned back just in time to dodge a header. It was a close call, because whether it was some chiseled Roman stone or just a piece of studio handiwork it would have cracked open this farm boy's thick skull and left him a souvenir he never bargained for.

I remembered the dark circles on Molly's neck and arm and I couldn't blame her for looking for a way out. Then just as I reached the exit a body stepped in my way and up went his hands as if to tackle me. All I saw was butter-colored hair and a plaid kerchief, and then I fired off a quick left jab and followed it with a full right swing to his cheek that caught him by surprise and sent him spiraling to the ground.

I was halfway across the track then and still felt like I was being followed. I dared a quick glance back, then stopped and swung around with both fists raised. But the track was empty, and when I raised my eyes to the sky a spear of cold terror shot through me.

A bearded giant peered down through the fog, its neck bulging with muscles like a real-life Atlas. But no globe was held on its shoulders, and it was too still to be alive. It was just another piece of Hollywood hooey, a make-believe colossus fashioned of concrete and plaster to decorate the track. There was no danger. It was just my own sense of guilt shadowing me.

How did I let myself get so carried away over poor Molly from Raleigh? How did I come so close to overpowering her, pressing my advantage over that helpless, moonstruck child?

It was not how I was brought up. Where I came from a woman was someone's wife or neighbor's daughter and you gave her all the respect you wanted for your own womenfolk. Out here on the edge of the country it was too easy to forget that. Things appeared different. Everyone you met in Los Angeles seemed to be just passing through. People stayed strangers, doing what they needed to do to gain some measure of advantage. There weren't many ought-to's about it—no great moral prohibitions, no preachers' codes of conduct.

In Hollywood, there were the Virginia Rappes and there were the Fatty Arbuckles. But mostly, no one gave a fig what you were up to if you could promise to get them in the movies.

CHAPTER TWO

The Organizer

Outside the arena waited stragglers from a routed army. The misty field resembled a charcoal rendering of Napoleon's retreat from Moscow or a view of the smoky aftermath at the Somme. Bodies sprawled in the dirt and propped themselves next to the burned-out frames of trucks. Around the smoke pots and campfires the lost survivors stared into tin cups as others wandered past working out the stiffness of a leg or stopping to tamp their first pipe of the day.

Lines were forming outside the new makeshift outhouses, each with its own plaque bearing the letters M-G-M nailed above the door. It was a welcome sight to me since I had been searching for a toilet ever since climbing down off Mrs. Addison's bicycle back at the studio.

The closest latrine had no waiting line at all but I could hear pounding from the inside. A waist-high length of two-by-four had wedged itself under the latch, and those close enough to hear seemed quite indifferent to the commotion.

I had only lifted up the board an inch before the outhouse sprung open like a jack-in-the-box. Out popped a wavy-haired man looking about as angry as a mud wasp for someone to sting. He quickly checked both sides of the outhouse before coming back to me.

"You see where they run to?" he asked.

"No, sir. I didn't see no one at all," I answered.

The man was dressed in brown trousers and the type of waist-length flying jacket favored by ace barnstormers at county fairs. He held tight to a clutch of papers, though it did not attract my notice at the time.

His anger was quick to disappear and out came a full sparkler of a smile just for me. "Thank you for the kindness, friend," he said. "You new to the business? Looking to pick up a little spare chink, is that it?"

I told him I had been hired to wrangle horses for one of the teams.

The stranger pursed his lips at that and gave me a quick once-over. "That so? Whose team would that be?"

"Fellow with a sort of funny name. Scranton. … Scranton Ardale."

"Buddy?" His smile expanded even farther. "Buddy's back? Well, damn! There goes the darn race."

"You know him?"

"Oh, yeah. It figures Buddy'd be here. Best damn teamster in Hollywood. We worked on—what the hell was it? 'Covered Wagon,' for one. Some piece of DeMille idiocy, for another. Can't remember what it was now. I always said he was too big a man to be bested by a bottle. *Shit!* Forget I said that. Come on, I'll help you find him."

My bladder was strong and it wasn't such a pressing concern at present. So I nodded, figuring it could wait until I found where I was going. Looking back, that might have been my worst decision all day. Funny how a man's life—hell, all of history—can pivot on such a small matter as where and when to pee.

"Will you have a look at that," said my wavy-haired friend. A small group was hunkered down behind a parked flatbed, waving fistfuls of money around and shouting to no one in particular. We stopped to watch as a man near the center pitched forward with a yell and then froze as the dice smacked against a wheel and tumbled in the dirt. There were groans and excited squeals as the cubes were handed along to the next man.

"Never too early for some," said my companion as we continued on. "Some folks just can't wait to throw their money away."

"Well, one of them might get lucky."

"Think so? Can't agree there. The only luck anyone has a right to expect is the sort we make for ourselves. I'm a union man, all the way." He looked at me and set off another Fourth of July sparkler as he stuck out his hand. "Name's Freddie Moore. Friends call me 'Moore the Merrier.' I always prefer looking on the sunny side, you know? What's yours?"

"Grover."

"Ah, Grover Cleveland, eh? Like the former president. Hey, I won't hold it against you. Yes sir, we all have a lot of respect for your man Buddy. Ex-cavalryman, you know. Fought there at San Juan."

"Really?"

"That's what I heard. Part of the Rough Riders. Teddy Roosevelt and all. You should ask him about it."

Freddie Moore didn't seem more than a year or two older than me, and our Great War had ended almost seven years before. So I figured he was too young to have done much serious flying overseas. In any case, his leather jacket was good as new. "You a flyer?" I asked.

He looked puzzled and raised up the sheaf of handbills under his arm. "You mean these? … Oh, I get you. You mean my jacket. I did my duty like everyone's supposed to. I took lessons, just never got the chance. They had that war sowed up before I could get there. So now I do some stunt flying and other stuff for the movies. A little of this, a little of that. Whatever's needed. … Here's Buddy."

Up ahead a tall, lanky man stood over a small campfire. He probably wasn't more than forty or thereabout, but he sure seemed older at the time. His skin had the orange-brown color of deer moccasins, and as he leaned back to swallow from a burnt tin cup he swayed a bit to the left, as if a critical muscle had been pulled once too often and wouldn't trust him with another chance.

I knew hired hands like him on ranches back east. Usually when they signed on you could count on them to getting the job done. But after a time, when they got closer to Buddy's age, they grew less mindful of the "whosits and whatsits," as my dad would have said. One morning we would wake up and they'd be gone, never to be heard from again.

A studio hand in paint-spattered overalls passed by as we came walking up. He had a bucket in each hand and gave Buddy a friendly nod. "Hey, Buddy! You livin' the good life?" he called, to which Buddy answered back without a pause, "Can't afford the good life."

"Buddy, my friend" said Moore the Merrier. "It's wonderful to see you back. You're looking fit and well. How's your missus?"

"Good. She's been good."

"Fine, fine. Good to hear. Buddy, I just wanted to make sure your new man got to you all right."

Buddy's eyes narrowed as he took my measure. "You're Grover?"

"That's right."

"Whereabouts you from, exactly?"

"Missouri. Near Everton."

"So, they have horses up there in Everton?"

"I learned one end from the other."

"That'll be useful at feeding time."

"Buddy," said Moore, "I hope you and your men can make it out to the meeting this Monday."

"What meeting's that?"

Moore licked his thumb and slipped the top paper off his stack, reaching out to put it in Buddy's hand. "We figure we got a golden opportunity here. They got this picture booked for Christmas and there's major work yet to do. Think of it. Less than two months to finish the shooting, editing, scoring—the whole bees' wax. Timing just couldn't be better."

"Better for what?

"We got the studio over a barrel and it knows it. Now's the time to present our demands."

"What demands, exactly?"

Freddie Moore looked flustered. "Well, that's what the meeting's for. The men respect you, Buddy. It'd mean a lot to them to see your support."

Buddy was studying the handbill. "You got some more of these?"

"Sure," grinned Moore, and began to gather more sheets.

"Let me have 'em all."

This time Moore hesitated before handing him the stack. Buddy took it and turned to drop them in the fire.

"No!" cried out Moore. The flames licked up around the browning edges. "Those things cost money, you know," he muttered.

"Mr. Moore, you got a wife?"

"Yes. I do. Why?"

"I just felt sorry all at once that some poor father might have ended up with such an asshole for a son-in-law."

"Now, Buddy, there's no call for—"

"Get this straight, Mr. Moore. I don't know what world you go to bed in each night, but in my world we need this studio a good sight more than it needs us."

"You saying you don't favor an equitable wage, safe conditions, covered doctor care?"

"If I felt like living on a federal reservation I'd become an *Injun.*"

"But if we all stick together, we can—"

"Like in Italy? ... Or maybe *Russia?* Is that what you and your people are angling for?"

"You could at least think a little about—"

"Go back to your meeting hall, Mr. Moore. Tell your people this ain't Italy. If any of them tries to shut this picture down I'll personally kick their fucking teeth in. Now go stick your nose in someone else's business, and stay the hell away from my team!"

Moore held up both palms to signal a truce and was instantly backing away. Just before turning to leave he gave me a small apologetic smile.

Buddy might have felt bad about losing his temper but he didn't say another word. As much as I was dying to hear about what happened in Italy, I figured it sure as hell wasn't the right time to ask now.

Thankfully, a booming voice quickly followed to shatter the awkward silence. "Who let him out?" it said. Up strolled a short, beefy-looking redhead carrying a packed cowhide saddlebag.

Buddy grinned at him. "You're up bright and early," he said.

"It's early all right, but I ain't no brighter'n when I turned in." He had on a buckskin vest and shotgun chaps with leather laces crisscrossed at the crotch. It was a movie-cowboy costume as far as I could tell, but it seemed to suit him. "So, what'd our pal Freddie want?" he said.

"The usual."

"Figures. Any java left?"

"Too late," said Buddy, turning his tin cup upside down."

The redhead nodded and dropped his saddlebags on a small rise, then eased himself down beside it.

"Don't get too comfortable. As soon as Squeaks is here we'll grab some grub."

"Sounds fine," he said, looking at me for the first time.

"Say hello to the new man," said Buddy. "Name's Grover, out of Missouri. Breezy picked him."

"Oh?"

"This here's Rusty Bigelow. You two'll be working together."

The man looked to be in his middle thirties, with a round face and a freckled complexion the color of corroded iron. He had a squat nose and when I offered him my hand he ignored it and just kept staring at me from under his white bushy eyebrows.

"You're friends with Breezy?" he said at last. His voice suited him. It was dry and raspy like a rusty hinge.

"No. I didn't know him till the day of the cattle call."

"How come he picked you?"

"Don't know."

"You ambitious?"

"I like to keep busy."

"Well, get it straight up front. You're a wrangler, a handler. You ain't no teamster. You don't even think about stepping up in a rig, understand? There's a set order to things around here. You put one foot inside a rig, you got a problem."

"You mean with the union people?"

"With *me*, pretty boy. ... Hey, Buddy, what do you think? You think Fisher would like to come meet our new pretty boy?"

"Let the boy be," said Buddy. "Hey, you hear about old Charlie Edelman?"

"I thought he died?"

"Oh. You did hear. Well, it was news to me."

"That was over a year ago," said Rusty.

"Still sort of sad."

Rusty had returned to staring at me again. He wasn't about to let up on me yet.

"So, Missouri is it?"

"That's right."

"*Farm boy*," he sneered, then scooped up a handful of dirt and let it slip out between his fingers. "What do you think of the soil here, farm boy?"

"Right here? In this field? ... Too much sand, too much sun. Not good for much but prairie mange and palm trees."

"And movies," interjected Buddy. "Don't forget the movies."

"Not much call for farm boys here," said Rusty. "Maybe we'll fix you up with one of our older movie fellows? Yeah, maybe Francis Bushman or one of those real old-timers with the red lips. I bet they'd be happy to take you under their wing."

"You driving one of the chariots?" I asked him.

"Me?" He snorted and reached down for his boot but unbuckled the left leg on the chaps and hoisted up his Levi's as far as they'd go. Below it his leg appeared pale and hairless, as smooth as porcelain. "Not anymore," he said. He gave it a hard rap with a knuckle and it made a hollow thud. "Buddy does all the driving these days."

"Airing our privates in public again, are we?" said a voice.

"Well, here he is," said Buddy. "What the hell happened to you?"

As happy as I was for the distraction, my sense of relief was short-lived. The newcomer was a young man with dusty blond hair, a swollen cheek and a split lip. He must have ditched the plaid kerchief to hide any sign of blood, but I had no doubt at all that it was the man I socked back at the spina.

"A bit of a disagreement," he replied in a lilting Irish brogue. "A wee debate it was we were having. I put forth my arguments, but how was I to know she had such a strong rebuttal?" He grinned and raised the back of his hand to his cheek.

"You should know to duck by now," said Buddy with a wag of his head.

"That I should."

"Grover, this here is Squeaks."

The Irishman reached out to pump my hand and appeared pleased to meet me.

"He's new here," Buddy said. "Maybe you can stick sort of close and show him what needs doin'."

"No bother, no bother at all," he said with another smile. "We'll have you tagged and primed in no time."

"You're called Squeaks?" I asked.

"There's a lesson for you. Never wear new boots to a meeting with cowboys."

"You're Irish?"

"Could you tell, then? My feet are planted in America now but my heart still beats for *Arland*."

I could tell almost instantly he would not be a threat. He must have known it was me who socked him, but his genuine warmth made me feel all the sorrier for it. Then I thought of the other man at the spina, the one coming with a limp to reclaim his wife.

It seemed quite likely all at once that he was the person I had just been introduced to, my hollow-legged bully of a teammate.

***

"Men, who am I but a fella with good news?" That was the way the young Irishman talked, in his own screwy way. "Today it is I stand before you to say our fortunes are assured."

"Are the books open?" asked Rusty, taking a sudden interest.

"They are."

"What odds do they offer?"

"Four-to-one, but I've heard as much as five."

"Whoa-hoo!" shouted the redhead. "I got to get a piece of that action."

Buddy's brow furrowed as he leaned in. "How they figurin' it, Squeaks?"

"From what I've been able to gather, they see the Ben-Hur outfit as even-money. He's the favorite."

"Fools," blurted Rusty. "Things don't always work out the way they do in fairytales."

"True enough," nodded Buddy.

"Still, the odds-men appear mighty impressed with those four matched whites."

"Then who, after that?" asked Rusty.

"It's Messala, naturally. Bushman's proven an old hand with a team. He did good in Rome, handling his rig. They figure that gives him the edge for second."

"Sentimental hogwash!" spat Rusty.

"Could be. But still two-to-one."

"Then it's Buddy, right?"

"Hunh-unh. They like the Greek. Another pro, not as experienced as Francis, but he had a good showing in training."

"He'll be tough to beat all right," said Buddy.

"And then us," said Squeaks with a knowing smirk. "That is—us and all them other fellas."

"What?"

"They don't know enough about Buddy, and not a thing about his sweet little ace in the hole. They lumped us all together at four or five."

"Ya-hoo!' cried out Rusty. "I'm counting my winnings already. Look, we should pool our money and have our bet placed before word gets out."

As they batted the idea back and forth a bit I stood there feeling confused. Moore the Merrier had said there was going to be a race but I thought he was talking about the movie race. It never crossed my mind that he could mean something else.

Finally Buddy broke off and wandered away to do some calculating of his own. Rusty struggled to get on his feet and came for me with his eyes ablaze with hunger. "How much you got on you?" he demanded.

"What? You mean money?"

He gave a disgusted scowl and waited.

"I don't know. Close to seventeen dollars."

"Well, give it here."

I must have looked as shocked as I felt. It was all the money I had in this world. "Buddy," I called out, "what's this about?"

He turned and came wandering back. "Aw, they're thinking there's goin' to be a race."

"That's right," snapped Rusty. "Just like Rome."

"But it was different there and you know it. No one is saying it will happen again."

"Stands to reason, though, don't it?" said Rusty. "There's more at stake now."

"That's what 'Moore the Idiot' was saying," said Buddy.

I couldn't hold back any longer. The subject of Italy was now fair game. "What happened there, Buddy?"

"Oh, we just getting started, runnin' some laps for the cameras. But those rigs wouldn't roll fast enough for some. So this A.D. pipes up. 'Let's try runnin' her for real, see what happens.' They put up a purse—a hundred bucks for the winning teamster and a night in a whorehouse for his crew. It got the attention of those dagos, all right. They started whipping the backs of their teams and driving like crazy men."

"Who won?"

"Those Italian nags didn't have no proper training. And the drivers couldn't handle them. You didn't have to hear the grunts to know the shit was coming."

"Did you see it, Buddy?" asked Squeaks.

"Nah. I was just focused on winning at the time. I just straightened out from a turn and I heard a loud crack and people started hollerin'. Someone must have cut in too close and his car bounced off the wall. He went careening off into the other teams. It was a mess."

Rusty had been listening closely. "I heard Bushman tell it. According to him, some of them Italians didn't walk away."

"Killed?" I asked.

Buddy tilted his head. "Let's just say no one got a night in the whorehouse."

"You think they'd ever try it here?" I asked.

"Sure they would," said Rusty.

"Maybe this time it'll be a whorehouse in Pasadena!" said the Irishman.

Buddy shook his head. "Breezy told me straight-out it wouldn't happen here. Not with all them executives watching."

"Look," said Rusty, "all I know is that chariot race is either going to make 'em or break 'em. Hell, they're human. They'll do whatever it takes to make it exciting."

Squeaks rubbed his palms together with glee. "Pasadena, here I come!"

Even Buddy broke into a smile at that. "Swear to God, Squeaks," he said, "if you didn't have a dick you'd have no sense of direction at all."

We all enjoyed a laugh and when it all grew quiet again, Rusty spoke with a far-off gaze in his eyes. "I got to say, I could sure use a chunk of a sizable purse. Could get myself a shotgun with a fancy stock and a leather case. Or one of them fancy field tents with a whatsacallit—a awning." He looked back at me and stuck out his palm. "Come on, Missouri. By dinner you'll get all your seventeen dollars back, multiplied five-fold!"

The idea of making a good return on my money took hold of me. Maybe it was meant to be. Maybe this was how I was going to climb up out of the hole I'd dug for myself and get back on track. With no more reasoning to it than that I pulled out my billfold and handed all the cash I had in the world to a man who would have just as soon killed me if he ever found out it was me that morning with Molly.

Rusty collected everyone's money and Buddy told him to meet us at the breakfast wagons after he got the bet placed. We were all feeling pretty confident as Buddy kicked some dirt over the smoldering remains of Freddie Moore's handbills.

"Let's go have some chow," said Buddy.

As we walked Squeaks asked Buddy if he had met the new A.D.

"Yeah. I met him."

"What'd you think?"

"Kind of full of hisself."

"Someone was tellin' me he might be an Englishman."

"Nah, he ain't English."

"Well, thanks for setting me mind at ease," said Squeaks, muttering something under his breath that sounded to my ears like, "I don't take *garters* from Englishmen."

A roll of white smoke hung over the next ridge, and the aroma of hot grease and coffee rolled on the breeze. I was so interested in food all at once that I didn't notice the sound of clanking metal and the pounding of hooves until they seemed close enough to trample me. I jumped aside just as a pair of dun-colored mares came to a sharp stop only a meter away. The two massive beasts reared up, straining against harnesses that bound them to the yoke of a gold-painted chariot.

An unseen driver wrapped his reins over the rig's railing and I heard a thud as he landed hard in the dirt. A thick-armed hulk of a man I had never seen before stomped out from behind the car coiling a whip in one metal-studded glove.

The chariot driver could hardly contain his rage as he stopped to glower at me. "You been whittlin' on the wrong stick, boy."

"Excuse me?"

"You been whitewashing the wrong neighbor's barn."

"Let me just say—"

"Shut yer damn mouth!"

"I can see you're upset. If this is about Mol—"

He wouldn't hear any more. "You thought you'd get away with it. I'm here to say it ain't so."

I didn't dare take my eyes off the angry driver, but I sensed Buddy taking a step forward.

"You stay back, Buddy," ordered the whip man. "This is between me and this cowardly little shit here." He gave me a contemptuous scan from head to toe. "You bring a gun?"

Now I knew it was over. I was a goner. I couldn't run, I dared not fight. Whatever was about to happen, I would have to be prepared for the consequences. "I'm unarmed," I told him.

"Rusty," he said out the side of his mouth. "Give him your gun."

Rusty had come out of nowhere and was slowly walking toward the madman. "Now you know you don't want to hurt no one," he said.

"I'm just goin' to whip the Bible-fearin' crap out of him, that's all." He straightened back his arm and the braided whip uncurled behind him with a hiss.

All the blood must have drained from my fingers because they were tingling now. I felt lightheaded and fought the urge to pee in my pants. All around us were men who had stopped where they were to watch what was happening.

"Look, just tell us what's this about?" I heard Rusty say. I braced myself for everyone's hearing the story of how I had lured a helpless young bride into some dark corner and took advantage of her. I might have thought of bolting out into the open field, but I had no real chance of escaping now.

"We don't abide heathens in these parts," the charioteer was saying. "This land was claimed by Christian folk, and by God we'll keep it free from your dirty Mormon kind!"

Mormon? My mind raced to understand. What did Molly say to him? Did she forget I told her I was from Missouri, or did she think that Missouri was where the Mormons settled? Was I about to have my flesh sliced to the bone because some silly flirt didn't know her geography?

"Leave the boy be," commanded Rusty with a tone of authority. I glanced away in time to see him push aside his vest and expose the wooden grip of a handgun.

The whip man pivoted slightly off in Rusty's direction. "You had better be prepared to make me," he said.

"I'm prepared."

"Okay, Russ, fellas," said Buddy. "That's enough, Fisher."

Fisher? That was the name of the man Rusty wanted me to meet. What was going on? None of this made sense. What did Fisher have against me?

I just stood there numbly, watching my accuser as his eyes wavered between Rusty and me. Seconds ticked by and suddenly the stranger raised his arm as if to bring his whip up whistling over his shoulder.

Rusty's right side cramped up and in a blink the gun was in his hand and with a kick it let go a flash of fire. A crack came from everywhere at once and Fisher's body spun back and sideways and collapsed face-down in the dirt. The horses reared back again with a frightened whinny, and the chariot rocked on its wheels.

Everything was stock-still for just one awful second before the crowd of onlookers broke into laughter and uttering and a light round of applause. Some started to turn and go on about their business as Rusty holstered his gun with a final look at the fallen body of the man named Fisher. Then even the dead man started to twitch with laughter and went to push himself up.

By now the two horses had worked themselves into a lather of sheer terror. They stamped and pulled at their straps until a man standing near them grabbed for the reins and missed. Suddenly the team broke free and lurched ahead at full speed. "Whoa!" yelled the man but it was too late. Fisher's grin changed at once into a look of horror. "Grab 'em!" he screamed.

I still couldn't fathom what had happened, though I sensed I'd been made the butt of some joke. All I knew for sure was that I was about to pee my pants right then and there, making my humiliation complete. I just wanted the earth to open wide and swallow me whole. And in that instant the empty chariot came bouncing by and I grabbed for the railing and swung myself up into its bucking lap for what I could only think was the last, sad flight of my short, wasted life.

As the men and the food wagons and the smell of bacon receded into memory, all I caught sight of was Rusty's dark gaze as it narrowed to a blood-red promise of vengeance.

CHAPTER THREE

Rugs and Hugs

So much for her steely determination. So much for her solemn vows to herself not to go even an inch out of her way to contact him. Let him find out from someone else that she was there. Let it sink into his distracted executive head that she was in no grand hurry to see him at all. Then watch as he came running to find her!

That was how she should play it. Male vanity was a woman's greatest ally, as Mother Edith often said. Men needed to know they had a woman's approval just as plants needed sunshine.

But here she had been waiting—what? five *minutes*? She was barely settled into her seat in the stands, and already she was on the move, racing up to his private box like someone's life depended on it.

What weaklings we women are! God has given us the tools, and yet most lack the good sense to use them.

Of course, it was not a healthy sign that he had sent no one down to greet her. There she sat, the awe-inspiring Cyclops Queen, deigning to make a public spectacle of herself, preparing to emerge from her polished ebony carriage and wave to the throngs at court.

Clutching the soft folds of a genuine reindeer morning coat between her imported Canadian fingers, she scooted the royal fanny across the tufted leather seat. The door had been rightly held by an attentive footman, but then ... Well, where were the crowds and the cheers? No red carpet? No trumpeters? And more to the point: Where was *he*? Where was her little Jewish prince with the sad, sad heart? Had he not been notified of her approach?

The only person there to greet her was another new assistant, the latest in a string of competent tryouts culled from a secretarial pool. The woman ushered her through all the gatekeepers and up to her section, then turned and left her to find her own seat. How could anyone be so uncaring? She plastered a pleasant smile on her face to satisfy the curious looks from the whisperers in the stands.

There they all sat. The retinue and their hangers-on. The latest ingénue discoveries with their managers. That horrid knife-thrower and his wife! All those cigar-butt gnawers from the casting office. Horrid! They would all be ambling over to her in time, once they were sure she was unoccupied. It had been a mistake coming alone. People would think she was wanted company, and that she could have no possible reason for wishing to avoid them.

How wrong they all were. These were the last people on Earth she wanted to be buttonholed by on her one free Saturday morning all month!

She had come too early. Why did she ever believe the times that were put on invitations? These shoots were the worst, especially the ones involving animals and stunt people and multiple camera crews. They were always logistical nightmares, delaying everything.

By all accounts, this would be the biggest shoot Hollywood had ever seen. And here she had come *early*. She deserved to be stuck in the stands with a lot of studio drones and no-talent cousins with names that no one was even expected to know.

There was Miss Nothing standing in the aisle just below her section. No, she had spotted her, and then she was waving, moving back to the steps and starting the sure climb toward her.

That made it complete! A stock, cardboard invitation … and then this visit from a paid minion. Mr. Bottom Line was too busy to come, but Miss Nothing could come in his place to help make her feel truly neglected.

So she bolted for the aisle and headed up—up toward the covered rows and the private stalls with canvas flaps made for those household faces and well-known names in need of the highest levels of privacy.

"May I see Mr. Thalberg?" she asked yet another new go-between, posted there to safeguard the recluses.

"Whom should I say is asking?"

"Tell him it's Norma. … *Miss Shearer*," she added, just to make sure the Boy Wonder didn't mistake her for the other Norma, sister of that *other woman*. It would be a brutal blow to her ego if he emerged to greet her and even the faintest flicker of disappointment crossed his brow.

But tragedy was avoided once more. "Norma," he said, forcing his way under the canvas flap. That boyishly unlined yet masculine face lit with a genuine happiness to see her. He stepped up to gather both of her slim hands in his own. "It's so wonderful that you came. This is going to be a day Hollywood will never forget."

He started her down the aisle to a spot at the front railing, away from the blasé assistants and the overworked secretaries and the assistants to the overworked secretaries with the especially big ears.

She admired his neat blue pinstripe suit with a tan tie and shoes to match. Not for him any of the ridiculous costumes of the studio bosses and the bejeweled robes of the wives who thought it all just another New Year's romp.

"Listen, Norma, I must ask your professional opinion on something."

"Only professional?" she wanted to reply, perhaps giving him a saucy blink in the bargain. But that would be far too forward of her. It would not be in character. He would probably fail to see it anyway. So she said merely, "Of course."

It was flattering, was it not, to be consulted on a professional matter by the vice-president in charge of production?

"This fog—?"

"Yes?"

"If it shows up on film, would it be a distraction?"

That was all that concerned him? That's what he wanted to ask her? He wasn't asking her advice on the choice of a costar, or on the ladies' fashions or the holes as big as Moby Dick in the script? In an instant, though, she had answered merely, "Surely there was fog in ancient Rome."

"But you see, we've already shot some footage. Some of the race is in the can. Crowds arriving, close-ups of horses and faces—you know, wheels and things. All of it quite sunny. It all has to match. You just can't start the race and then there's fog."

"No, no, I suppose not."

"I was thinking about bringing in some big fans—airplane motors with oversized propellers—powerful things—and just blowing it all out of the stadium. What do you think?"

"Would that work? I don't know. It seems to me that fog would just roll back in. And then again, big fans might whip up a sand storm. It could end up looking worse."

"Hmmm. Well, thank you."

"I'm sure it will burn off by ten or eleven."

He might have forgotten what they were talking about. He looked at her blankly. "How's that?"

"The fog. It will burn off. It always does."

"The trouble is, time is precious. Everything has to be shot today. I mean, where the race is concerned. … Well, it's not your problem."

Ah, an opening! "Nonsense. Whatever affects the studio is my problem as well. And naturally, that includes you. I do worry about you, Irving. You are the studio's single greatest asset."

The Boy Wonder may have blushed, but his skin was too tan to tell. "Thank you again for coming out, Norma. I appreciate it. I know Mr. Mayer does too. It's above and beyond."

"Did I help you … clear up your fog?"

"You did, you did. You're a godsend, Norma. Stop by the office Monday. Everything should be back to normal then. Good-bye."

With a parting peck on her cheek, he turned to duck his head back under the executive flap and was gone.

Dismissed until Monday? No second thoughts? Why couldn't he have said, *Oh, why don't you join me, watch everything from my private booth?* Maybe he was expecting … someone else. … Oh, Lord! Did he really just say she was a *godsend?* Could there be anything less sexual than that?

She took a glance around her. The fat department heads were trying to be discreet but they were watching her, stealing quick looks from under their bad hairpieces. They knew she had just been dismissed by the boss. They were probably weighing the benefits now of coming up to offer her their nuggets of advice. Odds are they were hoping to establish a new front for their own romantic attempts.

The wives were nearly as bad. They refused to be caught looking but they were just as aware of what had happened to her. They were probably biding their time for the right moment to come over and give her their warm though not overly affectionate "also-ran" hugs.

Holy Mother! How can I go through with this? Hugs and rugs—that was what Hollywood had come to. The men in power wore the rugs—badly stitched mats made from other people's hair, paid for with other people's money. Their rugs had just one role in life to play. Deception. And mostly, they did a damn poor job of it.

The hugs came from the wives and secret mistresses and the occasional fashion designer with her own endless gallery of assistants. Their hugs were just as insincere as the men's rugs. They also were intended to deceive and usually accomplished the opposite. At least a hug didn't cost anyone anything.

By the time Norma was halfway back to her seat, she had made up her mind. She would make her escape at the earliest opportunity. She would send a note to Dougie to tell him she was not feeling well and couldn't stand the noise and the dust. Then she would find a discrete exit and send word to her chauffeur where to find her. No one would miss her anyway, once the so-called action started.

And so descended the Cyclops Queen from her rightful place among the gods, banished to the lower levels of the merely mortal. She wanted to cry. She wanted an unstoppable trail of tears to flow from her one good eye so that no one would mistake her for just another serene, unflappable beauty, as that awful New York critic wrote of one of her performances.

She told herself, *Time to calm down now, Norma. Get a grip on it, girl, as the Americans were fond of saying.* Ramón might stop by to see her soon, and he always made her feel better about the uncertainty of things. She shouldn't allow herself to get carried away by these emotional tangents. She should try to save them for her plum screen roles.

Still, the farther she got away from Irving's box, the more she was filled with polarizing impulses. Sometimes she felt like she deserved it all—the twelve bedrooms, the waiting staff, the drivers, the fawning attention of the magazine writers. She had made over a dozen feature films, worked for a half-dozen directors, and gotten more good notices for the studio than anyone thought possible. But at other times she looked at men like Irving and Mr. Mayer, and at what they had built and were creating out of contracts and dreams and pure moxie, and she felt like a stand-in, someone there to wear the right clothes and makeup, and to take the place of the star while the lights were being strung.

Irving and Mr. Mayer were truly in the eye of the hurricane. She and all the others swirled around them with an endless cloud of questions, demanding to be told how many? of what color? from which period? Why? Where? Who? Irving and Mr. Mayer were the holders of the answers. They would be remembered when she and the rest of the askers and the takers were all gone. Those two men would be remembered and it was right that they should be. They were all that truly burned and sparkled in the dark cosmos of Hollywood.

She worked her way down through the milling extras in fake Mediterranean finery, past the stands of press agents in peacock feathers and borrowed tiaras, trading smiles with janitors pretending to be rajahs and blowing kisses to make-believe Hebrew princesses being impersonated by real-life Hebrew princesses.

Things had not really changed much in two thousand years, she thought with a tinge of amusement.

With a sigh of relief she settled back in her own section, looking to see which of her colleagues had come. Scrawny "stone-faced" Buster Keaton was down on the racetrack, showing off with a net and a prop spear for anyone too bored or feeble-minded to hold up one end of a conversation. A few rows farther up sat Douglas Fairbanks, alone again, as he usually was in public on days when Mary had fallen off the wagon. She always enjoyed Douglas's company but even he could be an oaf at times. She didn't blame Mary for her addiction. Being married to all that good cheer and teetotaling bravado might have driven her to drink as well.

At least Douglas wasn't a mama's boy. He didn't need women to tell him how to behave. To Norma, Hollywood was one big bird's nest of chirping mama's boys. They themselves knew it, and recognized it in one another. That's why they tended toward ostentation when given enough rope. She was convinced it was the private bond between Irving and Mr. Mayer.

Louis B. revered his mother, though perhaps what Irving felt for Henrietta was something closer to awe. His Henrietta was a force of nature. She had once forbidden Irving to marry because she feared it would be fatal to him, given his weakened heart and all. One time she had marched out onto a tennis court and pulled the racket from poor Irving's hand. Irving respected his mother, just as Louis B. Mayer respected his. It was a useful thing to know for a woman. One could control men like that. Once you found the key, they would transfer all that mother-love to you.

Playing to their weaknesses, though, that would never do. That she was certain of. You simply couldn't allow yourself to come off as more needy and helpless than they were. Poor Constance was using a tactic that end in victory for her, not in the long run. Coquettes may rule the night, but it took a truly competent and commanding woman to win the day.

Maybe she should stay and play it out, see where the day took her. Even a man like Irving, a man who held all the answers, was thrown by the occasional surprise.

The reminder of Henrietta pulling the tennis racket out of Irving's grip made Norma smile. He must have stood there dumbfounded, but he wouldn't have had a chance of holding on. Irving had thin hands, small hands. Oddly enough, Mr. Mayer also had small hands, though they were anything but frail. He had come up the hard way, bending others to his will. Irving had to do it the smart way.

Other mama's boys in Hollywood were the opposite of Irving and Mr. Mayer: They had big hands but tiny ambitions. They would not be remembered as long. She couldn't think of a single reason why they should be.

So Norma eased herself back in her seat and interlaced her fingers in her lap. As a small signal of defiance to male indifference and weakness, she doffed her own royal reindeer morning coat and exposed her hand-embroidered chiffon dress to the world. Then she sat back to allow the new day a chance to bask in her radiance.

CHAPTER FOUR

King of the Hill

What the hell was I doing? It's not like hopping aboard a runaway chariot was a useful plan of action. But turning around and heading back now was just too plain humiliating for me to think about. Then again, I couldn't keep going and expect to outrun my troubles, either.

My money was tied up in a race no one could say would even happen. What I had jingling in my pocket might get me a bus ticket back to Mrs. Addison's bike, but she would want her rent soon, and the prospect of a job seemed as far off as Missouri.

Maybe I could return the rig and make a few bucks as an extra in the stands. There might be a race after all, and my bet could pay off for me. But honestly, I knew there was a better chance I'd be murdered by Rusty Bigelow once he learned of Molly and me.

The only thing that gave me comfort in my current situation was finding how much fun it was to drive a chariot. Most people would have found it challenging to stay balanced while pulling back on two panicked horses at full gallop. But I started helping with the harvests before I was nine, and sometimes I would stand in a wagon and drive my team from one row to the next. This one rode lower and faster than anything I ever drove before. But it was no problem getting the hang of it, and that was mainly thanks to an old crazy uncle of mine.

Old Uncle Ches had never married and didn't mix socially with the other ranch families. He kept to himself in a small shack out beyond the fruit orchards. Holidays were the only time he came to sit for dinner with us all, so I saw him mostly when he was out chopping logs. The mountains of firewood just got taller and taller around his cabin, all in preparation for an endless winter that he was sure was coming.

His thoughts must have been full of worries because he never stopped for small talk or paid much notice to us kids like other grownups did. He was a busy, busy man. And that just made it more surprising one day at school to hear a rattling commotion out in the schoolyard that turned out to be our Uncle Ches driving up in the old Conestoga.

All Miss O'Leary's kids went running to the window when he stopped at the playground and unhitched his team. We watched him fold his coat and set it on a swing, and then he pulled a sledgehammer out of the back gate. He proceeded to knock the hell out of that old wagon's sides and struts.

Broken timber was flying everywhere, and long after Miss O'Leary ordered us back to our desks I sat blindly there trying to fathom the reason for the hammering and sawing going on outside. When the recess finally came we ran to see what sort of mess my Uncle Ches had wrought.

It turned out he salvaged enough of the buckboard to fashion a platform about five-foot square. By the time school was out he had mounted the floor to some half-buried railroad ties by means of the wagon's iron axle springs. I don't know where he got the idea, but he called the contraption a "pitchin' board" and said it was for us kids to bounce around on. Between lessons our favorite pastime was playing King of the Hill on Uncle Ches's pitchin' board. I got good at it, too, learning how to best distribute my weight while I fended off challengers.

That old Conestoga was the same one that brought great-grandfather Daniel and his family out from Pennsylvania a century or so before. The canvas top was eaten away by now, and its spokes were splintered and frail. So it was of no use to anyone anymore. But the wood had held up through a couple of Indian wars and the battle over the Confederacy. It always amazed me how much of our frontier past was still lying around in those days. That's how young America was only back as far as when I was a boy.

So old Uncle Ches wasn't half as crazy as we thought. His endless winter never did come, but his pitchin' board was exactly what I needed to learn how to handle a runaway chariot.

***

My team of racers had taken me past the parking lot and we were out in the field bearing down on a paved city street. All that stood between me and the low foothills was a half-dozen tin house trailers parked in a row. I knew I had to make up my mind fast about what direction my life was going to take.

That decision was made for me when I heard the sputtering of a full-throttle engine closing hard on my tail. The driver was a fair-skinned man in eye goggles and gloves. As he hunched over his handlebars he traced a circle above his head with two fingers, like a cop signaling me to pull over. But he wasn't dressed like any cop I knew, and his motorbike was one of those pre-war holdouts barely able to stay a yard ahead of choking in its own black cloud.

Hell! I swore to myself. All I needed was to get my ass hauled before a judge and have him calling up my record.

I tugged hard on the hand break at the side of the car and coaxed the horses to slow down. They were pretty winded by that time anyway, and had probably forgotten why it was they were spooked. So my golden chariot rolled to a rocky halt and I waited for the motorcyclist to skid up behind me in a lather of dust.

He planted one leg down and kicked the stand into place before cutting his engine. He couldn't have stood more than five-eight or five-nine, but he appeared fit enough to wrangle a mountain lion if the need arose. Snapping the goggles up on his forehead, he looked me over as he walked up closer.

"Step on down there, sergeant," he said. There was a scar across his left eye that cleaved an eyebrow and pointed down to the tight smile on his lips.

"You a police officer?" I asked.

"Name's Burr. Delmer Burr. I'm a second-unit A.D. here."

I wrapped the reins so they would stay this time and climbed down to meet my pursuer.

"This here's one of the parade cars," he said, glancing all around us before pushing his face closer to mine. "Where's the parade?"

I told him how I was hired as a wrangler and how I had jumped into the chariot when the team got scared and took off without a soul aboard.

He pulled off his right glove to fetch a folded paper from inside his work shirt. "Your name's Grover, you say? Like Grover Cleveland?"

"Yes, sir."

He scanned down his paper and stopped. "You're supposed to be with Ardale's team."

"That's right."

"Tell me, Grover, who was it fired off that hand gun?"

"Gun? No. I mean, I can't tell you."

"Can't, huh?" He stashed the paper back in his pocket. Then fast as lightning he had balled up a fist and gave a quick jab that caught me just under the ribcage. He might have been the runt in his mother's litter, but Delmer Burr sure knew where to land a fist to knock all the fight out of a fellow.

I fell back, reeling against the side of chariot and gasping for air.

He seemed to instantly lose all interest in me then. He slipped his hand back inside his glove and checked to make sure his goggles were in place. "A wrangler's got no business driving a rig," he said flatly. "You get this one turned around now and take her straight to the livery, hear? I'll check in on you later ... *Grover.*"

He straddled his bike and pushed it forward to unlock the stand. As he settled back on his seat he called out to me, "Maybe you'll remember who fired off that round." Then he stomped hard on the pedal, dropped his goggles over his bridge, and spun away in a cloud of dust and smoke toward the stadium.

I struggled to gather in enough air to straighten up, and I wobbled over to the side of a house trailer to pee. I couldn't hold it any longer and no one was around, so I had just started to fumble with my buttons when there came a pounding from the window above my head.

A muffled voice yelled at me, "No, no, please, do not do *eet*," and I saw the curtains fall closed. A second later, the trailer door opened and a man stood at the top of the iron steps.

"Please, do not *peece* on my trailer," he said. He was small and tidy, with dark shiny hair. He was wearing a smart silk bathrobe with a cloth tied at his neck. I didn't want to upset him anymore than he was.

"You got a toilet?"

"Of course, of course. Please come inside. *Por favor,*" he said, holding the door wide.

Most of the work sites I ever saw had offices in trailers for the managers. But nothing compared to this. I stepped out of a clotted field into a swanky living room with a clean sofa and padded chairs. It had a carpeted floor and curtains to match the throw pillows, all done in the same bright reds and yellows as the bowl of Mexican peppers in the kitchen.

My host pointed me toward the toilet, and I hurried through a narrow hallway past photographs and mounted horseshoes and numerous displays of Southwest bric-a-brac.

I stood for the longest time over the toilet bowl, struggling to let go of what I'd been holding onto for so long. That surprise punch to my gut had left me a bit dazed still. If Delmer Burr was typical of these studio overlords, then maybe Freddie Moore was right. Maybe it was time for everyone to rise up together and put an end to the bullying. The world had too many of these little Delmer Burrs in it. People had to stand up sometime and show them they couldn't get away with it any more.

My muscles began to let go, and as my bladder emptied I filled with a new resolve: I would go back and do the job they hired me to do. And if I found a way to even the score with Mr. Delmer Burr along the way, so much the better. It might be worth braving whatever taunts and humiliations the day still held.

In the alcove behind the toilet was a framed photograph of a large Mexican family posing in a courtyard. Most wore embroidered finery as they gathered around the seated figure of an older gentleman dressed in a black coat swirling with patterns of metal studs. His whiskered face was cast in shadow by a large *sombrero* fringed with hanging balls. As stern and proud as the others appeared, the man at the center was sternest of all. Together they suggested a loyalty and respect for something greater than Hollywood.

The trailer door open and then slammed, and I heard a male voice booming in the front room. "What's with the chariot outside?"

"Never mind. Tell me, what *deed* you learn?"

"It's like I thought. He'll be reprimanded, maybe loaned out to another studio. No one thinks it's the end of his contract."

"Well, that's a relief."

By the time I dried my hands, the two were speaking in a lowered tone. I stopped in the hall to look at some of the photographs. In one, my host with the shiny hair was being honored with a plaque from a fat lady in a flowered dress. Next to it he was caught smiling in a lineup with businessmen. One frame held nothing but a canceled check made out to one Jose Ramón Samaniegos. He must be important, I thought. From the size of his trailer, he could be one of the producers or a local rancher who was renting them his horses.

But the next photograph told the story. It was taken on the set of a movie, and in this one Jose Ramón Samaniegos was made up to look like a South Seas native, wearing only a loincloth and giving a smoldering look to a dark-skinned woman in a sarong. Toward the bottom was a signature in white ink: "To Ramón, My Favorite Islander. Forever, Alice."

That's when it dawned on me: Jose Ramón Samaniegos was none other than Ramón Novarro. Yes, the man who let me use his toilet was Hollywood's Judah Ben-Hur, the star of the whole movie.

In the front room, Ramón leaned across the arm of the sofa almost to where his male visitor was sitting. They both looked slightly startled when I staggered out.

"Feeling better now?" asked the star. His dark eyes and groomed lashes were no doubt irresistible to his female fans. At some angles, though, his head appeared too large for such a slim frame and his small mouth seemed cockeyed. But he was handsome enough, I thought, and his tailoring was impressive, from his fur-lined house slippers to the top of his fragrant pomaded hair.

"Right as rain," I told him.

"And who's this you've been hiding?" asked the other man. He was about the same age and build as the actor, but to me he wasn't half as warm and gracious.

"Herbie, *thees* is the young man who came to use my facility."

"All the way from ancient Rome, I take it," responded the other and blinked his eyelids twice.

"You're Mr. Novarro, aren't you?"

"That's what they say. *Sí*. Although my father would have different thoughts about *eet*."

I asked if the photo in the bathroom of the proud older man could be his father.

"*Sí, con mi familia*. That was when we lived in Durango—no, no, I am mistaken! That was in Mexico City, after we moved. I am the oldest of thirteen children, can you believe *eet*?"

I think I muttered something about what a handsome family he had. Later I wished I had asked him about other things. But all I could think of at the time was getting the chariot back and trying to set things right.

"Well, thanks again," I said.

"*De nada*. Here, let me see you go," he said, jumping up to open the door. As I passed by he placed a hand on my shoulder and gave a somber stare. "I saw *heem*," he whispered so softly that only I might hear. "That bad man. I saw what he *deed*."

I smiled at him dumbly and pushed by. I didn't know what to say.

He followed out on the steps. The morning was looking less gray now, and the horses were calmly grazing as if nothing at all had happened. "These second unit people," said the actor. "Some of them are brutes. Believe me. *Eet* means nothing. Do not let them have your goat."

I check the harnesses and the wheels as Novarro pulled out a pouch and sprinkled tobacco into a thin slip of paper. "What is your name, my friend?"

"Link. Grover."

"Hunh. You know, Señor Grover, I was noticing that you *haf* a very musical quality to your voice. Do you sing?"

"Sometimes, sure."

"Maybe you would consent to join us in one of our *leetle* theatricals. I *haf* a theater, you see—nothing too ambitious—but we *poot* on shows. Do you take singing lessons?"

"Lessons? No."

He swiped the rolled paper across his tongue and proceeded to mold it as he spoke. "Oh, *amigo,* you must *haf* a vocal coach. Remember: Luck favors the prepared." He placed the finished cigarette between his lips and searched his pockets for a match. "I am going to be an international singing sensation. How do you say, a concert singer? I take lessons each and every day."

"Well, good luck to you," I said, stepping up into the chariot and disentangling the reins.

"May I ask you, Señor Grover, where did you learn to handle a team? A circus, no?"

"On a farm."

"Oh. Well, you do not drive like a farmer. If I may offer a little advice, please—?"

"Sure," I said, and almost instantly he had sprung as softly as a cat off of the steps, landing next to me in the wagon bed.

"You handle the reins very well, but you are too tense. You must relax your body. Lean back on the legs, like so. ... Do not lock the knees. Keep your feet square, planted, understand. Now let your body ... *float.* See?" He acted out each bit of advice as he was speaking, using his cigarette as a pointer. I was struck by how precise each movement seemed, and since acting in silent pictures back then was mostly pantomime, I could see why he had found such success at it. He watched as I tried to do what he showed me, then he hopped back gracefully down to the ground, struck a match and let out a quick puff of smoke before shaking the flame away.

"You know, these Hollywood people are just like horses. They are useful and entertaining, but they must be taught to respect you. Once they see how you handle a team, I think they will give you no more trouble. I will look for you out on the track, *amigo.*"

"You'll be in the race?"

"Naturally. Well, the close-ups, that is. And the big triumph scene when I ride into the winner's circle."

"I've been told there's gonna be a real race."

Ramón looked surprised. "You mean, like in Rome? No, I don't *theenk* so. There is enough danger in just running around the track."

"How can they let you do that? How can they risk something happening—to their star?"

"Maybe that is why they wait until the end to shoot *thees* chariot race. Who can say?" He took a drag on his cigarette. "*Thees* is indeed a crazy business, my friend. The studio heads, the front office, they say I must never *ever* do the dangerous stunts, because *thees* is how the insurance papers are written. See? So I must not drive the racing car or the motor-bicycle. I must not dive from high cliffs, or even go galloping away on a fast horse. It is all written there in the contract. But when it comes to the final scene in Mr. Mayer's *beeg* picture, when the director says I must be seen on the track driving a four-horse team in the most dangerous stunt of them all, then the studio lawyers all agree—*thees* cannot be what the papers mean."

Ramón shook his head and smiled. "Sometimes I think it is not the meek that will inherit this Earth," he said. "It *ees* the *neet-peekers.*"

I saw Ramón's father described in movie magazines as an important civic leader, a politician or even a well-placed diplomat. In truth, that stern patriarch in Ramón's photograph was nothing but a dentist. Still, in Mexico he was considered an educated professional, and he commanded great respect. He accumulated property and had some influence over the government. He had always hoped his first-born son would follow in his path and be a dentist, maybe marry a respectable young lady and present him with a flurry of grandchildren.

But Ramón rejected a future full of other people's bad teeth. Private schools showed him the worlds of dancing and acting and musical performance, and he grew up wanting only to pursue those interests.

Pancho Villa's revolution arrived before a real rift could open between Ramón and his father. The esteemed Dr. Mariano Samaniegos found himself branded an enemy by his own people. He received death threats, and finally decided his oldest son would be safer for the time being with relatives in El Paso. Ramón was just seventeen, but even at that young age he saw that Texas was not the answer for him. On the map it was but a short trip west to Los Angeles, the new Mecca for stage actors and performers of every nationality on Earth.

Driving away from his trailer that morning I felt like I had made a friend. I genuinely liked Ramón Novarro. He was the first stranger in Hollywood to take the time to show me a little compassion. There was nothing in that for him. He set himself apart from all the hand-to-mouth brutes that only wished to bully or humiliate me in Mr. Culver's city.

Many times in the next few hours I would think again about Novarro's words of advice as he smoked his hand-rolled cigarette. I would talk to him only briefly once more that day, and then I would not think about him much at all for decades, until the day in October 1968 when I read that his body had been found bludgeoned to death in his Laurel Canyon home.

The world spends so much time talking about its famous people, going over the intimate details of their lives in magazines and books, year after year. And then something happens and we see we never even got a glimpse of the truth about them. For all those acres of words and oceans of ink, we don't know them any better than we know any other stranger. One thing I can say about Ramón Novarro, though: No way in hell did he deserve the hand that fate had dealt him.

CHAPTER FIVE

A Farce to Be Reckoned With

The chariots were kept in a fenced section beneath a tin patchwork roof near the southern rim of the stadium. It should have been easy for me to ditch the rig there and get away unnoticed, but the only way in was between two fence posts, and by the time I spotted them it was too late. There was nothing I could do but circle around up ahead, and before I knew it I was in the open, driving toward the field of chuck wagons.

A dozen or so of the shiny food trucks sat there parked along a crescent ridge. Their sheet metal fronts were propped open to let out the smoke, and inside I could see chubby ladies in hairnets and colored men in aprons passing tin plates piled high with fluffy mounds of egg and charred chunks of 'taters.

Hundreds of hungry workers sat outside at folding tables covered in white linen, and as I got close I heard a cheer go up at one of the tables. I spotted Buddy at the center of some men, and Squeaks standing over them giving out a war whoop and waving that red neckerchief of his. Others stopped to give their own whistle calls and rebel yells. Even some waiting in line for their food stopped to look back and grin.

I made sure my knees were unlocked the way Ramón had showed me and tried to look like I knew what I was doing. There's no denying it made me feel good to see that no one there seemed to hold any grudge.

The guard on duty back at the livery was younger than me. He was probably some director's son, happy to pick up pocket money on a Saturday while his pals were out running after balls or taking in a Hoot Gibson western. The boy signaled for me to bring the team forward, then raised a hand to his freckled mouth to be heard above the racket. "What happened to Mr. Fisher?"

"I told him I'd bring it for him. Just leave it here?"

He shook his head violently and pointed deeper inside. "See that fancy pink rig at the end of the row?"

"Yeah."

"Leave her there. Next to Mr. Bushman."

"Mr. Bushman?" I said. "Francis X. Bushman?"

The boy waved me along, hiking up his shoulder blades to show he'd spent all the time he cared to waste on me.

Mrs. Addison! What a button-eyed dummy I'd been! Here I was sitting on that silly autograph book all morning and it never crossed my mind to pull it out. I could have gotten Ramón Novarro to put his name in it and that mortifying obligation would be over. Maybe I could find old Francis X. Bushman and get him to do a guy a favor.

Bushman's "pink rig" was actually more of a lavender, which made sense because I read somewhere that lavender was his color of choice. He was famous for smoking custom-made lavender cigarettes, and he traveled through Hollywood in a lavender Marmon limousine with his name on the side embossed in gold.

His chariot car was a real beauty, decorated with swirling vines around a raised silhouette of a peacock, or something like it. No one was there to ask, so I tied off my team and went to have a closer look. The carriage was wider and sat higher than my little two-horse parade car. They called those big four-horse racing rigs *quadrigae* in old Roman days. They could take the punishment from a team of runners strapped haunch-to-haunch to a neck yoke. From one wheel hub to the other, the axle looked like it measured eight feet, and each of the wheels rose up to my ribcage when I was standing beside it. The wagon body was made of wood but it was set down in a welded metal frame.

The wood felt solid when I rapped it with a knuckle, and instantly a fierce head shot bolt upright on the other side. It gave me the same start I got that morning at the spina when the stone giant fixed its eyes on me. "Who the devil are you?" it demanded.

"Sorry." There did seem something familiar about him though. "You wouldn't happen to be Mr. Bushman?"

"If you're here for an interview, you will have to be brief. I am not a stationary target. You young people think you have me in your sights but I am on the move, never in the same place for long. By the time your prose appears, I might be thousands of miles away, and your wrinkled fish-wrappers will be tumbling over rails a dozen stations to my rear!"

It was him all right. While I didn't know a thing about Ramón Novarro before we met, the whole world knew about Francis X. Bushman. He had been making movies since 1911, and had starred in over two hundred feature films. At one point he was said to be earning a million dollars a year, and with his wavy brown hair and athlete's physique, no one ever challenged his billing as "the handsomest man in the world."

He was motion pictures' first masculine sex symbol, fielding marriage proposals from every quarter of the globe. That came to a sudden end, though, when he was caught in an affair with his "Romeo and Juliet" costar. Then the newspapers found he had a wife back in Baltimore, where the Bushmans bred Great Danes on their estate, not to mention five children. His marriage in tatters, Francis was soon free again to marry his Juliet. But female movie-goers had moved on by then. They found a new, mysterious breed of sex idol like Rudolph Valentino more to their liking.

Bushman's contract with Metro was part of the baggage included in the studio merger. When he was cast in "Ben-Hur" as Messala, the bold Roman villain who sells out the prince, magazines called it a comeback vehicle for "the old man"—which was how everyone except Mrs. Addison thought of Francis X. Bushman in 1925. He was, after all, forty-two years old.

I hurried to correct his impression of me. "No, sir, I'm not an interviewer. My name is Grover. My landlady, Mrs. Addison, she's your biggest fan." It was dumb, yes, but I had to lay the groundwork for handing him her book.

"Indeed? No doubt a charming lady. With sophisticated tastes."

"Yes, sir. Well ... *maybe*."

"Don't tell me—you are new at this studio?"

"Yes, sir."

"Suddenly everyone is new here except me. Do you know I used to have to put on a fake mustache and dark glasses when I went out of my house? Everyone knew who I was. My face was known the world over by producers and directors—even emperors. Now they've moved along, get the point? Now I come to read for some flat-chested casting secretary and she asks me what types of roles I've done."

"I'm not from casting or anything."

"So, what is your role here?"

"I'm just a hired man. One of the horse wranglers."

"Well, Grover, nothing to be ashamed of. That is honorable work, yes indeed. I always adored working with animals myself. When I was growing up, I adopted creatures of every description. Rabbits, snakes, finches, fish. I loved them all, and they would all come to the front of their cages and aquariums when I entered the room. I would get up before dawn and run down to Lafayette Market, and everyone saved me scraps and whatever had not sold the day before, because you see, they knew I had all these animals to feed. It was the most astounding thing. I was only nine. But everyone loved me. I was such a beautiful boy. … What do you know about these undercarriages?"

He must have read my confusion at his sudden change of subject.

"Look here," he said, wiggling his finger for me to join him beneath the chariot. He pointed to some empty holes drilled under the assembly. The axle blocks had clearly been repositioned to a place four full inches higher. "Why do you suppose they raised the car?" he asked.

"Make it run faster?"

His eyes widened. "Smart lad. That is exactly what I was thinking. Someone must have decided they weren't swift enough there in Italy. Of course, since then they've added the metal and the frames. They were all wood in Rome. They were sleek and low to the ground and very fast. But it cost one poor man his life. I watched it happen. He broke up just like that wooden wagon."

He motioned for me to lean closer, as if to share a secret. "Don't look immediately, but when you have a chance, there are two men watching us from a pillar in back of you. Don't look! Let me know if you recognize either of them." Then he pulled back and straightened to his full height. He must have stood six feet, which was taller than average for men in those days. Without a beat, he continued on in his grand manner.

"Then I became interested in bodybuilding. I became a very popular sculptors' model. Have you been to Baltimore? Well if you go, pay a visit to the Francis Scott Key monument on Eutaw Street. That is me in my prime there. I am also Cecil Calvert on St. Paul, and Lord Baltimore. They tell me I appear in more bronze and marble in more American cities than any man in history. On Wall Street I am the torso of George Washington, and at Harvard, Nathan Hale. Great patriots, all. And all of them courtesy of my body in its post-adolescent prime."

While he was going on in that vein, I glanced back across my shoulder. Two clean-shaven strangers were indeed waiting off by a post. One stood a good head taller than the other, but each wore the same style thin-brimmed hat. They tried to look like they weren't interested in us at all, but clearly they were.

"No one I know," I told Bushman when he stopped for a breath. He nodded slightly before going on.

"In the old days, a studio would take care of the problems that arose. They would arrange transportation and lodging and handle the publicity. Now everything is on one's shoulders, and one must pay attention to everything."

He sighed deeply. "It's so sad to see what's going on today. This used to be such a wonderful business, you know. Putting on shows for people who hardly make enough to keep a stew on the stove. Somewhere the bosses forgot all that. They learned there were fortunes to be made. And so did the cheap hustlers, the sleazy nepotists and the hopheads and the sex fiends. Get the point?

"Who is thinking of the needs of the little people now? But I won't give in to them. I have not yet begun to fight," he said, raising his finger and striking a dramatic pose. "When your mother names you Francis, you learn how to fight at an early age."

"Mr. Bushman, before I go, may I ask a favor? It's about Mrs. Addison. She keeps this book of autographs, see, and she is your biggest fan, like I said. I promised her that if I ever got to meet you—"

"An autograph? Certainly. Let me have it. And how would you like me to make it out?"

He was being way too friendly all at once, and I felt like I should carry on the chit-chat while he was scribbling his name. I told him how Mrs. Addison liked to follow the latest studio gossip, and then I told him her opinion that "Ben-Hur" was being financed by a lot of Jewish money back East because it was a Jew that wins the race.

Bushman added a swooping flourish to his name before stopping to respond. "No, that is horse shit—pardon my language," he declared. "General Lew Wallace wrote his book to discredit such a sentiment. The character I am playing, this Messala fellow, he was steeped in the anti-Semitism of his own day. It existed in Rome long before the Crucifixion, believe me. That Crucifixion happened because of the hate that was there.

"General Wallace wanted to repudiate such intolerance. The point was not that a Jew wins the race. The thrill for readers was to watch Messala get his comeuppance. In the long run, hatred, you understand, is by its nature self-defeating. I hope you will tell that to your Mrs. Addison," he said, closing the little book and slapping it in my hand. Then he gave a smile worthy of any bronze hero, adding, "With my warmest regards."

As I hurried away I looked around for the two strangers in the thin-brimmed hats, but they were gone. Instead I noticed a single figure up at the livery gate, flapping his arms for me to hurry. It was Squeaks, the Irishman, and he was standing there next to the tilted body of a baby-blue chariot, all trimmed in white.

"What's up?" I asked as I drew near.

Squeaks always had this funny way of framing his answers as a sort of negative question. "Could it not be Buddy's own car?" he told me. "And will they not be expecting it now on the track?"

"Shall I not run and get the horses?" I said.

"It's the *harses* now, is it? Filthy wild beasts is what they be. In due time they'll come, in due time, so never you mind. Just grab hold of the other side and we'll be off."

Raising the two sides righted the chariot on its wheels and made it easy for us to roll. Squeaks said he hadn't noticed the suspicious men I described, but that it didn't surprise him a bit. He said I should be wary about who I was seen talking to and not to be caught in private with the wrong people.

"Who do you mean, exactly?"

"Oh, you'll know 'em when you meet 'em. Now, you take Francis Xavier Bushman," he said. "Surely he was a *farce* to be reckoned with in his day. But what went on in Italy, it sticks in the craw of some."

"What did he do?"

"The country's been torn in two since the election of this Mussolini chap. He's been lowering the boom on the labor strikes, and most people just want to keep their jobs. So when the strikers got around to protesting the production there, our people found themselves sitting by for months with nothing to do. Francis took the side of the strikers and used the shutdown to squeeze the studio for a fatter paycheck. For himself, of course."

"Sounds cagey."

"But his timing didn't sit well with the big cheeses who were on the hook for a lot of salaries and not getting a thing in return.

Then Francis decided since he wasn't being used at all he would take his entourage and go off on a sightseeing tour of Europe. A couple months later he returns as the guest of none other than Mr. Mussolini himself. Francis is now praising the *fascistas* for getting things done and crushing the labor strikes."

Squeaks shook his head in pity. "There are grievances coming due just now. People are divided, and some are ready to fight for what they think is true. There's plenty of ill will left over for those living high off both sides."

I knew Squeaks was leveling with me then. It made me want to confide in him and hear what he had to say about my own situation. First I had to come clean about throwing him that punch.

"No apology needed," he responded and raised a hand to the red scrape on his cheek. "It gets me more sympathy from the ladies."

I made him promise not to tell Rusty how it had been me there in the dark with Molly. Then I told him about my run-in with Delmer Burr, and he got a laugh when I told him Novarro had called ordinary movie folks a bunch of brutes.

"Sure I'd be lying if I said there weren't brutes amongst us here," he said. "Were you there for the dust-up at breakfast today?"

"No."

"Of course. That's when you were out on your ride."

He told me how they had just settled down with their food when they heard a big ruckus back at the line. A beggar had tried to cut in with his tray for something to eat, and a studio henchman had straight-armed him away.

"Someone at the table muttered, 'Ain't that old Walt Altskellar?' and we looked hard," said Squeaks. "Sure as we're standing here, it was he. Old Walt Altskellar, once a leading player over at Vitagraph before it got sold to the Warners. He was a fine horseman and a stunt rider, too, until he broke his hip doing a leap on a moving train.

"It was a bad setup, no denying it. So Walt had sued the bastards to pay for his bills, and he never saw another day's work in pictures. It looked like he could use a square meal, but those goons were not having it," said Squeaks.

"Before long here come more studio thugs to give old Walt the boot, and Walt was taking a pummeling from all sides. Buddy and me were getting up to go down there, but before we could raise a leg across the bench the fists were flyin', and this time it was the real thing.

"Walt folded up in two and went down on his knees, shieldin' his head from the blows. Then one of the henchmen went flying backwards, and someone new was in the fray, wailing away at the studio goons with his handy uppercuts and quick jabs to the belly. All I could make out was a pair of shotgun chaps and a bit of red hair. Then I knew, it was our own darling Rusty, pumping and pounding like a steam piston in the midst of the melee.

"Both his fists were on fire, they were, until the bloodied goons raised up their hands to call it quits. Buddy helped old Walt to his feet and handed him a tin plate, and some of the others helped him up to the front of the line."

"I wish I'd seen that."

"It was a sight to behold, I tell ya. There's none better to have on your side in a scuffle than Rusty Bigelow."

"What do you think he'd do—if he found out about me and Molly?"

"It wouldn't sit well, I expect. Then again, it's not something he never heard of before."

"What do you mean?"

"Rusty knows she's a handful. She's a wild filly, for sure, just like Rusty himself."

"How long has he been married?"

"Couldn't say. Long enough to have two young 'uns."

"Kids?"

"Does it surprise you?"

"Yes, it does. Molly's still so young."

He looked at me oddly. "But Elizabeth's and he are near the same age."

"Who's Elizabeth?"

"Rusty's wife."

"Wait. I thought Molly was his wife."

"Hah! Well, no wonder you were worryin'. No, little Molly, she's his baby sister. Out on a jaunt from North Carolina, she is. Trying to break into the picture racket, like thousands of other lasses. Only she may be a wee more determined. She's a hellcat, that Molly."

We had hauled Buddy's chariot to the southern gate by then, and I couldn't help noticing an old ice truck parked there by the wall. It was freshly whitewashed, with a red cross stenciled in a circle on the side. "What's the ambulance doing here?" I asked.

"The studio bought itself two or three of them old ice buckets now. They keep 'em around for the big shoots, just in case."

Two guards at the gate waved us through and we maneuvered the chariot down a long channel under the bleachers and came out in the open arena. In the full morning light the coliseum looked more massive than ever. Three water trucks were busy smoothing out the tracks, dragging heavy iron frames over the sand. It would take them four or five laps, I figured, to complete the job. Ahead of us was my old stone friend, Mr. Atlas, still struggling to get to his feet and kick the ass of whoever had run off with his globe.

Milling about in the bleachers were a good six hundred people, some waiting on benches and others gathered in small groups to shoot the breeze. Most everyone was dressed in white or tan togas of one type or another. Some wore fancy braids or Arabian head-dresses, or appeared more like commoners and slaves. Here and there I made out the wine-colored cape and silver breastplate of a Roman centurion.

"Wow, where'd they all come from?"

"You wait," said Squeaks. "In another hour, the stands'll be filled to bursting."

"How much you figure it cost for all these folks?"

"Most of 'em won't cost the studio a dime."

"Aren't they paid extras?"

"Hunh-uh. Gamblers, fan club presidents, newspaper editors, magazine writers. Contest winners. You name it. All manner of riff-raff shows up for a thing like this. Just point 'em to a free lunch and they'll sit and wait all day long."

"Wait? For what?"

"Maybe to see if M-G-M's going to lose its shirt. Or maybe—" He stopped.

"What?"

"Maybe to see our blood."

CHAPTER SIX

The Trap

Innocence. Was there anything on Earth more stimulating or enticing—more laughably sweet and irresistible—than a young man's blushing innocence? Norma was surprised at how seductive she found it. How exciting.

It had only been a momentary encounter but her own reaction overwhelmed her. Suddenly the day was alive again with possibilities.

And here it had all just fallen in her lap. Well, not her lap, precisely. But a hole. Yes. A trap, a typical Hollywood trap.

Perhaps that's what made her feel also halfway guilty. He hadn't seen it coming and didn't suspect it was there. In some way she was responsible for him falling. And that just reinforced her sense of what a truly naive innocent he was.

She had experienced her share of traps in her day. Perhaps she could teach him what she knew about snares. Just not at the moment. She was enjoying this feeling too much. There was nothing maternal about it. It wasn't the way she felt about Irving. No, it was more like the spider and the fly. She had come along at just the right time, when he was weak from struggling.

Oh, stop it, Norma! Are you mad? You know this has nothing to do with that boy. It's only this day, this awful wasted day in this predatory town. It was all this grotesque vanity business of making images. That was the trap, and it consumed everyone it attracted.

It would consume her, too, in time. She was no spider, for Lord's sake. She was every bit as much the victim as that boy!

Of course, she always knew what she was selling. She knew when she came to Hollywood that it meant sacrificing herself to the god of the camera lens. It would drink in her youth and her dreams and her entire future, if it was allowed to go on. That camera and its minions. That was the right word for them, wasn't it? That was Milton's word for Satan's helpers. Whatever she chose to call them, they had control of everything she was or ever would be now.

At one time her job had been to explore a role, learn her lines and work through her motivations. Now it was only to appear fresh and dewy-eyed, cleansed and oiled for her sacrifice to the camera god. She had to stand nude under the lights and allow each second of her life to be sliced into twenty-four frames and packaged like tissue paper for the runny-nosed masses.

"Hello, Norma. I hope there is a good dirty joke that goes with that naughty little grin."

Oh, God, it was Douglas. The "Son of Zorro" himself.

"I'm sure there are no smutty jokes you haven't heard already, Mr. Fairbanks," she said.

"Well, I live in hope. May I join you a moment?"

"Please."

Such a handsome man, but so weak. He did a tango in his last picture, but that hardly made him Valentino. With Rudy, the dance had become all about seducing his partner. But poor Douglas only seemed to use the dance to compete for attention.

What's he saying now? Something about the sky and the fog? Oh, he should go see Irving about that. They could have a wonderful chat together about the weather. Of course, Irving would take it seriously.

If only all those fans of Zorro could have seen him like she did, sobbing at sun-up in the sand at Malibu. No one could understand what he had to put up with, he wailed. On and on he poured out his heart to her until the last titter of laughter from the striped tents was lost in the coming of the tide.

"Son of Zero," she thought bitterly and smiled, feeling instantly ashamed over her lack of charity.

It was really funny how wrong everyone was about the two of them, Mary and Douglas. They all believed that Mary was the weaker of the two, because she was the one with the drinking problem. Her and Jack both, sister and brother. Some said their mother was the same. Alcoholism certainly ran through that family.

But nearly everyone drank too much now—even more since the horrid Volstead Act was passed. Now people took bigger risks to get a bottle, and that made the drinking all the more ceremonial. It was a rite of passage for a charter membership in The Good Life. Showing up drunk in public was like an act of civil disobedience. It was almost held as the duty of any good citizen.

But that wasn't the case with Mary. "America's sweetheart," indeed. With her, it was not status nor fellowship nor a simple leisure time pleasure. It was an illness.

It bothered Douglas but he could never help her. Maybe no one could, but Douglas was especially ineffective. He was used to doing whatever the studio asked. The rest of his energy went toward playing, as far as Norma could tell. Mary had been the one with the business savvy. She was the impetus behind the whole United Artists thing, back before it became such a fiasco. She was more than Chaplin's equal when it came to vision. Each of them was shrewd in their own way. But Douglas—no. He was mainly good at tennis and at walking on his hands.

Oh, stop talking, Dougie. I will speak with you later about all that, yes, yes. We will, we must. Anything you say. Now go away like a good boy. You are depressing me. You make me think of how magnificent you looked at your peak.

Douglas and Mary, my God! No one was more popular than they were during the war. There had never been a bond tour like theirs. The whole world put aside its problems for a time to offer them a hug. Some feared it would squeeze the life out of them both. Afterwards, they were like royalty. Wherever they went in Europe, everyone turned out for a glimpse of the reigning fairy book king and queen of the movies.

It began to dawn on people that the entire planet was addicted to motion pictures. Yes, Chaplin was big, but he was clearly just an entertainer. He appealed to people who liked clowns and underdogs. Douglas and Mary were so much more. They inspired people, and their marriage was one of those seismic jolts that move whole continents. It inspired people in hard times to reach higher, dream deeper, and keep hoping for something greater than mere survival.

To think of him how he was now, keeping up appearances and putting on a show, while sweet, bloated Mary sat holed up in Pickfair with her bottles and her astrological charts—it was beyond sad.

"You might have seen me sitting over there all alone thinking," said Douglas. "You know what I was thinking?"

"I couldn't begin to guess."

"I'll tell you. I was looking for an answer to a riddle a fellow told me."

"A riddle, huh? I'm pretty good at those. Shoot."

"What is the difference between European royalty and Hollywood royalty? ... I'm timing you."

"Hmmm," she said. "Oh, it's easy. European royalty is more likely to die while still on top."

Douglas's delighted smile yanked up his whole face. "Wonderful. You know, I think that must be it. Well, I've got my answer."

"Glad to help," she said.

"And now that I have been thoroughly deflated, I can fit back in my hat." He pulled an English walking cap out of nowhere and drew it comically low on his forehead, then produced a pipe and tossed it up and caught it in his teeth. "Tak' car', ma swee'."

And there he went, knowing that every set of eyes was on him and would stay fixed on him all the way back to his seat.

***

All of these fabulous directors and movie idols. How grand their smiles, how happy they looked. But what they all knew was their time was limited.

When their run was over, if they were lucky, they might have some family left to take them in. But that was the tragedy of Hollywood, wasn't it? Family was always the first victim of success. The celebrity stakes were so high, and appearances too important. Along the way there were too many snubs and affronts, and they left too much hurt in their wake.

Wait, wasn't that Gloria—oh, what's her name? They were in "Way Down East" together—well, off in the background, really. "Way Down East And Off in the Background," that should have been the name of the movie they were in. No, it couldn't be her. Why would she be here in Hollywood? She would never choose to leave her precious New York, her *the-ater*. Oh, well, couldn't remember her name anyway.

Still, it would have been fun to talk to someone who had been there, someone who had also been with David. Not that anyone but her ever called him David, of course. It was D. W., or Mr. Griffith. That's what Miss Lillian still called him. He was as "old South" as you could get.

He had once told her—it was late at night, after finishing her small part in "Way Down East"—and he had started to tell her about getting stranded as an actor in northern California. His repertory company ran out of money in the midst of the tour, and they had had to cancel the remaining dates. The troupe was let go without pay, and David was forced to harvest hops with migrant workers and Mexicans. He had turned the experience into a play. What was it called now? He was going to be a playwright then. But that was before he got back to the east coast and found he hated being in front of a camera.

But D.W. was one of the first to see the importance of the flickers. He began to think that directing them might be what he was meant to do. He was pretty much a teetotaler then, a polite social drinker if anything. Then came "The Birth of a Nation," and he really had nowhere to hide but in a bottle. The last anyone heard of him, he was living in a transient hotel and turning down all invitations from friends. *From hops we come and to hops we go,* she thought. She could never make such jokes out loud to anyone, but it was funny to her, in an awful way.

Oh, there's Buster again. No doubt Natalie was nearby then, or soon would be. And where Natalie was, sister Constance could be as well, slouching her way toward Irving. Mother Talmadge had given birth to three baby octopi. It was her way of getting her tentacles into everyone's business.

Well, Natalie was more than welcome to Buster. Always jumping around with props, trying to get a laugh. Couldn't he ever just relax? Those heavy, hound dog eyes of his. He might benefit from old Dr. Bates' muscle exercises. Keaton looked a little like Dr. Bates, now that she thought of it. Too bad she didn't think of it sooner. It might have made those long, dreary appointments seem more of a comedy. Maybe that's why she never particularly liked Buster—that and the way his clothes always stunk of tobacco and mothballs, the curse of being raised in a trunk.

Well, something was finally starting to happen down there. The cameramen were checking their canister, and men were running on the track with different colored flags.

Oh, no! There was that awful Dottie woman from costuming again! Please don't come over here, *please don't.* I know I can't wear my lovely chapeau once the cameras start to roll. I'll be good, I promise.

"Oh, Norma!"

She's seen me. She's coming. I'm doomed.

"Don't forget what I told you."

"What was that, Dottie, dear?"

"Your hat. They didn't have anything half so elegant in ancient Rome."

"Rome? I thought I was in Antioch, silly me."

"Your delicious shift is fine. At this distance, no one will see. But just remember to remove your hat."

"Yes, ma'am."

"If it showed up on screen, I'm sure all the ladies in the audience would forget the race and wonder where you've shopped."

"Cross my heart," she said like a chastened schoolgirl, adding to herself, *And wish to die—with a big Roman centurion on top!*

Dottie instantly launched into her next topic, about some man she didn't know whose wife passed away and how awful she looked in her open coffin. She went on and on about it, saying she had instructed her daughters that she would never want an open-coffin funeral for herself. It would be simply too appalling to have the world staring down at her little imperfections and not be able to raise even a finger to prevent it.

Was that really what Dottie was troubled about this morning? As if anyone would care a whit about her flaws on such an occasion.

"You needn't worry about these things, Dottie," she said. "You're still young and vital." She bit her lip and stopped. If she were being truthful she could have added, *Dottie, darling, you should welcome all the world to view your corpse and see what you had to contend with your entire life.*

But she would never say such a thing out loud. It would not fit her image. Her minions would not approve.

Luckily, even an open coffin would not reveal her own private flaw, her *amblyopia*. It was her wonderful gift from nature, a congenital case of *esotropic strobismus*. Or as Dr. Bates would put it, her *lazy eye*. Let it point wherever it wanted after she was gone.

Wasn't it The Great Ziegfeld who first remarked on it? Wait, no. Flo didn't like her *legs*. It was Mr. Griffith who did not care for her eyes. He was the one who said she had no future in the movies. Not only did the right eye come late to the party, he told her, but both her pupils were the wrong shade of blue. They would not register on film, and moviegoers would not be sure where she was looking or what she was feeling. That was the professional, considered opinion of the formerly prepossessing, currently predisposed David Wark Griffith. *Have another one on me, D.W.*

Of course, Mother knew better than the experts when it came to self-improvement. She wasn't about to give in without a fight. What did the appraisal of people like Florence Ziegfeld and D.W. Griffith mean? What did they know about her daughter's special *allure?* Hadn't she won a beauty contest at only fifteen? And that was despite the cast of her eye and without a decent leg to stand on! she crowed. Edith believed there was no finer beauty in all of eastern Canada than her little Norma. And besides, what did beauty have to do with it when your daughter was a born musical prodigy, destined for greatness as a concert pianist?

Mother saw to it that she had the best music teacher in all of Montreal. He was a frequent visitor to the Shearer home until the nasty crash of 1920. That changed everyone's plans. The Shearer construction business convulsed and went belly-up, and Edith whisked both daughters away to New York City in search of a more productive future.

As far as Norma was concerned, God had a good reason for giving her that lazy eye. It was there to remind her not to be too quick to believe everything she saw. It was a divine blessing to have an extra millisecond to perceive the world as more than a menu of tasty dishes.

The idea comforted Norma, though it was no match for the brutal reality of a New York winter. Bad enough those daily rounds of casting offices. There were nights, too, when the madness of a million blinking marquees kept everyone from getting any sleep.

Edith was there through it all, pushing her into all those dead-end movie roles. Even if the masses were not paying to see those pictures they were stopping for a gander at her modeling efforts. One day it was posing with laundry boxes, the next beside an automobile tire. Who didn't enjoy her curves as "Miss Lotta Miles," the Springfield Tire gal?

Libraries, it turned out, were full of books on how to improve one's posture and tone an unshapely leg. Then Edith found Dr. Bates and his natural technique for retraining the eye muscle. Norma's diligence paid off and she was soon getting small roles in better movies. There were other secrets the professionals would share about offsetting physical flaws and stressing one's strengths.

In the end, even Irving Thalberg looked beyond her drawbacks and saw only her assets. He signed her to contracts, not once but twice, and she was on her way to sunny California.

Too bad she couldn't squelch those early missteps, the stories of her extended "fling" with Victor Fleming. They bothered Irving a good deal. He and Victor were friends, after all, and unlike the movies then, men were known to talk.

Oh, Victor. Who would ever thrill her like that again? Other lovers paled, like those upright men at the midway who paid for a sledge-hammer hoping to impress by sending the lead weight all the way up the pole. Victor didn't need to ring any bells for her. He was all man. Everyone else in Hollywood was like John Gilbert, underfed and insecure, or like Ramón Novarro—well, enough said about that.

At least Ramón and she could chatter away like girlfriends. It was rare to find that in either sex any more. He spoke to her the way she spoke to herself. Once she had told him what she really thought of his latest friend, that horrid Herbert Howe. She could see that Howe was not to be trusted. She recognized that all those articles he published about traveling with the star were nothing but advertisements for himself. Ramón would not hear it. "Oh, Norma, you are a *sheet*. Just keep your eyes on your own affairs—or, rather," he added, "your good eye."

Ramón had pleaded with her to come today. It was going to be his day, he said. It would mark his arrival as a genuine star. He was terrified of failing, and it would give him courage to see her in the stands.

When he did finally ride out on the track, she could hardly believe how majestic he looked. She teared-up with joy. There in his sparkling chariot, standing behind a magnificent team of matched white stallions, he was so proud. He wore a brimless cap and a cutaway leather shirt that showed off his bare shoulders, pumped up and oiled. To her he did indeed look like a film star for the very first time.

She jumped out of her seat and went racing down to the front railing. She wanted to make sure he saw that she was there. She envisioned him calling her down to the track, and she would go and give him a long hug. People would speak of it for days—how Norma Shearer had openly shown so much love and magnanimity toward M-G-M's newest fellow star.

That would get tongues wagging, all right. It might counteract some of the damaging rumors about Ramon and the awful Herbie. It might even replace the gossip about her and Victor or ... *anyone else.*

She was almost at the rail when her second thoughts set in. What if the sand was soft and deep? What if her heels sank and she tottered as she felt herself falling? How magnanimous would she appear then, dropped in the sand on her skinny Canadian backside?

So she slowed a bit and took her time, and when she looked up Ramón had moved on and was turning the team around. He never saw that she was there for him.

And then came the boy. She noticed him out of the corner of her good eye. He was backing toward a pit dug to hold a camera, and he was putting one foot behind the other, not looking at all where he was headed. All too rapidly he reached the edge and fell flat backwards onto a billowing tarp.

She had no more misgivings then about looking bad or of sinking in the sand. She was the closest person to the boy and she worried he was hurt. So she hurried down to see if she could help.

When it was over, she was proud of herself for her impulsive act. The boy wasn't really a boy at all. He was quite the attractive young man, and he did appear so blushingly innocent. She had clearly impressed him with her concern. And she felt something stir within her that she hadn't felt in months.

Did anyone else notice? It didn't matter. She didn't care. But she wouldn't mind if on Monday morning the studio was buzzing about it. Maybe the story would get up to Irving's private office. He would hear how Miss Shearer had leapt from the stands and come running to the aid of a poor fallen cowboy.

No, she wouldn't mind that sort of gossip at all.

CHAPTER SEVEN

The Lost Angel

Whatever else was in store for me that day, I was determined to ride it out. There'd be no more running away for this farm boy. Good or ill, boom or bust, I was resolved to be there for it.

Squeaks and I had rolled our rig around to the backstretch, behind the spina and out of the eyes of the V.I.P. stands. That would be the staging area for the race. Other crews were getting their horses cinched up and strapped to their yokes, and I was expected to fetch ours next. So it was a surprise to hear the Irishman announce loudly, "Ladies and gents, here comes the winning team."

Rusty Bigelow was moseying down the track leading three good-looking mares. Close behind was a black man bouncing a tangle of big wooden blocks and harness gear off his shoulders like they had no weight at all.

"Colored fella's name is Powder Keg," said Squeaks. "He's our other mate."

"Where's the fourth horse?"

"Never you mind. She'll be along shortly."

The colored man appeared to be solid muscle, but I'd seen bigger. "Why do they call him Powder Keg?"

"Couldn't tell ya."

"He got a quick temper?"

Squeaks blew air out around his tongue. "Nah. He's a pussycat. You have any objection to working with coloreds?"

"Maybe you didn't hear the news over in Ireland."

"What's that?"

"Civil War's over."

Powder Keg unloaded everything next to the chariot and hardly looked up before setting to work untangling the straps.

"Are you going to introduce us?" I asked Squeaks.

"What for? He's stone deaf and never talks, neither. But Buddy won't accept a job from anyone unless Powder can come too."

Rusty was off getting the horses ready for the harnesses but he must have been listening to us talk. "Where is Buddy?" he called back.

"They sent him to wardrobe. He told me the A.D. came around and said he had to go."

"Which A.D.?" asked Rusty. "What's his name?"

"New man," said Squeaks. "Calls himself Delmer. Delmer Burr."

"Delmer?" said Rusty, rubbing his chin. "Seems I heard that name before."

"Not one you'd forget. Nice fella. Came up and introduced himself to Grover here, real polite and friendly like." The Irishman's eyes twinkled to see me scowl.

"Delmer Burr. Don't know why that sounds familiar," said Rusty. "Well, let's get these animals strapped up."

Buddy's chariot was much the same as Bushman's rig except its body was painted light blue and its shield was covered with white vines and curlicues. I grabbed a big knot of leather straps and sat down to help Powder Keg. Everything was going well until Rusty went to connect a harness block. He strained to force the cotter pin through but it wouldn't go, and when his grip gave out he tore some skin off his knuckles.

"Goddamn it!" he swore. "I can't figure out what's wrong with the fucker."

"Let me try," said Squeaks. "You hold it up and let me shove."

The pin still refused to slide into place, and now Squeaks was grunting and muttering Irish curses under his breath.

"Should be nothing to it," said Rusty, stopping him to check the alignment of the holes.

I had begun to suspect it had something to do with the changes that Francis X. Bushman found. But I didn't think it wise to bring up Bushman's name again, so I held my tongue and waited to see who would figure it out first.

"Give Powder Keg a poke, will you?" Rusty said to me.

"What?"

"The colored fellow—go give him a poke."

It turned out Powder Keg had stopped what he was doing and was coming over.

Rusty pointed at the block and the pin and then shrugged his shoulders.

"What do you think's wrong, Squeaks?"

"Don't know. Maybe they give us the wrong blocks.

Powder Keg had stuck his head under the chariot by then and he was back up, pressing his left shoulder against the side. Once the wheel was off the ground the pin slipped in easily and Squeaks gave out a cheer. "Atta fella!"

"That did it," said Rusty. "Good work."

Powder Keg moved to the other side as a shout rang out from the next team, "Hey, Rusty, can we borrow your Negro?"

"Screw yourself, Pedro," Rusty called back.

"Aw, come on," said a small smiling man in a stained fedora and tight shirt. "You can haf two of ours for *heem*."

"Powder stays with me," came a new voice.

It sounded like it must be Buddy, but I didn't know for sure until Squeaks let out with a cackle. "Hey, gorgeous, what're you doing after the race?"

Walking straight toward us was the nastiest looking old Roman I ever hope to see. He had on a rat's nest of a dark wig and a rumpled white toga not half long enough to hide his hairy legs and knobby knees. With his face coated in white and his eyes outlined in tar, he made for a downright comical sight.

"What're you staring at?" he said to me. "Never seen a charioteer before?"

"Whoa, Buddy," said Rusty, "Where should we send the flowers?"

"Hey, pretty mama!" shouted Pedro again from the neighboring rig.

"All right, y'all have your fun," Buddy spat. "How're things here. You got things set?"

Rusty told him about the problem with the blocks, and we were all trying to describe it that we hardly noticed a horse bearing down on us at full gallop.

She stopped before us on a dime, snorting and stomping and about as lathered up as her rider. Pint-sized Delmer Burr sat high up in the saddle bristling with anger. "Goddamn it, Ardale! Where the shit's the rest of your team?"

Buddy brushed some wig hairs out of his face and managed an innocent smile. "I hear she's on her way," he said. "Should arrive any minute."

Burr stretched up as high as he could in his stirrups and looked off in both directions, then plopped back down. "Well, you get those nags cinched up and ready to roll, hear me? Mr. Eason says we'll get started as soon as we see some sun."

I hadn't paid much attention to the sky before he mentioned it, but the grayish light was falling softly through the haze.

"You got it, cap'n," snapped Buddy, touching his forehead in a sort of mock salute. Delmer Burr gave his mount a jab with his heels and slapped his reins. "Hee-yahhh!"

As I watched him ride off, Rusty sidled up to Buddy. "Someone ought to remind that bastard about manners."

"He wouldn't dare talk to a feller like that out on the trail," agreed Squeaks.

"How long you been in America, Irish?" said the old horse soldier.

"Eleven months now, or near-about."

"Well, things ain't what they used to be 'on the trail.' Hell, things never were much how folks say."

"He's got a funny accent," said Rusty. "Where d'you think he got it?"

"Boston, maybe."

Rusty looked mixed up. "They make movies in Boston?"

"No," answered Buddy. "Boston's where nephews come from."

Squeaks was still sulking. "All I know is there should be laws against a half-pint squirt like him talking that way to a war hero."

"No one's putting a spur under my bedroll today, Irish," said Buddy.

Whatever misgivings I had were forgotten with the sound of a sudden, high-pitched squeal. "Grandpa!" shouted a little boy barreling full-speed into Buddy's bare legs.

The old soldier lifted him up and swung him around a time or two before putting him down for a hug. "Hey, Pirate, how you doin' today?"

The boy stared at Buddy's painted face a moment. "Is it Halloween, Grandpa?"

"Nah, that's just a little Hollywood dirt, that's all. Washes off real easy." Buddy gave the boy a stern look. "Now Pirate, have you been growin' again?"

"No."

"Come here and let me take a measure." He pulled the boy straight against his side and held a palm on the kid's tousled hair. "Lord, lookee there. You done too growed on me! You're a good two inches taller."

The boy squirmed with pleasure.

"Now, you know the deal. You can only get another inch or so taller and then you're gonna have to go out and look for work. You're goin' to have to cook your own food, and do your wash."

The boy's smooth grin was giving way to a fretted brow, but Buddy kept going.

"How you gonna pay for that fancy automobile, Pirate?"

The boy's fear became a shy grin as he realized he was just being joshed. "Grandpa," he giggled, "you know I don't have no car."

"You don't? Give me a dime and I'll let you drive my chariot."

"I don't have no money."

"Okay, you can have one ride on account. Go on. Just don't take her far," said Buddy, sending the boy off with a push on his bottom. We watched him climb up and roll into the bed before dashing up see through the front.

An attractive young woman in blue jeans and a wool shirt had stepped up out of nowhere. She was holding the reins of a tall, shiny-coated bay. "Hi, Papa," said the girl.

Buddy broke into a bigger smile. "There's my darlin' lady," he said. He burst forward past the newcomer to get straight to the horse. "That's my beautiful Polly, that's my girl. How you doing, hmm? Feelin' like a little race maybe?"

"Like this, Grandpa?" called out the boy, pretending to slap the reins against the rails.

"That's right, Pirate, that's how it's done."

"I gave her a good warm-up," said the freckle-faced blonde. She appeared a little older than me but she sure caught my attention. I never could resist the bangs and the spunk of a good-looking tomboy.

"How you been, Lace?" asked Squeaks softly.

"I been okay, Squeaks."

"Lacey, this here's Grover, from Missouri."

"Howdy."

"Pleased to meet you."

"Grover's the new man."

She smiled and then looked in the distance to Rusty. "Hey, Rusty, think you and I can have a word?"

"Sure thing."

She called up to her boy, "Stay here with Grandpa, hear me? Mommy'll be right back."

Her son was far too busy to answer. He was clearly in the middle of fending off an Indian attack.

Buddy was off in his own world as well, making hard swipes through his horse's coat with a currycomb. When he got down toward her belly, I could hear a patter of sand falling on the track.

"She been for a run?" I asked.

"Lacey rides her along the beach for me. It's good for her legs."

"You must be proud of her."

Buddy grinned. "Oh, even as a filly you could tell she was special."

"I meant your daughter."

"Lacey? Oh, yeah, sure. Like her mom."

I was rubbing the mare's muscular jaw. She really was a handsome animal—fifteen hands tall, I figured, with intelligent eyes and a reddish-brown coat that glistened with health. "You raised her from a filly?"

"I might have known her father. He was the smartest animal I ever knew. In the army, I had any number of service horses. Mostly the best the country had to offer. When I got promoted, they give me my pick. I had my eye on this hot-blooded sorrel named Getty— short for Gettysburg. Man, that Getty was a fine animal. I took good care of that solder. I'd have brought him back with me except he was shot out from under me one day. I looked up his breeder, and got to know him. Turned out he had another fine chestnut filly, offspring of old Getty's father. I told this breeder I was about to be getting my discharge. I wanted him to let me know if that chestnut filly ever had a foal of her own. Old Polly here. Only thing I ever got out of all those years in uniform."

"If you don't mind my asking, what made you leave the service?"

"There's no honor left in war now. They got *iron* horses. The cavalry—that was just something they sent out ahead to test the enemy's strength. It's not right. Whatever people like that are fighting for, it's worth the life of a good horse."

"That's a good name. Polly."

"Yeah. I named her for Polidoxus—queen of the racehorses."

The name was unusual and I did not want to forget it. So I scribbled it in the back of Mrs. Addison's autograph book. Later I looked it up in an encyclopedia and found it was a famous racehorse in the days of the old Roman Empire. Polidoxus was celebrated far and wide for her victories in the coliseum. Ancient peoples valued strength in horses then, and thoroughbreds were imported from every part of the empire to compete in the games. Horses that proved their speed and endurance were almost worshipped. Not too long ago some archeologists dug up a mosaic tablet in North Africa. It had writing on it they said, "Whether you win or lose, we love you, Polidoxus!"

Now I knew what people were saying earlier about Buddy's "ace in the hole." Polly wasn't just for show or luck. She was strong and trained to run in sand. Buddy must have been counting all along on there being a race. And with Polly at the head of the team he was going to see to it that he took home that purse.

***

Things grew quiet once Lacey and the boy were gone. We were able to get back to what we were doing. Squeaks hung the harness around Polly's neck, and when I looked over he was lost in thought, gazing into space. "Hey, Buddy," he called, "you think Miss Barbara LaMarr might be up in the stands today?"

"Could be. I hear every actor in town got a personal invite."

"You know what I'm thinkin'? I'm thinkin' that all I need is someone to introduce us. That's all—a wee little introduction. After that, it'll be Barbara and me, me and Barbara, arm in arm." He gripped Polly's large head and pulled it to him by the chinstraps. He planted a kiss right there on the smooth spot between those dark eyes. "Ah, Miss LaMarr," he swooned, "you are the sweetest vision ever to walk on God's green *Arth*."

"Irish," chided Rusty Bigelow. "You goin' on about that damn actress again?"

"There's none in the world more wonderful, nor more high-toned."

"Try a dog whistle," cracked Rusty.

Squeaks roused himself from his dreamy spell to look at Rusty. "What did Lacey want with you?"

"Oh, just a little advice, a little advice."

"Advice on what?"

"On raising boys, mainly. You know, boys without fathers."

Squeaks considered it a second. "And what makes you the expert on kids?"

"Well, you may not know this, Irish," he said slowly, "but I'm one myself." With that he sprang at the younger man, swung him around and knocked him over, letting out a holler or two before Squeaks shook him off and got free. The two men sat gasping for breaths and chuckling, which somehow made me feel better too. Even Powder Keg was grinning, sitting by himself near the spina, oiling straps.

"Oh, oh, here comes trouble," said Buddy as he walked up carrying a water bucket.

Rusty turned to squint off behind him. "Well, get a load of that!"

A lavender chariot had rounded the north rim of the track and was rattling toward us at a medium clip behind a team of all-black trotters. I knew at once whose car it was and who that statuesque figure at its reins had to be.

"You see who is it?" asked Rusty.

"Must be our 'X' movie star," said Squeaks. "Old Francis Bushman hisself, here to save the day."

"Watch how he handles his team," said Buddy. "If you want to learn about chariots, he's the one to ask. In Italy he didn't use no stunt double. No one could have done it better."

"I didn't think they'd allow such a thing," said Squeaks.

"Mayer encouraged him. From what I hear, he was hopin' Bushman would break his neck."

By then I could make out the rippling of his tanned forearms in the wind and the flapping of his wrist guards. His head sprouted two golden wings, held there by a strap across his forehead. Behind the defiant set of his eyes was a conquering warrior, ready to spit in the face of any foolhardy challenger.

"I heard he didn't even want this part," said Squeaks.

"He didn't like the idea of playing the heavy, that's for sure," said Buddy.

"He's too old to play lover-boys anymore," said Rusty.

"I heard he went to see Bill Hart," said Buddy. "Old William S. Hart was quite the cowpoke in his early days. He played Messala on Broadway for some years. He told Bushman he'd be nuts to turn it down. Said it was the best damn part in the picture."

"Hey, you men there, stop your yappin'!" bellowed a familiar voice. Delmer Burr was off a ways, raised up in his stirrups and acting like he was in command of the whole darn field. "Get that rig rolling, Ardale. You don't want the job, I got others that do!"

We just about had all the horses strapped in by then. Polly was in lead position on the left. When it came to those sharp turns, Buddy said, it was best to let Polly take most of the force and reassure the others.

"Any of you ever work with this other guy, this Novarro character?" asked Rusty.

"Not me," said Buddy.

"Me neither," said Squeaks. "But Grover here met him, didn't you?"

"Just for a moment."

"He let you use his toilet, right?"

"Yeah."

"So tell the boys what he was like."

"I don't know. Like most people. A little vain, a little shy. That's all I know."

Rusty scowled a bit. "I heard Valentino gave him a plaster mold of his dick."

"What?" gasped Squeaks.

"It's what I heard. Take it for what it's worth."

"All I know about him," said Buddy, "is the ladies fancy him. Over in Italy, they would throw their hankies and undergarments at him when he passed."

"I wouldn't mind the ladies pelting me with their undergarments," said Squeaks.

Rusty grinned. "You wouldn't look half so sweet in 'em!"

"One thing's certain, I won't be fighting him for the favors of Miss LaMarr!"

My face by then must have been as twisted as a pretzel. I couldn't grasp what Rusty and Squeaks were getting at. "Are you sayin' Mr. Novarro's one of them ... you now, *sissy guys?*"

Rusty gave a snort. "What do you think, Buddy? You think Novarro's one of them sissy guys?"

"Not no more, he ain't," said Buddy.

Now Squeaks looked puzzled. "What do you mean, Buddy?"

"I heard he got hisself caught in an all-boy bordello with Bill Haines. Louie B. 'bout tossed a shoe over it. Called him in before him. Said he wouldn't have the star of his expensive new religious picture mixed up in a sex scandal. The studio was stuck with Novarro, but I expect it'll be the last we hear of Billy Haines."

The whole notion of an all-boy bordello was so foreign to me then I didn't know what to think. I was still pondering it as we swung the rig around and Buddy took a big leap up into the bed. But he misjudged the height and cracked his shin so hard against the ledge that the sound came echoing back at us.

"Ow! Damn! Good Jesus!" he swore and more like it, bending over to rub his ankle. There was a trickle of blood down his leg and Buddy pulled a wadded kerchief from his toga to staunch the flow. "Who in blazes raised the damn carriage?"

"I thought she seemed a bit higher," said Rusty. "Maybe that's what was giving us the trouble."

Powder Keg was already on the move, bending low to investigate the underside. When he bobbed up again, he signaled for Rusty to have a look.

"Hey, Buddy," said Rusty after a second. "Powder Keg's right. They got blocks raisin' the axle three, four inches. Looks like it's all been shifted forward some, too. You can see the old holes."

"Watch that first step," shouted little Pedro from the next team, "it's a *keeller!*" Then he brayed and waved his fedora over his head.

Buddy paced around a bit to walk off the pain, then pulled himself together and tied off the wound. "I'm okay now. Nothing busted. Rusty, anyone say anything to you about alterations?"

"Hunh-uh."

Finally I felt I had to tell them what I knew. Even Squeaks was interested now in hearing about my talk with Bushman, especially in what he said about the metal frames being heavier and how the cars had to be brought up to speed.

Buddy nodded as if he had just made up his mind. "Well, that's another matter I'll have to take up with Mr. Louis B. Mayer next time we have a sit-down."

A commotion rose up in the bleachers on a chorus of gasps and a flurry of hurrahs. There was a rumble at the north entrance gate and out came perhaps the most impressive sight I'll ever live to see. A prancing team of four white Arabian show horses appeared pulling a peach-colored chariot decorated in silver fantasy creatures. The proud thoroughbreds were something to behold, with their manes braided in yellow tassels that bounced as they moved. Standing there at the reins behind them was my Mexican friend, Ramón Novarro, looking lean and fit in a vest of leather and his shoulders glistening with oil.

"All right, let's do what we came for," called Buddy as he heaved himself up into his rig. He gathered the reins and called out, "Come on, Polly!" as he handed the team just a taste of his leather.

My job was done for now, and I was aware of Ramón's chariot growing closer. I thought he saw me too and he steered his team at more of an angle toward me. I edged my way back to the spina. All I needed was for the other men to see him toss me a wink or a knowing wave and I'd never likely live it down. I walked faster and had just ducked through an open archway as Ramón went rolling past.

Two silhouetted figures stepped in to the doorway behind me, block my escape. Even without seeing their faces I knew them by their thin-brimmed hats. They were the spies from the livery yard, only now it was no secret what they wanted. The shorter of the men pulled a leather blackjack from his coat and they both started toward me. I was not going to take them on alone in the dark, so bolted to my rear and headed for the patch of daylight at the other side. The thugs wouldn't dare try anything in view of the crowds.

The sun had finally begun to break through the haze, and I ran squinting onto the track. I could tell the stands were nearly overflowing now, with people swirling about in shifting patterns as men with megaphones screamed for them to follow their directions.

I shaded my eyes to look back at the spina to see if I was being followed, and I must have kept backing up because I didn't see I was coming to a covered pit in the track. I felt my heel give way below me and I plummeted backward as if in slow motion, as helpless as a babe in freefall. All I could do was brace myself to hit the bottom with an *oomph*. But there was hardly any impact at all. I had been caught and gently lowered by a loving mother's unseen hand.

Then the ground began to pitch and roll, and I struggled to get my foot on something solid. In the confusion I heard a voice shout, "Watch it! Get off! Watch what you're doing!" A canvas tarp had broken my fall, and there was someone under it as mad as hell. "For Chrissakes, move your ass!"

A blurred vision rose over me and then moved closer. It was the face of a tending angel, her head fringed in the purest of white, radiating kindness and concern from her two loving eyes.

"Are you all right?" she asked. But I could not answer. I could do nothing but lie there, immobilized by a dream of no mortal understanding. Even in daylight, there were stars suspended in her eyes.

"Are you all right?" she asked again, alarmed at my silence.

"I think so."

The pushing from below ended and I slipped farther until I rested on solid ground.

"Why'n't you watch where you're stepping?" barked a man who was suddenly there in the pit next to me. He straightened out his oatmeal-colored safari vest with its various pockets and stitched cartridge loops, looking quite annoyed with me.

"I'm sorry. I didn't see anything until … " I began, then stopped as I saw the man's eyes fill with awe. He saw it too! That vision of an angel that hovered over me.

"Lucky thing," he told her, "I think he missed the camera."

By then I knew I had fallen in a dugged pit, just wide enough for a man and a hand-cranked camera.

"I thought I knew all of the pitfalls in Hollywood," said the angel with a twinkle of a laugh. "You found a new one."

She sat a lady's white bonnet on her head and fastened it with a purple ribbon. I still couldn't be sure of much, but I could see was definitely real and mortal. She had to have been an extra in the stands.

I was a practiced hand at hoisting myself out of holes by then, and this one was no special challenge. I hopped up and stood dusting the dirt from my jeans as the lady asked again of I was all right. "Oh, yes. Take more than a little fall to hurt me." I apologized to the cameraman for falling on him.

"You really have to stay alert on a set," she told me. "You never know what sort's under foot."

"Yes, ma'am." She was shorter than me by a head, I guessed, and maybe a year or so older. Some men might have said her forehead was too tall, or her sky-blue eyes a bit close-set. But none of that mattered to me at all. She was my angel and my protector, and she could not have been more perfect.

"Are you new?" she asked.

"Ma'am?"

She offered me a perfect porcelain hand. "Please, call me Norma. Are you new to picture-making?"

"I'm sorry. I feel like I'm speaking to an angel."

She reared back and her magical eyes glittered. "Well, how disappointed you will be," she said.

"You're the most beautiful girl I ever saw."

"Oh, then you *are* new." She chuckled. "What's your name?"

The gods must have gone green with envy. "It's Grover, ma'am. I'm Grover."

"Well, Grover, keep your eyes opened and you will see plenty of girls here prettier than I."

"You don't have to worry about them."

"I don't. I'll tell you a secret. Ever hear the story of the tortoise and the hare?" She almost whispered the last, and gave a small wink that snatched my breath away.

Every school child knew the fable about how "slow and steady wins the race." I always found it hard to swallow. Without thinking I blurted out, "Where I'm from, that's a lie farmers tell their sons so they don't grow up expecting more."

Norma stared back and did not react, but I could tell she was caught off guard. Then the wall fell and she broke into a toothy grin and her pale blue eyes split like a bag of precious gems. "My, you're a smart boy, aren't you?" she said. "Where are you from?"

"Missouri."

"And where are you supposed to be?"

I told her I was working on one of the teams, and when I got a break I'd like to come and sit with her a while.

"With me?"

"You aren't … here with someone?"

"I'm not married, no."

"Maybe I could take you out dancing, or to a show?"

"We'll see," she said. "I've been given a seat—up in the stands, I'm afraid."

"I'll find you."

"Oh, no. Don't—don't get in any trouble on my account. Maybe I'll send for you. How would that be?"

"Promise?"

"Of course. Grover, I think you're a cheery fellow. And remember to look before you step. Ta-ta."

Cheery fellow. I remember the words she used, because it was the only time anyone ever talked to me like that. It meant a lot, too, coming from my guardian angel.

After the adventure with Molly from Raleigh, I should have gone out of my way not to get mixed up with another Hollywood girl. But Norma was a different breed. She seemed filled with something a lot … more. I didn't know what it was precisely, but I made up my mind right then that I would do whatever it took to find out.

CHAPTER EIGHT

They Call Me Runaway

"Well, here comes the gentleman from Missouri," Buddy called to the others when he saw me hurrying down the track. He was standing in his chariot, keeping hold of the hand brake.

"Sorry. Call of nature," I said.

"We thought you might have grabbed hold of another runaway rig," grumbled Rusty up at Polly's nose straps.

"What're we waiting on?"

"Just waitin' to be waitin'," said Buddy. "Rusty, show old 'Runaway' here what to do."

"Sure enough," responded the redhead. He didn't appear to be in a mood to taunt me just now.

The horses sensed that something was about to begin, judging by the way they were rearing and acting up. It's foolish to think a horse can ever be completely tamed. When it comes down to it, no amount of training can change its basic nature. A horse will always be unpredictable. When a certain nervousness builds and mental pressures mount, all their training goes out the window and animal instinct kicks in. These horses were bred as runners and they hated being yoked. Some stomped and bucked and could hardly be held in place. A few jumped high enough to get their hooves stuck through their harness straps. It was all that us wranglers could do to just keep them poised and ready for the race.

As Buddy predicted, Polly had a calming influence on the others, so we had it better than most. Rusty held firm to Polly's nose straps and massaged along the underside of her jaw. My job was to watch over the outside pacers, and Squeaks and Powder Keg were around back, steadying the rig until Buddy got the signal to go.

Besides us there were just four chariots on the track now. Squeaks said it was because all they were shooting was some close-up action and what were called "inserts." All they wanted was for the teams to drive down the track and come racing up past the bleacher crowds. Later on they would get all twelve teams on the track and shoot the long shots. But they wanted to give it a little more time first for the last of the morning fog to burn off.

The burly driver closest to us was a stranger to me. He was the one they called "The Greek," and he had been with the production in Italy. Then there was Fisher, the whip man who had given me such a bad time at breakfast. He was barely recognizable now under a dark wig and stuffed into some sort of broadly stitched Roman get-up with a studded leather belt. Ramón Novarro's matched whites were easy enough to spot, though I was surprised to see it was not Ramón holding the reins. One of the stunt drivers was standing in for him and doing his best to manage the four spirited stallions.

Finally there was Francis X. Bushman in his winged helmet, looking as commanding as ever. His falcon eyes stared steadily ahead as a red centurion's robe lapped his chest. When his four black Arabians grew unsettled and began to buck and nervously stomp their hooves, however, he swore aloud at them and cursed his tenders for losing control.

While we waited, Rusty looked over at me. "Did you hear what the Boy Wonder wanted?"

"Who?"

"Thalberg. Our brilliant producer."

I knew a little about Irving Thalberg, I guess, enough to know he was dubbed the Boy Wonder because he was overseeing movie-making when he was still barely out of his teens. When he reached his mid-twenties he produced a box office hit for Universal called "The Hunchback of Notre Dame," insisting on Lon Chaney as the lead.

Thalberg had come by on a tour of the track while I was gone. He was all in a tizzy about the fog, demanding that his assistants bring in some wind machines to blow it all away. The men got quite a kick out of it.

"That's your all-American Boy Wonder, for ya," yelled the young Irishman from around back. "Just power up some fans and blow the mist back to Catalina."

Buddy chuckled at that. "Well, anyway, that's what passes for brains in this outfit."

A whistle sounded in the distance and was answered by another. Then a nearby field assistant fumbled with a cord around his neck and stuck a silver whistle to his lips. The piercing blast caught the horses by surprise and they lapsed into a new frenzy of jitters.

Up charged little Delmer Burr, whipping his hat from side to side against his mount. "Take your positions! Charioteers! Take your position!" He circled around and pulled his mount up short to look behind. More whistles were heard along the entire length of the arena.

Bushman unhooked his robe and pulled it from his sculpted shoulders. He tossed it to a helper, then tugged at his helmet to make sure it was secure.

A group of men hurried out on foot front the spina, headed toward the chariots. There was Novarro at the center of the pack, his eyes outlined in pitch. He resembled a scrappy boxer approaching the ring for a final bout as he took the reins from his stand-in and sprang up in the chariot rig.

He and Bushman traded nods.

"On your marks, fellows," shouted a new voice. There stood the suntanned cowboy with the oversized Stetson from the cattle calls. Now I knew him as B. Reeves Eason, or "Breezy," as the men liked to say. He was the second-unit director, which meant he was personally directing the action sequences like the chariot race and any stunts involving the horses.

"Wranglers, listen up!" he shouted. "Now when I give the signal, you gotta clear the tracks. Everyone understand me? *Comprende?*"

Heads were nodding all over the track, whether they had heard what he said or not. "Charioteers! Here's what we need from you. Wait for my signal. You proceed down the backstretch here, heading south …" he pointed and waited until he saw more nods of understanding, then repeated himself—"south! Get your speed up, understand, and when you get around the curve, you give 'em all you got.

"Continue up the track, in front of the stands. Don't stop, for God's sake. And keep your eyes on your teams. There'll be lots of cameras trained on you and they'll see everything you do. Everyone got it? Any questions?" He waited a second, then nodded to one of his assistants.

"Okay, men, get ready," he shouted after a pause. "Remember, this is supposed to be the end of the big race. I want to see some pain."

I learned later that Breezy had been going through his own pain, the worst kind of pain that can befall a man. He got his start in the business as a Western star at Universal, but soon found he preferred life behind the camera. He was raising his little boy to follow in his celebrated footsteps, and by the tender age of six, B. Reeves Eason, Jr. had made dozens of movies and was given top billing on posters as "Universal's Littlest Cowboy." Both Breezy and his son were big favorites with Hollywood's small cowboy-actor community.

Then one day while shooting a Harry Carey movie, "Universal's Littlest Cowboy" got run over by a truck. Harry Carey sat vigil by his sickbed, praying for a whole day nonstop before the boy succumbed. Breezy couldn't quite accept his son's passing, and Hollywood had waited nearly four years for him to return. When he was offered "Ben-Hur," he accepted and was finally getting back to work. It couldn't have been an easy choice for him. And "Ben-Hur" seemed to present enough challenges for even the toughest of men.

"All right, this is it! Wranglers, clear out! Drivers, get ready …"

He stared off to the top of the spina and a distant spot high up in the grandstand. There was some delay and the horses were getting hopped up on all the tension in the air. They stomped and bowed their necks and sent their shaggy manes flapping to and fro. Buddy held tight to his hand brake and leaned forward to whisper something to Polly.

Then I caught a speck of movement in the stands and a yellow flag dropped and Breezy fired off a gun. There was a roar from the onlookers and all four drivers gave out a shout and snapped their reins, "Hee-yaw!"

Squeaks and I dropped the bridles and hopped away as the chariot wheels woke in their cradles and lurched ahead with a clatter. Dirt and sand rained down from every direction, and I squeezed my eyes and held my breath. Through the din I heard Delmer Burr gallop after the teams.

When I deemed it safe to open my eyes, I saw the chariots reach the southern end and vanish in the turn.

"Good job, men!" hollered Breezy, adding as a softer aside, "We're off to the races."

A roar of excitement rose from the crowds when the chariots appeared. Many of the wranglers dropped everything and ran off through the spina to watch the action. The memory of getting cornered inside there by the pair of thugs made me decide to stay put. I was safer where I was. Besides, it was just the first shot of a long race. Those of us left behind pulled out tobacco pouches or fired up tailor-mades to enjoy the peace before the teamsters returned.

That didn't take long. The chariots reappeared one by one at the northern bend, returning in a brisk trot to their starting point.

As soon as Buddy pulled to a stop, Rusty grabbed for Polly's chin-strap. "How'd it handle?" he asked.

"Felt a bit flighty to me. ... Grover, have a look at the mouth bit on that buckskin, would you?" Then he turned back to Rusty and Squeaks. "She just isn't holding the track like she did."

"Is it safe?"

Buddy shrugged. "Have Powder Keg check underneath, will you? Something's not right."

I watched the colored man dive under the wheel and disappear, and took the opportunity to whisper to Squeaks, "You sure he can't hear?"

"What do you mean?"

"I could swear he was listening to us."

"You're imagining it. He's just a smart fella and knows what's going on."

Powder Keg straightened up, shaking his head. He could find nothing wrong.

"Okay, men, stand by," called Breezy Eason. This time he was sitting on a platform high over the edge rail. He was holding a small megaphone and I smiled because it made a funny sight, that dude in a Stetson with a megaphone—like a college crooner at a square dance. "Stand by. They're getting set up for another run."

Curious stragglers were peeking from the spina. Some were low-grade studio people of some sort, but others were clearly extras that came down from the stands to talk to movie stars.

A sporty-looking man in a tweed jacket and brown hat broke out of the pack to hurry toward Novarro's rig. When he got shooed away there by Ramón's handlers, he ambled toward us. "Hi, guys. Fitzhugh Lewis, Hollywood Daily Citizen. How 'bout some words for our readers?"

"Beat it, Fritz," snapped Rusty.

"Well, excuse me, Mr. Thalberg," said the reporter. "Still a free press in this country, last I heard." Then he looked at me. "What about you?"

"Me?"

"Like to see your name in print?"

"No, thanks."

"Mr. Lewis!" called a voice from the spina. A sweaty-looking man in a business suit stopped his waving to come over in a hurry. The reporter did not appear concerned. He positioned his stub of a pencil above a notepad and looked at me. "What do you think of the trend toward Latin lovers? You think they're better at it than you and me?"

"Better at what?"

"What about this Novarro kid? He the new Valentino?"

"Mr. Lewis!" called the sweaty man, hurling himself between us. "I'm afraid this area is out-of-bounds to our friends from the press. You'll have a chance to talk to people later, I promise you." He wrapped his arm around the reporter's shoulder and began urging him away just as Delmer Burr rode up in a gallop and stood balancing in his saddle for a word with Breezy Eason.

"Hey, who's the fellah talking with Breezy?" asked the writer.

"That's just a new assistant," said the sweaty man.

"His name's not Burr, is it? Elmer, Delroy, something like that?"

"I couldn't say. Now if you'll just come along—"

"His name's Delmer Burr," called Rusty.

"That's it! Delmer Burr!" said the newsman.

"What do you know about him?"

"Could be a story in it, that's what I know. He's the guy they kicked off the set of 'Covered Wagon.' Can I have a talk—?"

"Yes, but not now. Later," insisted the studio man, making a big show of his exasperation. "We'll give you biographies, photos, anything you want. Now, I have to insist, please, come, come."

Buddy watched the two men leave the track and turned sharply on Rusty. "Don't you know better than to do a thing like that?"

"What do you mean?"

"Talking to the press! He sticks your name in some story the studio don't like, you'll never get any more work in this town."

"But I was sure I knew that name. Don't you recall? Delmer Burr. I just couldn't place it. He was the A.D. that got canned for shoving that horse off a cliff."

"What's this?" asked Squeaks.

Rusty looked around and waited for us so to come close so no one could overhear. "It was off in the prairies somewhere, out in Utah or something. They were shooting 'The Covered Wagon' for Paramount. Delmer Burr was an untried A.D.."

"What did he do to the *harse,* Rusty?" asked Squeaks.

"Well, from what I recall—you recollect the scene where that horse takes a tumble off a cliff? It made people want to gag, but most folks thought it was a fake. Well, this fellow says he was working on the set that day, and he said this Delmer Burr wanted it to be realistic, and he paid for some rancher's horse just to shove it over. Healthy one, too, is what I heard."

"You mean he killed it?" I asked.

"Didn't do it no favor."

The Irishman looked outraged. "What's wrong with the son of a—?"

"Gotta have a rat in your wiring to do a bum thing like that," nodded Buddy.

"Why would this studio give a job to a guy like that?"

"Maybe they didn't know," I said.

"Somebody knew," said Rusty. "They took him anyway."

"Look," said Buddy, "no one knows nothin' for sure. We should find out before we go making any charges."

Before I could stop myself I had blurted out, "I know a guy worked on that movie 'The Covered Wagon.' "

Everyone stopped to stare at me. "What guy?" asked Buddy.

"Moore the Merrier."

"Freddie?"

"He told me himself. Said he had worked on 'The Covered Wagon.' He thought maybe Buddy had too."

"Nah," said Buddy. "They was going off on location for maybe six months. No way I could've managed that."

"It wouldn't hurt to find out," said Rusty. "Runaway, you got to go and see what more he'll say."

"But don't tip him off," said Buddy. "He's part of that union bunch now. They're lookin' for something like to hold over the studio."

I was by no means sure I could do what they were asking, but it made me feel good to be asked. There was no denying I was part of Buddy's team now. For the first time since I got to California, I felt like I belonged somewhere.

***

When Delmer Burr finished what he had to say, B. Reeves Eason blew his whistle and held up his megaphone.

"Men, listen! Okay, we got to do some traveling shots while we got the sun. They're bringing up a camera car, and what we need from you is to line up your wagons in a row. We're goin' to do the same run as before. But this time you'll have the camera riding alongside you. Okay? Let's move 'em!"

Buddy nodded to Powder Keg and cracked his reins gently, and Squeaks and me walked the team into position.

The camera car was nothing but an open-topped Ford with two upright tripods bolted to the floorboard. The driver waited for the charioteers to get started, then kicked the Ford into gear and took off after them. The car rolled up next to Buddy's rig first, then up the line to the others. The two cameramen stood shoulder-to-shoulder, cranking their handles and trying to keep their cheeks from bouncing too far from their eyepieces.

Nothing held us up between runs any more. Each time the charioteers returned they went back to their starting positions and got ready to go again. From time to time there'd be a break for the cameraman to load up a new canister. By 11 o'clock or so we were all pretty weary of the routine.

The spectators were restless, too, and when they tried to steal down onto the track, the studio cops would gather them up like straying chicks and herd them back to the bleachers.

After one run, Delmer Burr hopped up on the fence to lay into the drivers about holding back. He said the teams weren't running full out, and that people were starting to ask when the real race would begin. "So here's what I'm going to do, men," said Burr. "I got a couple pints of apple cider, and I'm willin' to turn them over to the driver who gets back here first." He wanted us to know he wasn't talking of plain old apple cider, either, but the kind of "guaranteed eighty-proof" juice cooked up for those who knew the difference.

The drivers didn't think much of his offer. It wasn't the big purse they were hoping for, and they didn't like being told they weren't doing their best. Rusty said it offended him that Burr was offering them a bribe to drive faster than was safe.

It was Squeaks, though, who actually hollered out when Burr was finished talking. "How 'bout a night in a Pasadena whorehouse?" he called. I don't think he meant it as a joke at all, but everybody had a good laugh just the same, and it eased the tension.

"Oh, oh. Here comes Santa Claus," said Rusty.

That was the first time I paid any notice to that mysterious Italian. I might have given him a sideways glance or two, but I never stopped to wonder about him. He was attached to Fisher's chariot team, and he looked sort of foreign with his head shaved high around the ears. He was tall and thin, dressed in a long black duster. The way he walked was odd, as well. He just glided over the earth without heft or bounce, like some graveyard apparition out of a bad dime novel.

"Who is he?" I asked.

Buddy said he was just a poor Italian the company had brought back with them from Rome. He had a useful knack for tending the horses, and could soothe them down quick in a panic. He spoke almost no English, but when he tried, he had an accent so thick you could stand on it. When someone asked him what he did for a living back home he said, "Selling clothes." The men thought he said *Santa Claus*. After that, he was just Santa Claus to them.

For some reason I saw this Santa as another sort of omen—like a prophet sent to warn the righteous to mend their ways. Mark it down to a fear of foreigners or some type of premonition because I don't care. All I know is that it wasn't long after that sighting of Santa Claus that we had our first serious accident of the day, and I got a hint of what I was in for.

CHAPTER NINE

Pain and Pageantry

From where we stood the crackup sounded none too serious—just a heavy crunch and a splintering of wood, as if someone dropped a crate off the back of a truck. But it was met by a collective gasp of the crowd that was as blood-curdling as any shriek ever heard.

Everything froze for an instant as we listened, and then a couple of wranglers tossed their cigarettes aside and went running down the track. Others followed, and I joined a group taking the shortcut through the spina.

A bulge of bodies and wood lay about halfway to the stands. Onlookers were on their feet and gathering at the rail, or standing on a bench to have a better view. A dozen or so workers were struggling to right a wheelless chariot and free the fallen horses. Two animals had managed to get on their feet and seemed okay. Two more lay motionless where they fell, visibly panting and probably in shock.

It wasn't Buddy's car. That's the first thing I looked for. The old cavalryman stood waiting in his chariot farther up the track beside two other rigs. The team of four whites was easy enough to spot, meaning that Ramón was safe, and even at a distance there was no mistaking the ramrod-straight bearing of Francis X. Bushman. A little farther ahead, the Greek had stopped his team and was watching the rescue efforts.

That left Fisher, the whip man, unaccounted for. Buddy must have realized it at the same time I did, because he tied off his reins and hopped to the ground to come sprinting back toward the pileup.

A Roman soldier with a spear stepped up next to me. "You see what happened?" he asked.

"Charioteer must have hit a dip or something," I said. "Took a bounce and flipped."

Then I heard heavy panting and Rusty Bigelow came up behind me. "Who—?" he started, then stopped to take a few rapid breaths. "Who is it?"

"Must be Fisher," I told him.

With that he was off again, hurrying to the site in a succession of stiff-legged skips and hops.

A bald man in a dark suit hustled his way through the crowd holding up a black bag. As he pulled out a stethoscope I saw Fisher sprawled there in the sand. I remembered how he looked when he fell dead that morning, and this time he sure wasn't play-acting.

The doctor was still feeling for a pulse when the body twitched and Fisher's head rose weakly, wobbling from side to side. The men nearest straightened up at once and broke into grins, looking much relieved. "He's all right," mumbled the Roman soldier next to me, then strolled away carrying his spear on his shoulder like a fishing pole.

In another minute, two men were helping the driver to his feet. They and let him stand there on his own, and he raised an arm to the crowd and gave a solid rodeo wave. There was a new round of cheering and a smattering of applause before they all went back to their usual chatter.

Buddy had pushed his way through to lay a hand on Fisher's shoulder. The two men exchanged private words, and I saw Buddy smile and nod as he glanced around anxiously.

A large panel opened in the wall below the stands, and men came out with blankets to cover the horses. Next they hooked chains to the wrecked chariot and used a team of mules to drag it off the track.

Buddy had walked away from Fisher to confront a man in a brown business suit watching from the passageway. Buddy appeared to be doing all the talking, gesturing angrily this way and that as the businessman listened. After a minute, he heard all he cared to, nodded once, and turned to get away.

"All right," boomed a hollow-sounding voice from above us on the spina. I had to step out to see it was a man standing on an outcrop, pointing a large megaphone out toward the bleachers. "The driver's all right, ladies and gentlemen," came his voice. "These men are professionals, I can assure you of that."

Fisher hobbled his way off, and even the megaphone man sounded relieved. "How about a hand for our courageous stunt drivers!" he hollered, then waited for the cheers to die off.

He must have thought everyone already knew him, because he didn't bother to introduce himself. All I can say is that he wore a gray cap and a brown jacket with baggy puttees tucked into his boots. He lifted the funnel back to his mouth. "You extras, please return to your places. Everything's going as planned, folks. That's it for today's stunts.

"Now I want to introduce you all to the man in charge. No, not God," he joked, waiting for a laugh that didn't come. "But close. He comes close, I can promise you that. He'll be calling the shots from here out. Please give a hand to the director of M-G-M's grand new 'Ben-Hur' show. He's the man who helped Doug Fairbanks buckle his swash as 'Son of Zorro,' then sent him off with those three musketeers. I give you Hollywood's foremost director of romantic adventures … Mr. Fred Niblo!"

There was enthusiastic applause from the crowd as a man stepped up to take the megaphone. He was a large man with a round face and a manly brow, and he was wearing a tailored safari jacket and brown trousers with alligator boots. With his free hand he held up a carved wooden pipe to signal to the crowd.

"Hello, everyone. Thank you for your part in all this today. This is very exciting. I'm sure it will be remembered as the biggest picture ever produced. And it's being made right here at our own glorious Hollywood studio."

He took a thoughtful puff on his pipe and let the smoke curl free. "You won't see any more camera cars on the tracks. We don't want to spoil this once-in-a-lifetime spectacle. All of us are about to witness an event that hasn't been seen for two thousand years—a Roman chariot race." He waited as another round of cheers worked its way through the stands.

Without so much as raising one of his fancy, alligator-skin boots, Fred Niblo seemed to prance before that audience like an eager thoroughbred. Later I read what I could find written about him. These days he fancied himself more of an outdoorsman and an adventurer than a movie director. But he started out on the New York stage, making a name for himself on Broadway. He became a director and married Josephine Cohan, the singing sister of song-and-dance man George M. Cohan. Together he and Josephine traveled to Africa, filming his expeditions and turning them into travelogues on the vaudeville circuit.

When Josephine took sick and died, Niblo married an English actress named Enid Bennett, who encouraged his interest in making movies. He directed her in a few misfires before striking gold with those back-to-back Fairbanks hits mentioned in his introduction. Niblo followed them with "Blood and Sand," a bullfighter romance starring Rudolph Valentino. Then he did what others in Hollywood did when success went to their head—he formed his own picture company. He had a contract with the Metro studio to distribute his films. But business was not his strong suit, and he was on the verge of bankruptcy when Irving Thalberg phoned to talk to him about taking over the troubled "Ben-Hur" production in Italy.

The view from an executive office at the new M-G-M studio would have tempted any maverick director. But Niblo knew the Italian production was in utter shambles. He must have seen that taking on "Ben-Hur" was the Hollywood equivalent of standing before a charging rhino with a jammed rifle.

In the end, as he told reporters, it wasn't the prestige of the project that swayed him as much as the challenge. Now Niblo had one thing more in common with both the mightiest of executives and the lowliest of studio hacks drawn to Culver City that day: None of them could permit "Ben-Hur" to fail.

***

"Before going on with the race," Niblo shouted in his megaphone, "Mr. Mayer and Mr. Thalberg have arranged for a grand entertainment for us all." The director turned to an assistant who was getting a quick update from aides. "Are they ready?" he asked into the megaphone, then realized he didn't need to be heard, and puffed his pipe instead.

When he got an assured nod from his man, he turned to address the crowd. "*Cit-i-zens of Rome,*" he announced grandly, hammering each syllable like a tent stake at the big top. "It is our *honor* ... to present the esteemed *senators of Rome* ... and their wives!"

Horns blared from midway up the stands. Three men in circus tunics stood hidden in the shadows of a canopy, blow their tapered trumpets. Near them a gate opened in a tunnel-like passage and figures began to emerge from the darkness.

Portly men in festive robes and folded togas appeared wearing laurel leaf crowns. Respectable older ladies in jeweled dresses and elaborate headgear came accompanied by their entourage of slave girls and bare-chested Negroes with scimitars. One couple held fast to the leashes of tall, immaculate dogs, and another balanced colorful parrots on their outstretched arms.

One by one or two by two they made their way up the steps to special boxes, and when the last had cleared the gate, Niblo conferred again with his cohorts and lifted his megaphone. "Now welcome with us, citizens of Rome, the honored guests of the emperor. ... The royal military generals *of all the empire!*"

A new line of costumed figures was waiting at the tunnel. I could see breastplates bobbing and helmets glistening, but when I looked for a better place to stand I spotted Squeaks off by himself in a recessed alcove.

"Fisher's going to be all right," I said as I joined him there.

"But would you take a look at that now," he said, nodding down at the track to the site of the wreck.

While we had been watching what was happening in the stands, a number of studio hands planted poles into metal discs on the ground and were now hard at work wrapping bolts of drapery around the poles. Once they were finished, the fallen horses would effectively be blocked from view.

Two new trumpet blasts sounded, and Fred Niblo held up his megaphone to shout so hard I thought he might go hoarse: "Citizens of Rome! *All hail ... our emperor!*"

Now the crowd rose as one to its feet at the honor of it all. The seated senators and military officers stood again to see the royal entryway. Standing under the arch was a short, rounded figure in a regal toga and sporting a golden crown. He absolutely beamed, smiling at the masses through thick glasses with what appeared to be tortoise-shell frames. I took it as a stab at humor, a little joke staged for our amusement.

"Look, they got some burlesque clown playing the emperor," I told Squeaks.

"I'd laugh," he said, "but that's the man will be signing our checks at the end of the day. ... That's Mr. Louis B. Mayer."

The M-G-M president gave a shy, upraised palm to all his make-be-lieve senators and military generals. Then two young women took him by the elbows and lead him to his private stall.

Niblo was waving that megaphone around again. "And now ... Ladies and gentlemen of Rome!" he screamed. "The Antioch Coliseum is pleased to present ... the heroes of all the empire ... the mighty warriors and their champion racers ... in M-G-M's grand *parade of the charioteers!*"

A cacophony of trumpet blasts rang out from the south end. A half-dozen men in red robes stood in a row with long, thin horns at their lips. Under them was the gate from the livery stables, and in the opening an assembled throng stood in formation.

In that moment of anticipation before anyone could move, a hushed silence fell over everything. And suddenly there was a clatter of metal, and all eyes swiveled to the circle of curtains on the track. Out plodded two teams of mules dragging heavy lengths of chain. They were driven by large men with whips who whistled and shouted at the mules to hurry along. A wave of snickering rippled through the stands, followed by jeers and laughter. It was as though the mule-drivers were being greeted as the studio's big spectacle.

A man in the stands waved a yellow banner that was answered by another yellow streamer to the south. There sounded a new blast of bugles and a rumbling gargle of drums. A carpet was unrolled from the south gate and the hemorrhaging of marchers began. Every idle cowpoke and would-be starlet in Hollywood had apparently moved heaven and earth to be part of the parade.

Two lines of runners emerged dressed like Olympics torchbearers, followed by a platoon of trumpeters and banner-holders. Behind them walked a trainer with the lion that was M-G-M's mascot.

A prancing bevy of young topless women came next, wearing only flower necklaces and short skirts split to the waist on one side. As they strutted barefoot down the carpeting they scattered rose petals from earthen platters before the hooves of an advancing squadron of Roman cavalry.

The crowd was so charged with excitement by now that I couldn't hear what Squeaks was trying to tell me, something about a delivery.

I cupped a hand to my ear. "What?"

"I said 'Lord deliver us,'" he shouted. "That's Molly!"

The Irishman was pointing to the dancing girls, and instantly I saw he was right. There was skinny little Molly from Raleigh, skipping along in the pack of topless lasses, looking frail and almost boyish from this distance. I wanted to hurry down there and throw a coat around her shoulders, but she seemed so happy and unfettered, like she was finally running free.

"Well," I told Squeaks, "that's one way to get herself noticed."

"She better hope it's not Big Rusty doin' the noticing."

At last Ramón Novarro's chariot came rolling off the carpet behind its snow-white stallions. The sight set off new rounds of squeals and cheers as he drove his team closer to the stands to further tantalize the crowd.

Francis X. Bushman came next, glowering stoically out over the backs of his four ebony racers. I don't know if it was meant as a joke or not, but Bushman was followed out by a rodeo clown pulling a rickshaw with a midget in the seat. In any case, it made me laugh.

Next came an elephant and some camels, and a man with a bear on a long leash. Then an old Model-T careened into view on its skinny spoked tires. It was one of those boxy numbers with the extending fenders on both sides attached to running boards. Piled all over the car and holding tight to headlamps and hats were some dozen Keystone Cops in their trademark mustaches and thimble-shaped helmets.

The driver paused before the stands for a comical routine in which they pantomimed having engine problems. When they threw open the hood out popped a stowaway dressed like Charlie Chaplin. The police chased him around for a while and were all finally picked up by a fire truck pulled by a team of six tired plow horses. The crowd loved it.

Buddy and the other drivers began to enter single-file in their line of chariots. Each charioteer was dressed in native ceremonial garb with headgear representing the twelve major provinces of the Roman republic: Egypt, Sicily, Sardinia, Iberia, Greece, Crete, Illyricum, Macedonia, Africa, Asia Minor, Gaul, Syria and Rome itself.

It was the first time I saw all the chariots in motion, and together they appeared like a giant pull-toy. They glided along in their Easter-egg colors on a string of spinning golden wheels and pumping heads on a cushion of leather and fur. Surely I was not the only one there that day to feel the tickle of goose flesh.

As the parade passed along and headed toward the stately Gate of Triumph at the north, the pandemonium began to subside. It was then that Rusty Bigelow slipped up beside Squeaks with a big, dopey grin on his face. "It's on," he said. "The race. Just like we figured. We just got the word. They're runnin' her for real."

"What's the purse?" asked the Irishman.

"Details are being worked out," he said, "but it's gonna be big—" He stopped abruptly, and we looked up to find Rusty's smile froze as he stared off at the track. Delmer Burr had come out of the gap under the bleachers and was walking toward the curtained-off area. We watched him pull a drape aside and slip inside.

I think we all expected to hear a sharp crack through the din, and when we did it hung there a while, and then came another that echoed around a bit too. Seconds later Delmer Burr came out, pushing a handgun down in his belted holster. Through the curtains I caught a glimpse of the mule teams with their tentacle-like chains being attached to the corpses.

Rusty Bigelow mouthed a silent curse before glancing back at us. "Just like Italy," he scowled, then shook his head. "God damn!" Then he turned sharply to get away.

I suspect Rusty did not watch the end of the parade, so he missed the most curious moment of all. Following the last charioteer and another marching platoon, out stumbled a half-naked figure in ragged robes and wearing a crown of thorns. His arms were tied to an oversized length of lumber, which he carried like a yoke while a small band of Roman soldiers taunted him with spears.

Yes, it was clearly meant to be Jesus on His final walk to Calvary. Some in the crowd must have found the sight vulgar and tasteless after all the hoopla and dancing girls that came before it. I didn't know how to take it myself at first. But knowing what I did about General Wallace and his purpose for writing "Ben-Hur," it seemed okay. At least someone had thought to remind everyone again about the Prince of Peace.

The crowd grew quiet as history's most beloved martyr passed before it. Then someone at the front of the stands recognized the dressed-up actor as an old cowpoke named "Lariat" McCoy. He had evidently hit hard times, and when he heard his screen name called and the smattering of applause it brought, he couldn't keep the smile from his face. I think he may have even given a small dip of gratitude to his fans with the end of his crossbeam.

It was as if old Lariat forgot for a moment what he was doing and who he was supposed to be. Maybe he even believed he could be someone of importance in that town again.

PART TWO

CHAPTER TEN

Clinching the Deal

Oh, Ramón, how can you do it? How can you stand there so calmly in your freshly painted chariot and accept the plaudits and the cheers and let the rose petals rain down around you when *all those poor horses have just been killed?* Those lovely, healthy beasts, sacrificed in the name of our amusement and the carcasses dragged off discreetly in chains!

Norma had to think about this a bit.

"Where there's a secret, there's a shame," mother Edith always said. Now here they were, she and her powerful, educated beacons of culture and good breeding, yet all of them willing to plant lawn seeds over a new cemetery of secrets.

It wasn't all Ramón's doing, of course. He just happened to be standing chin-deep in it now. What sort of star smiles at such a time? Basking in his moment of victory, he was caught in a different light. He was more of a stand-in or surrogate—yes, a surrogate for an entire industry's willful blindness.

There he stood, arm raised high to the adoring throng. And just yards away lay the telltale ruts in the sand. Everyone must have seen it. They knew it. It's just that they had decided to ignore it.

Lord almighty, how the Cyclops Queen hated this business at times. Objecting was not an option, though, not in the scheme of things. There were families to think of, and futures. No one could afford to act selfishly in these harsh economic days.

So, did that mean they should all stand by with their arms and eyes lifted and accept the applause as if nothing had happened? Is that what was really meant by the term "silent stars"? Were they all taking money to keep their mouths shut?

Well, there was no clause in anyone's contract that said they couldn't question the way business was being conducted. A studio did not have to get signatures in blood to buy a few souls. Ink worked just as well. And once it had its contract, no actress could ever again be sure how far she might go—nor even if she would ever say "no" again.

The only ones who were not hypocrites were whores long before they stepped off the train. Girls like that new one they were grooming from Missouri or wherever. That Lucille LeSueur. She had tried to get chummy with everyone on the set of "Pretty Ladies." She said she had been a chorus dancer on Broadway. But privately people said Lucille had made more money as an after-hours escort than at dancing. The gossips said she had even been picked up for prostitution once in Detroit or somewhere.

Now they had straightened her teeth and given her a new name? It was Joan something—Crawford, yes! That was it. It sounded like crawfish, low and slimy. But at least *Joan* had arrived with the proper skills. There were no blurry moral lines for her, nothing to cause her to strain those big, oversized eyes.

No one could accuse her of hypocrisy, because she knew what she was when she first got to Hollywood. She might be a star some day, if the right part came along at the right time and she was smart enough to grab it. One thing was certain: No one would ever have to twist her arm to clinch the deal.

There would never be any reason for her to escape in a bottle or to put some freelance druggist on her payroll. Like poor Barbara LaMarr.

Well, there went Ramón. He had finished with his victory bows. He had made his grand gestures to the crowd and accepted his winner's wreath. The cameramen appeared satisfied. Now he could drive his chariot out of everyone's sight, turn it over to some assistants, and was free to collect his salary.

It was probably the last she would see of him today.

There were so many sad, lost souls in this town. Where could that sweet boy have gone to? *Grover.* He wouldn't just stand by and let them hurt the horses. No one had bought him yet.

God, it was exciting to watch the men down there on the track. Those were the real men, the family providers. They had such an innocent belief in the importance of their labor. They were not like these Hollywood men with their schemes and their idealistic drivel, making deals and leaving others to do the dirty work.

Poor Barbara LaMarr. But she had known the score. She was the first to tell her what the male executives expected from their contract stars.

"Reading the fine print is one thing, Norma," Barbara had told her over lunch, as casually as if she were discussing a menu item. "But after spending their time and money on you, they want something to make them feel good about their investment. Believe me, after a tough negotiation, it's not a *pen* that most of them want to slap in your hand."

All these male executives, so driven and full of life, holding such horrifying power over other people's destinies! And all the ladies, so damned beautiful and yet so wracked with doubts about their standing. It was no wonder everyone walked around all day on edge, looking to blow off some steam. That was the way Barbara had put it to her.

"So we give them a little *handshake* when called upon," she said. "Really, no harm done, is there? The wife's still happy at home. Boyfriend none the wiser. Business gets done so the front office is happy. Everyone walks away feeling a little more ... relaxed, a little less insecure."

The Cyclops Queen had to stifle a chuckle. There was just one thing the men had that ladies didn't. It figured they would always be wanting to rub it in our faces.

Maybe there should have been a special float in that parade. After all the marching troops and slave girls passed, they should have wheeled out a giant phallus in a long wagon. At its base would lie a tangled mass of pubic hair made from a thousand shredded contracts. And Mr. Mayer could have his throne there behind it, waving with his fat cigar with *that* poking up at the crowd. That would have gotten some knowing laughs from those toadying "yes" men and "why not?" dames.

Of course, Barbara had a lot to say about the latter. "Don't think the gals don't get just as much out of it as the fellows," she said with a smirk. "This whole beauty game, it's mostly for us ladies, don't you know. You think the men need any of that *window dressing*?

"Truth is, the women who get as far as a screen test don't need much help. But once they've got their hair done and their lipstick perfect, they're as game as the gents. The so-called 'casting couch' is way overestimated, in my experience. No one has the time to deal with anything as messy as a pregnancy, and the ladies don't want to spoil their makeup. So that's how we show them our respect. Call it a professional courtesy. Everyone does it, and don't think it isn't fun for us, too—sizing a fellow up, so to speak.

"The ladies I know, the ones who've been around, they carry a hand cream in their purse, if they've got any compassion. You never know the toll. Some casting directors see two go-getters by lunch. If they both got dry hands, he might not be able to pee standing up for a week. You certainly wouldn't want him cursing you as he's standing there holding his raw johnson. Those of us who know the score, we come prepared. We even have little ways of letting a man know."

"Like a secret code?" she had asked. She still cringed at the memory. *Honestly, Norma, at times you can sound like such a dull Canadian rube!*

"More like bridge," Barbara went on. "You know, table talk. I might say something like, 'I always take extra cream with my coffee,' or, 'Mind if I fix my lipstick?' Something like that. Just enough to let the fellow know I'm ready."

It all made the Cyclops Queen extremely thankful she wasn't starting out in the business now. ... Not that Mr. Thalberg was the type to ask for any easy gratification. He didn't even put his name on *his films*, for Lord's sake!

She had signed two contracts with him before she even knew what he looked like. When he was with Universal he just sent a letter saying he enjoyed her in some movie or another. Then when he moved to Metro, he offered her a better contract if she would come to Hollywood.

She had heard stories about him, but she was not prepared at all for their first meeting. He was standing in the outer office and she thought he might be someone's secretary or an office boy. Then he took her into Mr. Thalberg's private office and had a seat at his desk. She was about to chide him for his presumptuousness when she realized it must be the man himself, and that all that talk of a "Boy Wonder" was true.

In a world divided between the users and the used, Irving was neither. He had managed to rise above the corruption, like a treasured gift passed from one adult to the next above the dirty dealings of their peers. The young man had been born blue, with a poorly functioning heart, and the doctors said that he probably would not live past his mid-twenties. But his grandmother was a neighbor of Carl Laemmle's long before "Uncle Carl" had even *seen* a movie, let alone dreamed of starting his own business. He would later christen his picture company Universal after a name he liked on a passing milk truck. But he knew from the start that he didn't have the education to succeed at finding and packaging sure-fire stories.

That was one thing Uncle Carl had in common with all the studio heads, it seemed to Norma. They all had low self-esteem due to their limited education. But Irving impressed Mr. Laemmle as someone who did know the difference between a good story and a bum one. He had the benefit of years and years as a shut-in holed up in his bedroom with books. This sickly, sheltered mama's boy actually had true value to offer a man whose business was telling stories.

In a few miraculous evenings Irving was able to avoid the resumé tango, the front office shuffle, and all the high-stepping compromises on the dance floor of success. He was like the prince in one of his own storybook romances, bred and raised on the miracle food of fictions.

Uncle Carl may have been grooming Irving to also be his son-in-law. Daughter Rosabelle Laemmle was cultured, well traveled and socially savvy. But Irving's mother Henrietta thought her son could do much better.

By the time he got to left Universal for Metro and that became M-G-M, Irving had outgrown Rosabelle and was used to staying aloof and playing the field. He eventually got around to asking Norma along on one of his executive's social functions, but by then he had grown quite smitten with "Dutch" Talmadge, the youngest of the Talmadge girls.

Constance Talmadge had acquired a reputation as the "wildest" of the three Hollywood sisters. Natalie Talmadge had limited success in the movies, and had given up on acting to marry Buster Keaton in 1921. Norma Talmadge was the serious beauty of the family, and was one of the most popular actresses in Hollywood.

But it was Constance who projected a devil-may-care air that was perfectly in sync with the times. When World War I deflated the idealists and left a so-called "lost generation" in its wake, Constance expressed the true Jazz Age spirit of "What the hell, let's have some fun!"

Norma could understand how easy it was for her to turn the head of someone like Irving. A man like him, who had spent his young manhood talking in parlors to a lot of stuffy adults with Old World accents—a girl like Dutch could catch him in her spell without taking her gloves off.

There were stories about Irving sitting outside Dutch's home in his automobile, waiting in the dark to see when she got in from a party. She was mercurial and flighty, notorious for her habit of picking up and disappearing for months at a time. There would be sightings of her in Monte Carlo or Istanbul, and always there would be a handsome beau in the picture. It drove Irving crazy.

Dutch was in town now, however, and Irving was sure to be fully apprised of that. No doubt he had sent her a far more personal invitation to come today.

The Cyclops Queen had just advantage when it came to Irving. It was Henrietta. Mrs. Thalberg did not like Dutch at all. She was not the sort that any mother would want for their sons. Henrietta made no more a secret of her disapproval of Dutch than she had of Rosabelle.

Thank God for over-controlling mothers! Just as men could sense a commonality of weaknesses among other men, Norma was sure that women sensed their common ground with other women.

Henrietta was much like her own mother. Both she and Edith watched over their children and did not leave their futures to be determined by happenstance. Irving did not know it yet, but both Edith and Henrietta had cast him to be Norma's real life co-star. The ending would turn out the way those single-minded mothers had decided it would, or it wouldn't be the ending at all.

But for it to succeed Norma had to play her part well. She had to figure out a way to get Irving to accept her in a new role. Once he had done that she could count on Henrietta to be her fiercest ally.

There was nothing she could do now but wait, like Irving outside Dutch's house. No use getting wound up over the deaths of a few horses. Did she want to end up like Athole? Her only sister had taken to moping around the house for so long that doctors finally diagnosed her condition as "war neurosis." Athole, they said, suffered an acute depression over all the fine young men from Westmount High who went off to fight and never returned.

Even years later and in the sunny surroundings of southern California, Athole had not recovered. She was still too much the recluse, and no one could snap her out of it. Such a fate was simply not an option for Mama Edith's older girl.

CHAPTER ELEVEN

The Golden Purse

The chariots were up getting a final check outside the Gate of Triumph, back where Molly and I had met only hours before. To me it seemed more like a month because of all that had happened.

I was in no rush to rejoin my team or to get on with the race. All I cared to do was stay close to the stands and maybe catch a sight of Norma to prove to myself she wasn't just a dream.

What chance did I have of winning the heart of an angel like her? No chance at all, I figured, until I improved my circumstances. But still I couldn't bring myself to move on.

"What are you waitin' for?" came a raspy voice behind me.

It was Rusty Bigelow, and I knew I couldn't tell him the truth. "Someone told me they saw Tom Mix up there in the stands."

"Mix? Hunh-uh. Tom Mix is on his ranch in Colorado this month."

"I thought you'd be up with the wagons."

"I'm headed that way. You haven't seen Molly anywhere, have you?"

I didn't know for sure what Rusty knew, so I thought I better just play dumb and shake my head. "Sorry. Maybe she's at the wagons."

"Maybe. You coming?"

"Yeah, sure."

We started off and walked in silence for a ways.

"So, I hear Molly's your sister. That right?

"I promised our folks I'd watch her. I've been doin' a piss-poor job of it so far."

"I wouldn't want that responsibility."

"Exactly."

"I grounded her for a month once. Caught her ditching school to watch 'em make movies. I told her I'd bring her today if she stayed in the stands and didn't get in any trouble. She asked if she could be in the parade. I said sure. ... That didn't go the way I thought. Now she's run off again."

"I'm sure she'll show up," I told him, but I wasn't sure at all.

We found Buddy's chariot right off but Buddy wasn't anywhere to be seen. Squeaks was holding onto Polly's nose straps and Powder Keg was tending to the hobbles on the pacers.

"What's going on over there?" asked Rusty, nodding to a group of drivers having a fairly heated debate with a couple of studio men. I recognized one of them as the man Buddy spoke with after the crash.

"Is it not a bloody rebellion in the air?" said Squeaks.

"Cut the crap," said Rusty. "What's it about?"

"The drivers are apparently convinced now the studio's done something to the cars. They feel they're no longer as safe as they were. Some of the want to call off the race until the problem's fixed."

"What?" blurted Rusty. "That's our money they're talking about! I know who's doin' it. It's them troublemakers from the union. They've been achin' to whip up support for a strike!"

"Could be malarkey," said Squeaks. "Then again, if Fisher can't handle these rigs, who can? What do you think, Runaway?"

"Well, it could be time for union help. Someone's got to take the men's side—I mean, if the studio won't."

Rusty considered it a second. "Maybe so. But I never wanted—" He happened to glance up and then stopped suddenly. "Hold on. Here comes Buddy."

We waited for the old soldier to get a little closer and then Rusty shouted out, "What'd they say, Buddy? They going to shut it down?"

"Okay, here's the scoop," he said. "They definitely raised the cars some, and we think that made 'em top-heavy. The studio won't stop the race but they agreed to make a modification."

"What sort of modification, Buddy?"

"They're going to add weight to the front, enough to hold the wheels on the track. We figure fifty-pounds of sand'll do it. They'll come around and attach some heavy straps to the floor behind the shield. They sandbags are on their way. We should be ready to shoot after lunch."

"Fifty pounds enough?" asked Rusty.

"That's what they calculate. Might still be a problem for some in the curves. Lighter fellows like Pedro and Johnson could have a disadvantage. But they'll be faster on the straightaway, so it works out."

I don't think any of us had ever heard Buddy talk so much. It gave me new respect for him. While we were all off arguing about possible problems, Buddy had buckled down and got the real one problem solved.

Just then we heard a man calling out from next to the big archway. "All right, fellows, can you all give me your attention here?" The conversations all died off as the men recognized B. Reeves Eason. He had climbed up on a wooden crate at the front, and everyone edged forward to hear what he had to say.

"You men know me and I know you, and I think we've grown to respect one another over the years. What we're about to do together now is maybe the most difficult thing we ever tried. The few of you who were with me in Italy know that anytime you run chariots there's gonna be danger. Two rigs, four rigs, even six rigs has been done before, and those was doozies. Today we've got twelve rigs, each pulled by a four-horse team. For those of you who didn't get as far as me in grade school, that's forty-eight horses. Some of you drivers are going to be tempted to do things that ain't safe. Others are going to want to hang back and keep out of the fray. But neither of them things is going to happen, not on my set.

"This studio has put its money on us, fellows. We're going to come through for 'em. We're going to give 'em a race they'll never forget!" he shouted, and the men responded with cheers and whistling. After a while, Eason signaled for them to quiet down so he could continue.

"Now, men, just to show you what kind of respect this studio has for us, it sent one of its top executives down to address us here. So listen up. I think you'll be glad to hear what he has to say. I'm proud to present the M-G-M production manager, Mr. Joe Cohn."

With that, Breezy hopped down off the box and a wiry little buzzard of a man stepped up. He had a nose like a shark fin and bushy brows and a couple of saddlebags under his eyes. Most people called him J. J. Cohn, one of those front office whizzes who could plan movie budgets and draw up shooting schedules.

He had been opposed to shooting in Italy from the start. But Mr. Mussolini wanted those big Yankee bucks to fill his war chest, so he made a special appeal. His Italian representatives managed to get a Metro vice president named "Major" Edward Bowes drunk enough to sign his name on a contract and filming was committed to be in Rome. Two years later when the defeated film company dragged itself home with little to show for the effort, J.J. Cohn was hailed as a prophet and Major Bowes was sent packing to radio to host an amateur hour.

The studio workmen stopped by to install our straps and it was my job to keep the horses calm, so I only heard parts of his speech. He wanted us to know what a big movie "Ben-Hur" would be. Not only was it booked for the Christmas holiday at Sid Grauman's Egyptian Theatre, it was set to play there a full year with options to extend. It would be at New York's Knickerbocker Theatre, too, for two years. He acknowledged there had been troubles on the production, but he repeated he was sure that with our help it would come in on schedule and "under the wire."

Then he shouted his prediction that "Ben-Hur" was going to be "the biggest goddamned religious picture ever made!" That raised some chuckles from the men.

"Now, fellows, I've got one last thing to say," he continued. "I've said what this picture means to M-G-M. And for my money, this chariot race today is the very heart of the picture. For that reason it's got to be exciting. It's got to be real. Every one of you here has got to put all you have into it, your dreams, your blood.

"We need good old American determination, boys. So I've checked with our accountants and the front office, and they gave me the okay to offer a purse. We're going to run a real race here today, boys, hear me? The third place driver will get a bonus of two hundred dollars. Second place will get three hundred. And the winner today will get a banker's check for one thousand smackeroos! How's that sound?"

Excitement rippled through the crowd, but there was a hesitance to celebrate yet because there were questions unanswered.

"Only for the drivers?" whispered Rusty, loud enough for several others around to hear and nod their agreement. The majority waited to learn if there would be anything in it for them.

J. J. Cohn teased them with a smile. "And let me just add, each and every member of a winning crew will get himself a payroll bonus of one hundred dollars!" With that a small pandemonium broke out, with cheers and shouts and spontaneous dances of joy.

This was more money than many of these people ever thought of seeing at one time. In 1925 you could buy a new automobile from Henry Ford for less than three hundred dollars. A thousand bucks could buy a small house in the valley outright, or make a sizable down on a bungalow up in the canyons. What J. J. Cohn was holding out was not just a reward, but an entry ticket to the kind of life any rough-and-tumble saddle-puncher could only dream of.

All at once we were laughing together and trading grins and catching each other's hats in the air. But I had to wonder: What would become of all that jolly camaraderie once the idea really took hold and we were facing off, team against team, down at the starting line?

***

"Now, men, listen up," shouted J. J. Cohn as the excitement crested. "We're going to take a breather now before we get started. Mr. Thalberg is not happy that there's still empty rows in the bleachers. So we're sending our buses and cars around to scout up more extras. The fog's burning off, and there's some work needs to be done on the chariots. So you men go and get yourselves some lunch at the chuck wagons. You'll find soup and stew and drinks there, all on us. Take a break, and we'll all meet back at twelve-thirty sharp for the greatest chariot race the world ever saw!"

Another cheer arose as Cohn and Breezy Eason went off together, and I saw Molly from Raleigh with fresh flowers in her hair, lost and sort of wandering through the crowd.

"Well, hello, cowboy," she said when she turned and saw me. "I was looking for you." She was still dressed in that slave girl get-up, looking like the party had just up and left without her.

I pulled her with me into a corner. "Listen, it's not a good idea for you to be here now. Rusty's been looking for you and I think he's mad."

"Oh, bosh!" she said. "He's not my father."

"No, and he's not your husband either."

"That was mean of me, Grover, I admit it," she said with a pout. "But honestly, you have to admit you were no gentleman. You simply *must* forgive me, though, Grover, because I really need your help."

"Help doin' what?"

"I just can't seem to meet the right people, and time is flying by. If I can just get an introduction, maybe I can get a shot at a *real* part."

"What can I do?"

"You could introduce me to your famous friend."

I was sure she was going to start that business about Breezy Eason all over again. But it occurred to me she might mean Ramón Novarro. Calling him my friend was a whopper even by Hollywood standards, but if taking Molly to meet him would make her happy, I didn't have a thing to lose.

"I'll introduce you, but that's it. Anything after that is on you."

"Of course."

I grabbed her hand and we went zigzagging through the chariot teams, paying no attention to the jibes and cackles of the men. Ramón's four white stallions were getting their shoes checked by a studio blacksmith. Ramón was bent down and poking at the new sandbag strapped in his chariot.

"Ramón," I called, giving Molly a push forward. Only it was not Ramón. The man was dressed in Ben-Hur's vest and leather cap, but it was none other than the man called Fisher, looking fully recovered after his crash.

"Well, howdy, Mormon," he said, then turned to give Molly a full body once-over from head to toe. He gave her a lopsided grin. "And hello to you, too, sweet little miss."

"This is Molly, Rusty's sister," I said flatly. "Where's Ramón?"

"Don't know where he is but I do know where he ain't. And that's here."

Molly crossed her arms with great impatience and rolled her eyes.

"Well, why are you dressed in his clothes?"

"Anything you want to give to him, you can give to me," he said. "I'm Mr. Ben-Hur from here out." He gave Molly another leer.

That was it for her. She yanked her arm free of my grip. "Let go!" she screamed, and went storming off.

"Never mind," I told Fisher and hustled to catch up with her. "Hey, slow down! Stop running!"

Molly halted and turned to face me with fury in her eyes. "I ain't kidding with you, buster."

"I'm sorry. I thought it was Ramón. It was his car. I thought you wanted me to introduce you."

She stared at me, and tapped her foot. "Ramón Novarro?"

"That's right. I didn't know he was gone."

She crossed her arms again. "You know Ramón Novarro?"

"Sure. He's a nice fellow. He gave me some tips on driving chariots. Honest."

I could see her mental gears whirring. "Oh, you're the most exasperating boy, Grover. You knew darn well it wasn't Ramón Novarro I was talking about."

"No, I didn't. Did you mean Mr. Bushman? Frances X. Bushman? Come on, I can introduce you two for sure."

I reached for her hand but she jerked it away. "I don't want to see another washed up old man. I already got to meet Mr. Lionel Barrymore and that was enough for a life time."

"Well, I swear, Molly, I am truly at a loss to know who you—"

"I'm talking about your little tête-à-tête with Miss Shearer."

"Who?"

"Norma Shearer, that's who. Don't you pretend like you don't know her, because I sat and I watched you two on the track."

I felt like she had reached into my gut and pulled a plug. My little reserve of optimism for the future was gushing out where I stood. Norma Shearer had made such a big splash in pictures lately that even I knew the name. "That girl on the track?" I said. "Why, that wasn't Norma Shearer." But even as I said it I knew Molly must be right.

It all made sense now: How calm and experienced she seemed, how in charge of everything, the way the cameraman treated her with respect. She couldn't have just been some unknown extra from the stands. How could my own personal guardian angel have turned into an idol to millions? Up until that moment, I never knew a dashed dream could weigh so much.

"It most certainly *was* Norma Shearer," Molly was saying. "Haven't I seen every picture she ever made? 'He Who Gets Slapped,' 'Lady of the Night,' 'A Slave of Fashion,' 'The Secretary' ... and all the rest? I certainly know her when I see her, which is more than you can say. What were you two talking about anyway?"

"Never mind."

"No, really. What?"

"It wasn't anything."

"Well, what'd she say to you?"

"Nothing."

"And what'd you say to her?"

"Nothing.

"That was a fine private conversation with Norma Shearer where neither of you said nothing!"

"Yeah."

All the time that Molly was pounding away at me, I had an odd feeling. It was the same feeling I had at the livery yard, the sense that someone was spying on me. I glanced through the crowd, looking for a clue in strangers' faces, finally shrugging it off.

"Well?" said Molly.

"What do you mean?"

"Are you going to introduce us?"

The drivers were all tying off their reins now and handlers were fetching buckets of oats for the animals. I saw Squeaks standing all alone next to our chariot. "Look, if I can help, I'll let you know. I'm not sure I'll ever see the lady again. But I'll do what I can. I got to run."

"Well, dandy," she answered as I hurried off, shouting out after me, "Maybe Ramón Novarro will come by and give you a ride!"

Until my talk with Molly I had been looking forward to a good lunch. I missed one meal already and I was feeling hunger pangs deep in my belly. But I didn't much care about eating any more. All I could think about was Norma, and how now she would never belong to me.

Buddy came up beside me along the way and he could tell something was going on. "You okay?"

"I'm fine. What's up?"

"You hear about the purse?"

"Yeah. I saw Fisher."

"How'd he look?"

"Good as new. Did you know he was taking over the Ben-Hur team?"

Buddy nodded. "He's a good driver. But those white nags are just for show. They won't be much competition."

"Hey, Rusty!" called out Pedro, passing by wearing that same stained fedora. "You got your bets down?"

"We're counting our winnings now."

"If you feel like celebrating, I know a guy selling hooch. Two bucks a bottle!"

Rusty came up out of nowhere in a foul mood. "Get the hell away from us, Pedro. For Chrissakes!"

Pedro looked stung and turned to Buddy with remorse. "Sorry, Buddy. I wasn't thinking."

"It's okay, Pedro."

"I don't mean nothing," he told Rusty. "Sorry."

We were almost to the chariot then and Squeaks was standing by shaking his head. We got down to business but a little later I leaned over to whisper in the Irishman's ear. "What was that about with Pedro?"

"He can be a wee rash at times. He should've known better, is all I'll say."

Rusty plopped a bucket of water down under the nose of a rear runner. He straightened up and said loud enough for all to hear, "Some folks around here could have a little problem with their drinking."

"He means me," said Buddy, strolling out from the back of the wagon. "Only drinking was never the problem. Seemed more like the solution. What say we go and tie on a feed bag?"

We were halfway to the food trucks when I heard there was someone asking around for me. It turned out to be a slender, pale young man with dark glasses and the withdrawn air of a college boy.

"You Grover?" he asked me.

"Yeah."

"I was told a 'guardian angel' wants to see you."

"Where is she?"

"If you're free I'll take you."

It turned out the messenger's name was Douglas Shearer, and he was my guardian angel's older brother.

CHAPTER TWELVE

The Two Dougs

There's a nightmare I had in my youth that I always remembered because it made such an impression. I'm lying in bed with just a sheet over me on a summer night too hot to sleep. There's a tapping off in the woods, and it's so loud I'm sure it must be some big old woodpecker hammering at a fruit tree. It seems to be getting madder by the minute, and suddenly it occurs to me that there's this hole in my window screen. I worry that this big angry bird is going to find its way to that hole and squeeze through to peck at me.

And that's what happens, too, except I jump out of bed and I'm standing there when its beak comes poking in, and I grab its head and the bird goes wild, squawking and flapping in my hands. And then I see it's no woodpecker at all. It's just some riled up little hummingbird, and I smother its head with my thumb until it goes limp and its wings stop moving.

That's what I was thinking about on my way to see Norma. I could never fit in some movie star's world. I was so poor even in my sleep I was cutting corners and making do with hummingbirds in place of woodpeckers.

What did I know about stuff like contracts and private secretaries and promotional tours? How could I ever understand life in a mansion with butlers and chauffeurs? My heart beat a mile a minute as the distance between us kept shrinking and the gap between us got wider.

At least Douglas Shearer was normal enough. He was no pampered movie star. I would have been amazed, of course, to learn he was about to lead M-G-M into the era of "talkies" and leave his name on every important film the studio would turn out over the next four decades. But even that ordinary-looking college kid could talk up a storm. Right now he was fired up about how the most expensive movie in Hollywood history was carrying on "like it was back in the brushes with D. W. Griffith," as he put it.

"Megaphones!" he said in disgust. "For crying out loud! We've had radio with us for five years already and these guys are still hollering through megaphones! Semaphore flags and *wigwagging!* What's next, you think—smoke signals?"

There were exciting things happening in science, he told me, and a revolution was brewing. The war for Americans' attention would be won with stuff like transformers and speaker horns and vacuum tubes.

"Radio is bringing concert music to people's homes. We can hear the voices of kings and actors and sports reporters—all there at our own fireplaces. Movie houses have to be ready to compete. People aren't going to go out to a theater for a night of parlor piano and pantomime. But you'll see crowds around the block at the first theater that lets 'em hear the thunder of horse hooves."

He said amplification was the biggest challenge they faced. They could put big radios in theaters but they'd still never be loud enough. As soon as there was a practical way to push sound out to an auditorium full of people, silent pictures would be done for. "And so will the studios that make 'em," he added.

Douglas Shearer had found his way into engineering when studying telegraphy and signaling back in Canada. He tried to join the Royal Air Force but he was too young and the Great War ended, so he took an engineering job with a power company in Montreal. When Norma found success in movies, he followed her and his other sister and their mother out to California. He had just landed an engineering job at Warner Brothers in recent weeks, and he was preaching the gospel of sound to anyone he could collar.

Doug Shearer was a good example of an everyday kind of guy in the right place with the right skills to leave a big mark on the world. At that moment, though, the only world I could think of was the one inhabited by his big sister, Norma.

"What's it like having a movie star for a sister?" I asked him.

He smiled. "She said you didn't know about that. ... Well, funny, but I don't see her that way. She's just 'little sis.' She took piano lessons, and had pets. One time I watched her lay into a whole group of neighborhood bullies for teasing a stray cat. Now I look at her up on that screen, and it's not really my sister at all."

We mounted the steps past rows of extras and others with lunch bags and soda pop bottles. Then we crossed an aisle and reached some railed boxes and a cordon guarding a purple canopy. Two guys dressed like Roman centurions stepped up to question us, then the taller one unhooked the rope for Douglas and me to enter.

Only a few of the people inside the canopy had bothered to wear costumes. The men wore light linen trousers and coats with a European cut. The ladies were mostly dressed in cotton smocks, and several had bobbed hair with those flapper hats. Some of their faces looked familiar to me, like ones I might have seen in magazines at the barbershop. All of them stopped to see if Doug and I were anyone, then turned away in total disinterest.

Norma was seated alone in a railed-off stall, and once I saw her, my worries and fears no longer mattered. She had been chatting across the divide with an older lady, but when she turned to me her pale, perfect face lit like a shooting gallery at dusk.

"Ah, there you are, Grover," she chirped gaily. "Here, come here. Have a seat with me," she said, patting the empty chair. I edged up closer with utmost care, afraid to frighten off such a rare and delicate creature. "Will you stay with me a while?" she asked.

"A whi—while," I stammered. She was as perfect as I remembered. Her beauty was not the store-bought kind. Below the pinwheel sparks of her pale blue eyes was a thin mouth that was almost schoolmarm-ish in a way, and her curled lips held the secret wisdom of the ages.

I lowered myself into the chair next to her.

"What do you think of Dougie?"

"You two don't look much alike."

"Well, I wish I had his brains. We expect huge things of him, Mother and I. *Huge* things."

"Yes, ma'am."

"Please, it's *Norma*. Just plain old nobody-from-nowhere Norma."

"He *knows,* Sis," said Doug Shearer. He clearly had little patience with her games.

"What?"

"He knows who you are," he said.

Her eyes fell with disappointment. "Oh. ... *Pity.*"

I must have been staring because she suddenly seemed to grow shy and self-conscious. She dropped her gaze before remembering that Douglas was still standing there. "Thank you, Dougie. Thank you for bringing Grover to me."

"That's all right, Sis. Glad to do it. See ya later."

We watched him step over the cordon and then Norma turned to me with a tinge of regret. "You were looking at my eye, weren't you?"

"What?"

"It's all right. You can tell me the truth."

"You have the most beautiful eyes I've ever seen."

It just came out like that, like a statement of fact that no one could deny, because they were and that was what I thought.

She shrugged her soft shoulders and whatever it was that had bothered her was gone. It was the sunny Norma I knew who smiled to ask, "So, who told you?"

I stammered again, not knowing just what she was asking.

"You spoke so easily to me this morning. I hope you're not one of those people who can only talk after falling in a hole."

"No, ma—. Norma."

"That's better. So, what were you told, exactly? That I am a very *scary* person?" She watched as I shook my head. "Just too famous?"

"Well, you are," I said.

"Grover, I'm the same person I was this morning. Now isn't that so?"

"Yes."

"And you're the same you. At least, I hope you are." Her eyes winked without moving.

"But it's not," I said. "It isn't just you and me at all."

"It's not?"

"There's thousands of people all over this world who see your pictures. They follow what you're doing, and they want to see your photos."

"No, Grover, you're wrong. There are *millions* around the world," she said and gave a small chuckle. "I will tell you something I learned about being famous. Want to know?"

I must have nodded.

"When I first started to become known by strangers, I was invited to all the best parties. So many famous people there, Grover! And I thought to myself, 'Norma, you have made it.' But the more I got to know them, the more I saw how insecure and unhappy they were. That thought infected me like a virus. I caught whatever they had, and after that, I could never be sure if I moving up or it was them on their way down."

She stopped and smiled at me, but it didn't make me feel any better. She decided to try a different tack.

"Grover, don't you know that all any woman really wants is for just the one *right person* to feel like that about her?" Then she leaned her face closer until it was nearly touching mine. "Kiss me," she said.

"What?"

"Just a simple kiss. On the mouth." She puckered up and shut her eyes.

Her dark lashes fluttered at me as she waited, but it was nothing compared to the back flips my heart was doing. It took me ages to meet her face and press my lips to hers. If I hadn't been sitting down, I'm sure I'd have fainted. But all at once the bad feelings disappeared, and I was just sitting and smooching with a classroom sweetheart.

"There," she said, opening her eyes. She gave me a soft, knowing grin. "That was nice. You see, I'm just a woman, no more, no less." Then she straightened out her icy blue dress and settled back in her chair. "So, tell me about all the work you do."

"The work?"

"The other men—what are they like?"

"They're okay. They're straight-ahead guys, mostly. Except for this one guy. He pretty much hates my guts, I guess."

"That's a very strong word, Grover. Why does he hate you?"

"I guess he thinks I'm after his job."

"Oh. Well, that would explain it. And is he the one who told you about me?"

I shook my head. "I don't think he goes to your type of pictures."

"So who told you I was such a *scary* famous person?"

"A girl I met. Molly from Raleigh."

Norma's thin eyebrows arched knowingly and she drew her lips in a bundle. "Oh. ... The 'other woman.' And who is she?"

"Just a young actress. No one, really."

"Well, that's not too flattering. Is she your girlfriend?"

"No. I mean, I hardly know her."

"And yet she mentioned me? That's odd."

I felt a little sheepish then. "She was asking for advice and she wondered what you might tell her."

"About what?"

"About having a career in movies. Getting noticed and stuff."

"You could tell her that no matter what she's told or who it is offering the advice, she must not become discouraged. She must keep moving forward, despite what anyone says. That's what I would tell her."

"Thanks. I'll tell her you said so. She's really interested in this business, and thinks you're aces."

"Tell me, has she said anything about our Mr. Thalberg?"

"Thalberg? Not really. But I know the men don't like him much."

Norma looked surprised. "What have they got against poor Irving?" she said with a chortle.

"They think he's a little ... simple-minded, I guess."

"Simple-minded?"

"Stupid," I corrected.

At that Norma roared with laughter, rocking in her chair a bit. "That's so funny, Grover," she said, then stopped suddenly in a frown. "But you are serious. Why do the men think that?"

I told her the story I heard about him coming down on the track and asking if wind machines could blow the fog away. She clapped her delicate fingers to her lips, as if stifling a laugh. "Oh, my," she said, "that doesn't sound very bright, does it?"

Then she bit her bottom lip in thought and I saw some dark emotion play across her brow. I knew she was thinking about Irving Thalberg, and I felt a twinge of envy. "You like him, don't you?"

She gave me a steady look. "I like *you*, Grover," she answered. "A lady can only have one beau at a time. Besides, Mr. Thalberg is my boss and he has a girlfriend, so that's that. I also don't believe he thinks I'm quite as wonderful as you do."

"Well, then," I said, "he *is* stupid." With that she turned her face away from me, apparently pleased with my reply.

***

People in the boxes around us were taking more notice of Norma and me. I saw them looking, and it bothered me no end that I couldn't say why they seemed so familiar. They were like the distant relations one encounters at a family reunion, though these folks were generally thinner and handsomer than most people's relatives.

There was one man with a deep tan and a thin mustache looking at me from a box a bit behind ours. I was sure I had seen him in newsreels or somewhere. He had an oval face and a high, rounded forehead with thinning hair, but he simply glowed with good health and prosperity.

I leaned toward Norma to whisper. "That tan fellow back there— is that Al Jolson?"

"Heavens to gracious, no. It's far too early in the day for Mr. Jolson to be up and around. I see the resemblance, though. That's the other Douglas in my life. Mr. Fairbanks. Would you like to meet him?"

Without giving me a moment to think she had twisted in her chair to wave him over. "Douglas, I'd like you to meet someone," she called.

The handsome neighbor instantly uncrossed his legs and gave a nod. His smile sent that thin mustache rising like a curtain to reveal a dazzling white set of teeth. He leapt from his chair and hopped the metal rail to land in a squat behind us.

"I'd like you to meet Grover Link, Mr. Fairbanks," said Norma. "He's one of the brave new breed of stunt actors. Grover, this is Doug Fairbanks."

"Part of the younger crop, eh?" said Fairbanks, reaching an arm over the partition to shake my hand. "Happy to meet you, Grover. Say, what happened down there on the track? Everyone all right?"

"A driver got the air knocked out of him, that's all. Two horses had to be put down, though."

"Oh, that's always a pity. Any tips on the big race? I have a couple cards riding on Mr. Novarro. What do you think? Is my money safe?"

"Why'd you choose him?" I asked.

"I read the book, my boy," he said with another flash of his choppers. "Personally, I have nothing but respect for Francis Bushman. I know he can handle his team, and I'd like to see him win for the sake of 'old Hollywood.' But I'm afraid it's not in the script. Everyone is wagering on Novarro. He may be a bit green as an actor—and 'Scaramouche' wasn't much of a picture, in my opinion. But he's young, athletic. He's the future, is the way I see it."

"Well, the men mostly favor chariot number three," I said. "That blue-and-white rig with them golden vines. That's Buddy Ardale's car."

Fairbanks's face clouded over and he quickly pulled out his tip sheet to check the odds. "Four-to-one. What makes them think he stands a good chance?"

"Buddy drove in Italy and he had a strong showing at practice."

Fairbanks took that in. "But Novarro did, too, I'm told."

"Yes, but Novarro's done for the day. Someone else will be driving that rig, and Buddy Ardale's got a secret ace in the hole."

"What do you mean?"

"He's got Polly, his own trained thoroughbred. She'll be his pacer."

"Novarro's opted out, huh? How about that guy! I knew he wouldn't be up for the long haul," said Fairbanks, squeezing out the words as if to fit them through the tight squint of his eyes.

"My, my, four-to-one," he repeated, checking his sheet once more. "Thanks for the tip, my friend. Sounds like a good one. What's your name again? Grover? I think I'll go and change my bet while I can."

He rose and started to turn, then looked at Norma. "Miss Shearer, did I mention earlier how elegant you look? My love, as always," he added, lifting the back of her hand to his lips. Then he gave me a fast wink and made his retreat, bounding over a back curtain and taking the steps up two at a time.

I looked at Norma in amazement. "That was really Douglas Fairbanks? From 'Son of Zorro' and 'Thief of Bagdad'?"

She smiled back, a trifle distracted.

"He sure doesn't look like he does in the movies," I muttered.

"What you said about the horses being 'put down'—why must they be treated so horridly?"

"No one wants it. I mean, most of the men love horses like part of their family. But they don't want to see 'em suffer. Sometimes it's the kindest thing you can do, if they're injured like that."

"How did it happen?"

"The studio did something to the chariots. Raised 'em up, or something. Just to make 'em more exciting for the cameras."

"Oh, God, Grover," she said, "is that true?"

"Apparently, yeah."

"I can't stand to watch animals mistreated. I know some of the people here—they would like nothing better than to see crashes and injuries. But I hate it. I wasn't even going to come today."

"Why did you?" I asked. I think I hoped she would say she was feeling lonely, and if she did, I was going to grab her around the waist and tell her she would never have to be lonely again.

"Ramón," she said. "Ramón Novarro asked me to come. He wants me to do his next picture with him, 'The Student Prince'—the book, not the operetta, of course. Ramón would really prefer the operetta. He wants so badly to sing for people, the dear. He's quite taken with my brother. If the movies could talk, he says, then they could sing too, and people everywhere would hear his voice. That's his dream. Anyway, that's the way things tend to happen in Hollywood. You keep appointments, you attend the dinner parties and studio events, and somehow deals get *struck*."

She pronounced the last word like a bullet through the brain. All the time I could see her withdrawing into some private chamber where walls were closing in. I could hear the burden of her regrets. Whatever she desired from life at this point, it wasn't a new picture deal with Ramón Novarro.

Norma stayed in that forlorn place a mere second or two. Then as if on cue the sun overhead broke through the clouds and the fog, and bathed the whole coliseum in bands of sunshine.

"That's more like it," said Norma, lifting up a fancy pair of opera glasses to scan the track. "Gorgeous. Oh, look. Some of the men are taking off their shirts. My, what muscles, and—" She gasped and let the glasses fall in her lap. I tried to see where she was looking. One of the men stood close to the wall of the spina and I could see a wet stain growing on the fake marble facade.

I felt ashamed and personally humiliated. … It would take more than a few pleasantries to bridge that chasm between Norma's smart, upper-class set and my down and dirty clan of free-wheeling pissers.

A couple of chariots came rolling down the track and I knew lunchtime was ended. I would have to be getting back. How could I tell Norma goodbye now?

Suddenly she turned to me with moist tears in her eyes and she took hold of my hands. "Oh, Grover, why can't we just run away together?"

"What?"

"How I long for simplicity again. Just the basics. Food, shelter, a humble day's work. And love."

"You'd walk away from this?"

"*What?*" she asked. She was really at a loss to see all she would be giving up.

"Your fans, your career … security."

"Security?" she said, grabbing the word like it was a gate-crasher.

"Well, you signed a contract, didn't you?"

"That," she scoffed. "They can wiggle out of that when it suits them." She gave a twisted smile and looked down. "Ever hear of something called a morality clause? If your films fail or they think you're getting a little hard to handle, all they need to do is issue an official denial to the press: 'The studio wants it known that there's absolutely no truth to the rumor that Miss So-and-So was found wandering drunk through the streets of Tijuana,' or whatever. The press picks up the denial and the gossip begins. Soon there's a public outcry. 'We will not go to any more of the pictures that feature Miss So-and-So or anyone who dares behave in such a scandalous fashion!' So, the studio exercises the morality clause, and your contract is null and void."

"They would do that?"

"They absolutely do. Ask Mr. Arbuckle. The biggest names in pictures, they all live in fear of falling out of favor. It literally would mean the end of them."

I couldn't be sure but I thought I saw desperation in her eyes. She looked at me as if begging me to rescue her.

"Look," I told her, "I've got to go, but I'll come back when this is over. I want to—I mean, if you're serious—we'll go away."

"Dear Grover, thank you. I knew you were a darling. I'll wait, my darling. I'll hold on and we'll see where the day takes us."

"I'll be back," I repeated, standing to go.

Some voices yelled out from above and I saw a whole rowdy pack of young men barreling down the steps. Their shouts of "Tell us—" and "What do you—" and "We were told—" all came crashing in at me like an avalanche as they pushed and tripped to gather around. They were like drunken college boys, shushing one another and trading insults until one of the better groomed among them leapt to the fore.

"Doug Fairbanks said you'd tipped him," he blurted. "Be a sport and tell us, too. Which one should we bet on?" "Yeah!" cried the others, nodding and muttering as they squeezed into a cluster

"All I told him was that the men favored chariot number three. It's the one with—" but that was all they wanted to hear. "Three! It's number three!" they yelled as they peeled off one by one in search of the nearest bookie. Others in the boxes close at hand whispered among themselves, and several more men stood to excuse themselves and hurry away.

It was Norma's turn now to stare in amazement. "Gracious," she said.

"What can I do now?" I asked.

"You'd better go down there and make certain your number three wins."

I nodded and turned but before I got more than a step away she called for me to stop.

"And Grover?"

"Yes?"

"You can tell young Molly that Norma says *not* to give up her dreams—not until the pain of holding onto them outweighs all the pain of letting go."

CHAPTER THIRTEEN

Jinxed!

One foot after the other—that was the idea. That's what I told myself just to keep from spinning around and tearing up those steps again to breathe the same air as Norma. Every ounce of fiber in my being was screaming for me to turn back. So I had to keep repeating over and over how it was done. I didn't dare falter now or allow even the quickest of glances behind to test my resolve.

What would one of those old Roman soldiers have done? Would he have bowed to pluck and fortitude and continued on his way? Or would he have gone charging back for the woman he loved, let her kick and claw until she accepted the reality that she was now his?

Well, it only went to show how times had changed.

Lunch was over and the spectators were feeling fat and sleepy. All their nervous chatter and aimless wanderings had drifted off in a collective digestive coma. I reached the track and kept going, passing the spot where Fisher had his crackup. The curtain panels were taken away and all that remained to remind us were two moist patches of sand.

The next thing I knew I was under the Gate of Triumph looking through to the horses grazing lazily in their feedbags. Chained to their chariot cars they were just so many moored rowboats at low tide.

None of the men had returned from the lunch wagons yet, and the loudest sound was my own crunchings in the gravel. Then I heard a rumbling tune hummed by a masculine voice. It was a naptime lullaby that took me only a second to place. It was "Swing Low, Sweet Chariot," a melody I learned in Sunday school about a hundred years before: *"I looked over Jordan and what did I see-ee, coming for to carry me home ...?"* Yes, I knew that one. Only it was not the way our choirmaster taught it. This was more like a dirge, slow and drained, like a poor parched thing staked out on a hill to die.

A dark figure moved in the distance and caught my eye. Crouching down, I made out a black canvas hem sweeping the tops of two scuffed boots. I shifted to see more. It was that Santa Claus fellow, the mysterious horseman brought back from Italy by the crew.

It must have been him doing the humming, I thought, until I saw his lips were drawn and his neck still as he went about his business. When the humming stopped suddenly, he paused to listen, then turned to hurry away.

It was only seconds later that I felt myself tackled by some unseen force and knocked flat on my back. A large and heavy person settled on my chest, pinning my arms to the ground. "Let me up!" I shouted, but he didn't budge and squirming accomplished nothing. His face remained hidden somewhere atop his heaving chest.

Then up stepped a pair of black shoes and a man stood peering down at me. It was one of the thugs with a blackjack from back at the spina. Yes, it was the shorter of the two, and I no longer had to guess who was holding my arms.

"You've been quite a busy boy, Mr. Link," the upright fellow said.

"Who are you two? What do you want?"

"Do you know where you are, Mr. Link?"

"Culver City, last I heard."

"You are correct. You're in a tract in Culver City. More specifically, it is a tract leased from the Marblehead Land Company. The coliseum—your make-believe Antioch—that is different. It belongs to the M-G-M studio. Cost: two hundred thousand dollars. Sand, lumber, concrete ... even a measure of blood.

"Maybe you noticed how some sections of bleachers go up only so far and stop? Well, they will look much higher in the picture. Do you know how that is done? They fix a camera to a tripod and aim it down at the track through a large picture frame. In that frame is a scale model, like a dollhouse, all painted up to match the stands. There are even tiny human torsos there, attached to wooden dowels, and these can be made to rise and stand like spectators in the top-most rows. That is how M-G-M turns its two hundred grand investment in Culver City into the long-lost coliseum at Antioch."

All I could think was that I was at the mercy of some deranged accountant. I couldn't for the life of me see where all this was headed. "Come on, fellows, just let me up."

"You see, Mr. Link," went on the smaller fellow, "that is Hollywood in a nutshell. You bend over and look through the camera in just the right way—and magic! The design, the lighting, the model work, all of it. Pure art! But take one step back, or look from a few inches to the side, and you see the truth.

"Well, my friends and I, we've taken that other look. And you know what we've seen? A hoax. An illusion. A magic act for children. Much the same as America itself, I'm afraid."

"Look, what do you want from me?"

"We want to know what you've seen, Mr. Link. Just who exactly it is you're working for."

"I was hired by the studio. A guy named Eason. That's all I know. I'm just one of the wranglers for chrissake!"

He bent down very quickly and thrust his hand inside my shirt. "Where is it?" he muttered.

"Hey, stop it. What are you looking for?"

The small man straightened up and looked at his partner. "Check his pockets," he said.

The taller of the two now shifted his knees up over my arms and I could see his face. He grinned down at me with tobacco-stained teeth. He patted down the front of my Levi's and then slipped a hand back under my butt until he stopped and gave another smile. With a sudden tug he pulled something free and held it up.

At first I thought it was my wallet, but I had left that back in my room. Then I glimpsed a bit of the cover. It was Mrs. Addison's autograph book!

"Hey, give it back!" I shouted and squirmed hard to break loose.

The small man was thumbing through the pages, smiling to himself. "Very interesting," he said. "This is all for now. But we'll be around."

"Yeah" said the taller man, "and maybe we'll have a surprise for you and your cronies." Then he started to get off but paused and brought his whole weight down hard against my ribs. I heard an "ooph!" and for the second time that day I felt the air knocked from my lungs. I clawed and struggled for breath.

The tall man just chuckled and gave my cheeks two quick slaps before climbing away.

There came a cry in the distance. "Hey! You fuck heads, get away from him!" I heard running and both my assailants took off at a gallop. All I could do was turn my head and watch them vanish off between two parked trucks as I struggled to understand.

***

My rescuer had been no more than a blur, but now he came walking back to see if I was still breathing. "Hey, friend, you okay?" he asked. It was my old aviator buddy, Freddie Moore.

I fought to answer. "Where they go?" I wheezed.

"Never mind that," said Moore the Merrier. "What'd they want?"

"They took something."

"Your money?"

I weakly shook my head. "My landlady—her autograph book."

He gave a smile of disbelief. "That can't be what they wanted."

"You *know* them?"

"I hate to admit it. They're on my side." He shook his head. "Union hired hands," he said. "Buddy shouldn't have tried to go it alone. That business with the sandbags. Clever. But the organizers wanted to handle such negotiations. They want the men's respect. Buddy's stirred up a hornet's nest now. I was coming to warn him."

"Why'd they jump me? I didn't do nothing."

"Fellow walks in off the streets and finds himself with a sweet job. People got to wonder how a thing like that happens. They gotta think—maybe, 'studio spy'?"

"Spy? Me? It's those two—Mutt and Jeff—they're the ones doin' the spying. They've been following me since breakfast."

"You sure?"

"Ask Mr. Bushman. He noticed 'em before I did."

"Francis Bushman? What were you doing with him?"

"Getting' a signature for Mrs. Addison's book."

"The book again," he said, shaking the sand out of his head. "Wait. Well there you go! They saw you getting signatures. They probably thought you recruiting folks opposed to a union."

By this time I had my breath back and managed to climb to my feet.

"Feelin' better?" he asked me.

"No. Not 'til I get my landlady's book back."

"You sure?"

"Yeah."

"I'll come with you."

"On whose side?"

"Your side. The men's side. What d'you think?"

We followed Mutt and Jeff's trail back through the line of trucks and down a crooked path between parked cars.

Moore stayed quiet for a time, unsure still about what had just happened. Then he cleared his throat to speak. "I hate to see things turn violent," he said. "At breakfast, that dust-up over old Walt Altskellar. It was good to see Rusty put it to those studio goons. But what good was it? Tomorrow old Walt's belly will be empty again, and there won't be food wagons around to raid.

"The truth is, this motion picture business is big and it's going to get bigger. You know it's the fifth biggest industry in America?"

"Hunh-uh."

"Wall Street says it rakes in several million bucks each year. And all that goes in the coffers of some dozen companies. The fat cats are looking out for themselves, all right. But who's lookin' out for you and me and Walt Altskellar?"

"My dad used to say a man's gotta look out for himself."

"Well, sure. To a point. If you've got a beef, though, you think you can just stroll into Mr. Mayer's private office and spill your woes? No. Bosses are busy, maybe more than most. You need to be part of an organization if you want their attention."

"With the help of a few hired thugs," I added.

"We're just trying to do some good," said Freddie. "You look at all the suffering there is, the poverty. Average joes like you and me, they're calling. The great battle is waging, my friend, always waging. And we're up against some heartless S.O.B.s."

"What do you mean?"

"Anyone tell you what really went on in Italy?"

"Accidents can happen everywhere."

Moore's eyes wrinkled. "Accident?"

"The pile up ... on the track."

"A load of shit went on over there, no question about that. What I'm talking about is drowned dagos."

"Drowned dagos?"

"They were shooting this sea battle. You know, from the book. Sea pirates taking on a fleet of Roman ships. The way it was meant to go, there's this fire planned, see, and there's time for everyone to get off the burning ship. But those dago shipbuilders were late with the vessels, and the decks were still fresh with tar. So the shooting begins, and all at once the fire spreads lickety-split. Extras go diving over the sides. Only some of them Italians can't swim and others got metal breastplates on.

"By the time the boats get to them, they're not all accounted for. Then someone sees there's still street clothes on the racks at the end of the day. So the production chief orders them burned, just to put an end to any questions.

"That's what we're dealing with. The studio is looking to its bottom line. But our Italian brothers, they got a line on the bastards. They got organized and the battle is engaged. They're standing up to that Mussolini and his *fascistas,* and when they're done, Italy is going to be a workers' paradise. We got to do our part here, too. Then let 'em try to pull what they pulled on old Walt Altskellar."

We came out through the rows with a clear view of the whole north lot. There were cars parked all around but nary a sight of my assailants. Those thugs had had enough time to hop in a car or take a turn back to get lost in the stadium crowd.

"Well, I better get over to makeup," said Moore. "Did you hear they got me driving one of the chariots?"

"How'd that happen?"

"I was a standby. I took the training just in case they came up short a driver. Well, with Fisher taking over Novarro's rig, someone had to take Fisher's."

Just then came the slam of a trunk lid and I saw a figure standing in back of a sharp-looking gray Nash convertible. I recognized that waist-length jacket right away. It was Delmer Burr.

"Son of a bitch," I uttered.

"Who is it?"

"It's the son of a bitch Burr. He caught me off-guard with a real kidney punch this morning."

"What for?"

"I'd like to show him what-for."

Without thinking, I started off toward him but Freddie Moore grabbed my shoulder and held me back. "Are you crazy? You talk about trouble! That guy has connections."

"What do you mean, 'connections'?"

"That wasn't no spare tire he was looking at. I'd wager fifty dollars that trunk's filled with a bed of straw, making a cozy little nursery for a whole load of newborn moonshine."

"Bootleg hooch?"

Freddie nodded. "Prohibition's a godsend for guys like him. Every studio executive needs his suppliers. There's usually some way to put them on the payroll. Your friend Burr, you can be damn sure he has protectors in very high places."

"That explains a lot. Rusty Bigelow told me Burr got fired in the past. Out shooting 'Covered Wagon' on location. You know anything about it?"

"No. I was just in a few pickup scenes. Those were shot at the studio. You want me to see what I can find out?"

"It doesn't matter now. I know what I need to know about Delmer Burr."

True to his name, Moore the Merrier cut through the gloom and started to smile, then chuckled some until I had to ask him what was so amusing.

"You've only been working half a day and already you got punched by one studio goon and mugged by a pair of hired thugs. Can't wait to see who steps up next."

"Yeah," I said. "Number three should be quite the charmer."

CHAPTER FOURTEEN

The Race Begins

"All right, fellas, listen up," said Buddy, summoning up all his old military training. We gathered close around him here in back of his chariot car—all except for Powder Keg. He had gone off to eat with the other coloreds in a different part of the field and wasn't back yet.

"I'm about to tell you something you probably don't know. In all of life there's just two kinds of tracks," said Buddy. "You got your clockwise tracks and you got those that run in a counterclockwise fashion. Most people never stop to think what type of track they're on. So they end up running the wrong kind of race and wonderin' why they ain't getting' nowhere."

As Squeaks and I traded our grins I saw he had on a lady's fine white scarf in place of his old red neckerchief. He must have made a new friend at lunch, I figured, and gotten a bit farther with her than I had with Norma.

"Today we're bein' paid good U.S. dollars to know what we're doing, so pay attention."

Buddy stopped to gaze off a ways. "Okay, here comes Powder Keg now," he said. He waited a few seconds and gave Powder Key a questioning hike of the shoulders. The black man just waved a big hand his way and took a spot by the wheel.

"What we're standing outside of here is your classic, Olympic-size stadium—six hundred feet in length from end to end. Its oval track consists of six inches of decomposed granite packed and rolled to a solid surface, covered over in three inches of sand. It's a standard-issue clockwise track with a couple of tricky turns."

He went over the rules that had been laid out, which were simple enough to follow. The chariots would all start out in a diagonal line. There were no lanes. At the starting signal, each driver would have to depend on his own skill and cunning to keep his team in the running.

The race would consist of seven complete laps around the spina—two miles in total. Each lap would be marked by the turning down of one of seven dolphin figures at the south end of the spina. If the race had to be stopped for any reason, the distances between chariots would be noted so that the teams could start again from an equivalent position.

"Now, the inside spot is where one normally wants to be if he can keep the lead. It's the shortest way around, but it's also the most dangerous. The turns come sharper, and so do the other drivers. Some of them might have it in their heads to win. I figure if I can stay ahead of Bushman and Fisher, the rest'll be easy as rolling off a log."

We were all raring to get to it now. We helped Buddy up into the chariot and I saw him plant his feet firmly against the sides of the newly installed sandbag on the floor. We started walking the team down to the southern end, and a squad of mounted legionnaires in colorful robes and helmets galloped up to accompany us to the starting line.

There was a new murmur of excitement from the stands when we appeared at the bend. At last it looked like the race was going to begin. A last-minute surge of honored guests was filing into the privileged sections under the canopies. Somewhere up there Norma would be watching. Would her heart be pounding as she held her breath and worried for my safety? Maybe she was just as anxious as I was to see the whole damn thing wound up so that we could be united again.

Everywhere I turned I saw people darting around with empty equipment boxes, stashing them out of sight and handing people signal flags and such.

The cameras themselves were hard to spot. I was told there were some forty-six operators on hand, the best cameramen in the business. Most sat up high on platforms or shot from well-concealed positions like that camera pit that had been laying in wait for me.

"Goddamn It, Ardale, you cocksucker!" spat Delmer Burr as he rode up beside Buddy. "Who gave you authority to order those fucking sandbags? I should have every one of 'em torn out, you hear me? There's no time for that now. But you try goin' over my head again and I'll poke your damned eyes out with my thumbs! You got that, you scrawny old fuck?"

"Yes, sir," answered the old horse soldier, passing the reins into his left hand in order to give a salute. Somehow it lost its purpose on the way and ended up looking like he was swatting at a fly.

Squeaks was noticeably bristling across from me over Burr's crude insults.

As the twelve teams snorted and jostled to resist, we brought them into line. Of course, getting them there was one thing and holding them there was another. They kicked at us and bucked, probably reaching back to some ancestral vision of galloping on the plains unfettered and free. They didn't like standing in those heavy straps, yoked to a six hundred pound block of wood and metal tied to their tails by a confederation of human scum.

Breezy Eason came trotting up on a chalky-eyed pinto, with his oversized Stetson bouncing above him like a beach umbrella on a windy day. "Now, when you hear the signal, men," he called to the drivers, "I want to see some action. This ain't the time for holding back. You get them hooves pounding to beat the band."

Polly's sense of calm and confidence helped settle down our team. It gave me a chance to ask Squeaks about that dandy new scarf.

"Ain't she a beauty?" The young Irishman lifted it by to show off its pearly sheen. "Just a token of the affections of a fair-haired lass. 'Here,' she says, 'take this into yonder battle, and when you win, know that you have but to come and collect my heart.' " He patted it against his shirt with a tender touch.

At any other time this might have moved me with its romance. But I felt only spite and envy. Why couldn't Norma have sent down some sentimental token to me? If she had, I'd have been walking on air now, and what was to come would have been so much more bearable.

***

Now with the race about to commence let me clear away all other thoughts so I can set down events as they appeared to me. Let the ancient spirits guide my hand as I travel back to the searing memory of that day.

Down on the sunny track stands a jagged line of horse flanks, stretching over the sands like piano keys: white, black, white white, black, white, and so forth. I see the matchstick yokes shift as the chains clank and clatter from the agitated movements of the mounts.

Lined up at the starting rope the forty-eight steeds prance in place, lashing their tails against the twelve painted chariot cars at their rear. Wheels carve ruts deeper in the sand as the wagons rock to and fro.

Above this churning cauldron hover like fat bumblebees the heads of the charioteers, their eyes alert, their necks tensed, their arms and fingers intent upon the reins. Most wear headgear of one sort or another—Italian oarsman's caps or studded Greek headbands or plain Egyptian-cloth wrapped with leather. But what were mere costumes only minutes before are now the colors of contestants surrendering their fates to the prowess of their teams.

Francis X. Bushman stands as wooden as a cigar-store Indian at the nearest helm. Next to him is the Ben-Hur chariot with Fisher at its reins, dressed in Novarro's leather skullcap and vest. Then comes the Greek team, and next to it Buddy Ardale's rig, and the one driven by a man named MacNeil, and then Pedro and Freddie Moore, and so on.

Raining down from all sections of the coliseum are rose petals and laurel leaves, a colored mix of confetti on the breeze. In the pandemonium, last-minute wagers are placed, shouts of names and proclamations of favorites build on one another until the noise becomes a whirlpool of sound.

Then abruptly it subsides. All is hushed. Four men in fluttering tunics hold up poles with white banners. All eyes attend. In the lull the sound of whipping fabric grows deafening, and faintly in the air comes the metal grinding of hand cranks and the curious squawks of coastal gulls swooping overhead. In the distance is an oblivious putt-putting of motorists on empty Culver City streets as remote as tomorrow.

Then the banners tumble like axe blades and the rope is dropped. The teams are loosed like arrows from their battery of bowmen.

Spectators leap up their benches or go charging to the front rails. Every breast pounds in time to one hundred and ninety-two thundering hooves.

Bushman has somehow been the first to get his team to speed, and his chariot is the first to cross headlong toward the inner wall. Clouds of dust rise and expand as other teams shoot forward. Pedro is holding to a second position, a length or so ahead of Fisher and MacNeil.

Buddy's car has been caught in a backward roll by the starting flag and struggles to get off. Polly strains mightily into her yoke and reverses the slippage, and now the four snap to action. The team pulls as one as Buddy works to gain upon MacNeil as the spectators go wild.

Not all the drivers head toward the inner wall. The Greek and others think they can build momentum in the open and pass at the turn to the front of the pack. The race for leadership is engaged as some reach for their crops to lash the teams onward.

Bushman's four still hold the front as they push nearer the wall. Pedro has the speed now and leaves the pocket behind Bushman to pass him at his side. Fisher slips his chariot tight to the wall and looks for an opportunity to break through.

The neck-on-neck competition is between MacNeil and Buddy for third place at the wall. Buddy's team is making up for lost time. As the chariots approach the *metae,* or turning posts, the drivers brace for the force of the pull. Buddy hollers to Polly and the muscular bay lowers her neck into the task. The car surges forward and passes MacNeil's team to steal into third position at the spina wall.

Now comes the turn and Bushman allows his team to go wide rather than risk a flip. Pedro is forced to move wider yet to get around, and Fisher bears down on the prize of an opening. At the last minute, the chance is gone and Bushman swings around fast to close the gap, leaving Pedro stranded outside Fisher. The chariots at the middle make a broad arch in the northern turn and are passed handily by the cars at the spina.

In the backstretch the race resumes on the straightaway with Bushman, then Pedro and Fisher, now Buddy in a gallop. The rest follow them and for seconds all that can be seen from my vantage are heads and shoulders, which quickly drop from sight. The forerunners come wheeling around the crouching colossus of Atlas, and a game-marker on the division wall raises his stanchion to flip a dolphin nose down.

Six laps remain.

Now all the cars have had their turn around the course. Bushman, little Pedro, Fisher and Buddy are all lengths ahead. Those lagging behind face the full measure of the job at hand and map a new strategy. One of the drivers, a man whose name I later learn is Garrigan, has been whipping his team to breakneck frenzy on the outside track. In a desperate bid for position, Garrigan now yanks his reins to the left with such force that blood flies from the mouth of his lead runner.

The team zags to the left and the wagon's fragile wheels skirl and squeak. Just at that instant the cart seems to hit a bump and it bounces high. Its wheels spin madly above the track as the driver flies clear and the wagon wrenches to the left. There comes a clatter of screaming chains and the horses are picked up by an invisible fist and slammed nostrils-first into the sand.

By the time the wreck comes to an appalling stillness, the other drivers are well down the track with only the final few hazarding a quick look back. Thus the race continues for those in the lead while we who are standing by realize in a flash that there is only limited time to clear the wreckage from the way.

A hitched team of plow horses comes from nowhere and is whipped to the site of the crash, dragging chains and hooks. Other workers show up with a stretcher and hurry to the fallen driver. Garrigan is sitting up now and appears okay, but when I get to the wreck I see at once that the problems won't be quickly handled. All four horses appear hurt or dazed. At least one may be dead. The bodies are lying atop one another and buried in splintered spikes of lumber. Somehow they must be freed from the yoke and dragged away.

Out runs a worker with a huge cutter whose jaws are sent to bite through the metal. SNAP! answers the one and is followed in a moment by another. Workers frantically pull chains through iron eyes. Powder Keg and a half dozen others free the car and hoist its greased axles onto their shoulders and run it toward the stands.

The plow team has its hooks around the fallen horses. But time is out. The crowd spots the racers reappearing at the turn, and there is a massive cry of alarm from the bleachers. Bushman and Pedro are fighting for the lead but they see the obstacle in their way. They divert their teams to the right and drive them toward the outside wall.

Behind them, Fisher whips his team and steers them into the opening before spotting the wreckage ahead. He has only fifty yards to bring his chariot to a halt before his horses are crushed between six hundred pounds of hurtling metal and an immovable mound of flesh. Coming close behind, Buddy cannot see that Fisher is attempting to stop, and then it is too late. Buddy violently throws himself into the task of braking his wagon, but his horses have little space to slow and they come to a dead stop at the back edge of Fisher's car.

It seems that tragedy has been averted. When the dust clears, Buddy's team is intact and standing immediately at Fisher's chariot. The other drivers are far enough back to bring their wagons to a stop. Now that I can breathe again I become aware of warning whistles shrieking out hither and yon from the field directors.

The race is over for the time being, and the ear-piercing trills bring me back from my waking dream of eternal Rome to the here-and-now reality of filmmakers and studio bosses and hired extras who have put their lives on the line so that ticket buyers, too, can have their waking dream.

***

"Is everyone all right?" called Buddy when he saw me rushing toward him.

"Looks like everyone's okay," said Rusty. "How 'bout you?"

"Guess we made it, but it was a close one. Better check the team."

I told Buddy the fallen driver had gotten away safely. He asked why the wreckage wasn't cleared and I told him there just wasn't time before they all came bearing down on us from the turn.

We were all starting to trade relieved smiles again until Rusty stood up from inspecting the team looking stricken. He gave a slight shake of the head to Buddy. "I dunno. Polly took a hard crack against that car. Leg looks kind of serious to me."

Buddy turned as white as a picket fence and tossed his reins aside to jump down and look. Squeaks seemed nearly as pale, his head flying this way and that. "I'll get the doc," he yelled, and dashed off in a frenzy.

Rusty went back to prodding Polly's leg and when he touched a sore spot the mare whinnied in pain. "Easy, girl. Simmer down, Polly."

"All right, men, get your teams moving," ordered Delmer Burr as he came trotting up high in his saddle. "Get this area cleared and let's get back to work." Then he saw everyone gathered around Polly and he edged his mount closer. "What's wrong with your team there?" he called out.

"Looks like she took a whack on her leg," said Rusty.

"Broke?"

"We're waiting for the vet now."

Squeaks was leading back a funny-looking man in a Western-style tie and a silver buckle in the shape of a horse. He bent to his task but wasn't there a moment before he straightened up and looked to Delmer Burr. "It's her foreleg. Fractured, at least. Maybe broke. Can't tell here. She's through though," he said with a matter-of-fact squint.

Delmer nodded. "Tough luck, Ardale," he said. "You're out. Get your team off the track."

"Wait a second!" blurted out Buddy. "We're not through here."

"You are."

"No, I'm sayin', we're not!"

"The studio's paying for a race. That mare got any race left in her? We can't afford to wait for her to mend. So get her off the track, understand, or—"

"Or what?"

"Or we do what's necessary to get on with things."

"Do what's necessary?" repeated Squeaks. "Would you mind putting that into plain English for a dumb mick?"

"You know what it means," said Burr.

"Shoot her? Is that what you're requiring?"

"Calm down here, Irish," said Buddy. "We got to think about this."

Squeaks turned on him in horror. "You can't be thinking of doing this?"

"I got to think what's best. All I know is, I won't let 'em take me out of this race."

The Irishman turned to Rusty. "Will you listen to what the man is sayin'? You can't be in agreement."

"Don't ask me," said the redhead. "I got some bucks riding on our car, but it's only money. Polly's Buddy's horse. It's up to him to decide."

"What's her chances?" asked Buddy, "I mean, of her getting well?"

Rusty didn't have to think long. "She may knit, then again she might not. She'll never be the runner she was."

Buddy started to pace in a small circle, thinking on what he should do, as Freddie Moore came pushing up through the crowd. "What's the hold up?" he asked.

One of the other men said, "They want to shoot Buddy's horse"

Buddy stopped to look at Moore. "You're the expert here on workers' rights. Do I got to do this?"

Moore appeared stumped. "Man's calling the shots for now, Buddy," he muttered.

"Sorry, Buddy," said one of the workers, and his sentiment was repeated in the nods of a number of the others.

"I didn't raise Polly to be no saddle horse for kids," said Buddy. He looked up at Delmer Burr. "You find me another horse. I'm in this race to the end." Then he walked over to Polly and began gently unstrapping her harness.

"Burr," said Moore with anger in his eyes, "if you force this, there'll be a price to pay."

"Stop yer yappin' and give them a hand," he answered. "You men in the back there, get out to the paddocks and bring a fresh replacement. The rest of you, get those dead animals off the track. Move it, people. Time's runnin' low!"

Squeaks wedge his body in front of the old cavalry soldier. "Buddy, for glory's sake, think what you're doing. This is Polly," he said.

Rusty tugged on the Irishman's arm. "Let him be now. He's made up his mind."

Squeaks squared off against Buddy then and struck a defiant stance. "I won't be a party to it, understand? I wash me hands of you, Buddy Ardale!" And then he gave an explosive spin and stomped away.

Almost immediately Fisher stepped forward holding onto his coiled whip, glaring around at the men waiting there. "We could put an end to this now, if we all stand together. We can show 'em. They got to see they can't keep pushin' us around."

Delmer Burr's horse stomped and snorted. "Whoa, boy, settle down," he said. When it was calm again he glared at Fisher. "If you're thinking about shutting down this shoot, you'll have to go through me." He slid a hand up his trouser leg to the handle of a side gun poking from its holster.

Fisher's eyes darted this way and that for some back-up from the men. But he saw no movement and soon he had to bow to reality. He grudgingly tossed his whip in the sand.

Burr gave a victorious smirk. "Fisher, we've had enough of your demands. You've got yourself thirty seconds to get off studio property or there's goin' to be an unfortunate gun accident."

Fisher glared back a second, then pulled off his racing cap and threw it at the hooves of Burr's mount. He swiveled and went storming off the track.

"Mr. Burr," said Freddie Moore in a measured tone, "we'll be filing an official protest before this day is done. We'll ask for an inquiry into all of the irregularities and violations."

"What are you talking about?"

"We got no prior notice of the carriages being modified. Studio employees have a right to safe conditions at work. Then there's the mistreatment of the horses. There will have to be restitution for every one that has to be destroyed."

Burr gave an indifferent grunt and looked off at someone coming down the track.

Rusty leaned over to me and whispered, "Here comes Breezy. He'll put an end to this horse shit."

B. Reeves Eason came striding up on foot, looking none too happy. He demanded to know what was holding things up.

"A little disagreement, sir," said Burr. "I had to discharge one of the drivers."

"You fired him? Goddamn it, Burr! We're trying to film a twelve-man race here!"

"We got back-ups."

"We had exactly one back-up left. And I put him with the replacement rig."

"Why can't Garrigan do the driving?" asked Burr.

"Damn it, Garrigan's seeing double. He landed on his head and the doctor says he's out for the day. ... Who'd you fire?"

"Fisher."

"Fisher! My God! That's our Ben-Hur. *Mr. Mayer i*s betting on that rig! We can't just put anyone in her."

"We'll get our best driver in there. I'll see to it."

Eason nervously dug a pipe out of his coat and tapped it against his palm the way Niblo did it. "We're still short one driver."

"I know got some others with training."

"If it's handling the fours you're needing," called out a voice from the mob. Squeaks stepped forward in his blazing white scarf. "I can do it for you."

Eason stopped in the middle of opening his tobacco pouch to look up. "Did that man get the training?"

"The basics. Enough to be a stand-in."

Eason spilled more tobacco on his boots than he packed in his bowl. It was clear he had little practice with a pipe. The way he was fumbling with his pouch and his tamper might have struck me as comical at any other time. "Which team you with, son?" he asked the young Irishman.

"They put me with Buddy's rig. But it's ready I am to move on."

"Buddy Ardale?" said Eason, looking around for the old horse soldier. "Good to see you. ... This man telling the truth?"

"He's free to stay or to go," said Buddy. "We'll make do."

"Uh, Mr. Eason, sir," interrupted Rusty Bigelow, "we got ourselves another issue at the moment. We got a hurt horse here in need of some medical care."

Eason finished lighting up his pipe and was testing its draw. He gave several puffs and frowned. "Well, get a replacement for it, for God's sake."

"Yes, sir," said Delmer Burr. "We're seeing to that now."

"And if Buddy's man here wants to drive in Garrigan's place, let him. Let's just get all the rigs back on track quick as possible." With that Eason sucked hard on his pipe again and nearly turned blue before giving an exasperated scowl. He hammered the bowl against his heel until all the tobacco was dislodged, then pushed the pipe back inside his coat and went clopping off.

"You there," Delmer Burr called to Squeaks. "Get yourself outfitted proper and get your ass back here—*pronto!*"

Rusty Bigelow was still standing there in a daze. But before I could talk to him Powder Keg caught my attention. He was pointing frantically off across the track. A half-dozen workers were filing onto the track with metal rods and large discs and curtain panels. They were getting set to hide the hurt horses away from the sight of the audience.

Somehow I expected the whole coliseum to be watching what was going on. But most seemed to have grown impatient with the delay and were standing around in clumps, chatting among themselves. I spotted an ice-blue dress right up front at the railing, and I saw it was a woman in a ribboned sun hat. She raised her arm when she saw me and called out faintly, "Grover! Over here!"

My heart jumped. Yes, it was Norma. I had a reason for hope again. I whispered in Rusty's ear, "I'm going to stop this! Watch Delmer Burr. Don't let him do nothing before I get back."

So I went sailing off across the track, past the workers with their poles and blinds, until I could reach out to take Norma's perfect downstretched hand in mine.

"Oh, Grover," she said, "wasn't it awful? Was anyone hurt?"

I told her about the dead horses and about how poor Polly now was facing destruction as well, just so they could get on with the picture.

"I don't understand," said Norma. "Who said Polly must be destroyed?"

"Mr. Burr," I said. "Delmer Burr."

"How asinine!" she railed. "And who is he?"

"Assistant director. Overseeing the racers."

"A second unit A.D.?" she asked, totally appalled.

I nodded. "He's the boss."

"He's *not* the boss," she said. "I know all the bosses, and he's not—"
Then she stopped and the flash of a smile crossed her lips. "Grover!
Come with me!"

"You mean now?"

"I'm going to take you up to see Mr. Thalberg. Yes! Mr. Thalberg
will put a stop to this." The idea seemed to take hold in her eyes, like
a glass slide dropped behind a magic lantern. She pointed to a small
gate and steps leading into the stands, and she was there to meet me
and we were together again.

My joy lasted just a second, though, and a wave of terror filled the
void. "What can I possibly say to Irving Thalberg?"

"You will tell him what you told me, my darling. He's a kind and
sympathetic soul. You'll see. If anyone can save your Polly, it's the
Boy Wonder of M-G-M!"

CHAPTER FIFTEEN

Heart Trouble

"You know, there aren't many wild animals in Brooklyn. A little boy has to make a lot of bus transfers to find an elephant or a tiger," Norma was saying on our way up to the executive tier.

"This is only my own theory, of course, but I don't think Mr. Thalberg really cared too much about going to work for Mr. Mayer. And you can believe there were other offers. The man who got Universal to make 'Hunchback of Notre Dame'? *Insisting* on Lon Chaney for the lead? Believe me, a man who ends up turning that into a winning picture gets plenty of attention from other studios."

She stopped on a step to look at me. "And do you know why Mr. Thalberg said yes to Mr. Mayer?" She waited with smiling eyes for her answer. "Go ahead, guess," she urged.

"Because he loves animals?"

She seemed a bit taken back. "That's right! Well done, Grover!" She turned to continue the climb as she went back to her chatter. "Mr. Mayer had all sorts of wonderful animals at the time. Monkeys and zebras and tigers and a big lion named Leo."

"Sounds like a zoo."

"Well, it was. That was Mr. Mayer's first studio. It was the site of the old Selig Studio, on Mission Road. This was seven or eight years ago. Long before I arrived, of course. Colonel Selig made jungle pictures, and he found it was cheaper to buy animals outright than to keep renting them. So there were cages on the lot, and after a while Mr. Selig charged people to come in and see them. It became the Selig Zoo, and that's what Mr. Mayer leased to begin his own studio.

"I'll never forget my first visit, before they moved it all to Culver City. The first thing I heard was a lion roar. I felt like a doomed Christian. Mr. Thalberg was there by then, and he was so proud of those animals. He knew every one of them by name. He gave me a tour, and he'd say, 'This is Charlie, Miss Shearer, and Charlie's a boa constrictor. We only need to feed him twice a month.' He always spoke to them and asked the caretakers how they were doing. They always were given everything they needed."

We had arrived on a landing and Norma stopped as if winded from her talking. She meant to reassure with a smile. "There's no question about Mr. Thalberg's being concerned for your horse," she said.

The fact is it had occurred to me that none of this was really about saving Polly at all. Norma's spirits were almost too bubbly for any rescue mission. Something else was on her mind entirely, and I didn't have to guess what it might be. It was Irving Thalberg.

The landing led to four steps that dropped down to a private stall with a closed canvas flap. A costumed guard in a silver breastplate and a burgundy Roman cape recognized Norma and apologized for not letting her pass.

A woman in a severe-looking business suit jumped up from a nearby seat to rush over. "Why, Miss Shearer," she said, "we weren't expecting you."

"Hello, Myra."

"And what a smart outfit!"

"You like it? It's new. I love your suit, by the way. It does wonders for your eyes. Listen, I need to slip in for a quick word with Mr. Thalberg."

"I'm afraid he's with someone at the moment," she said. "Perhaps after the race ..."

"No, I'm afraid this can't wait. It's about the race, you see. This man has some very urgent information to share. It's really life-or-death."

The secretary looked at me askance, then nodded. "Let me tell Mr. T you're here. Excuse me."

The woman scratched on the canvas flap and called something, then vanished inside.

Norma squeezed her lips together in that way women have of smoothing their lipstick. Then she craned her neck about as if searching for something and I saw her eyes fasten on the guard.

"Excuse me," she said, fishing out a gold tube from her wrist bag. "Do you mind?" She bent close to see herself in the man's silver breastplate and made a fast repair, then wiped a pinkie across her front teeth. "Thank you very much," she told him.

My stomach felt like it was churning butter by this time. As much as I tried to convince myself it was hunger, I knew it was all just nerves. I mumbled something to Norma about not wishing to interrupt anyone.

"Relax, Grover. It's absolutely the right thing to do."

"But I heard he had fired a director once for holding up a production."

"One doesn't She straightened up to look straight at me.

"If you mean Mr. von Stroheim, yes, Mr. Thalberg had to take action. He's such a frightening man, keeping his head shaved and pretending to be a Prussian aristocrat. He was just a stickler for authenticity, and was costing the studio oodles. Well, Mr. Thalberg wasn't chosen to command a studio at age twenty for being timid. When he went down on the set and fired Von Stroheim he certainly got people's attention. It was unheard of. No director had ever been fired from his own picture before. The producer was suddenly king, and all directors were on notice."

"So why should he listen to me?"

She dropped her lipstick tube in her bag and pulled the drawstrings tight. "There's a life at stake here, Grover."

The flap flew open and I think we both expected to see the secretary emerge. But instead, out stepped a different woman altogether. She had striking dark eyes and raven-black hair that bounced in curls on her two pale shoulders.

"Hello, Dutch," said Norma.

The woman gave a sheepish smile and gathered the folds of her frilly lavender dress to negotiate the steps. "Norma, darling, what a pleasure seeing you. I told Irving you wouldn't miss it."

"Connie, this is Grover Link. Grover, meet Constance Talmadge."

She smiled and held out a long, slender hand to me. "Would you mind?" Taking her hand was like picking up a kitten and finding nothing there but a bit of fluff and wiggle. She held on as she stepped up onto the landing and smoothed her dress.

"I couldn't miss all the excitement, could I?" said Norma.

The beauty queen smiled awkwardly.

"Miss Talmadge has driven chariots too, Grover. Isn't that so, Dutch?"

"I was just telling Mr. Thalberg about that."

"That was years and years ago, of course."

"Norma, dear, you make me sound ancient." She turned to me confidentially. "It was a picture called 'Intolerance.' I was a Babylonian, and Mr. Griffith had me drive up in a chariot. Of course, the real driver was crouched down on the floor. I just had to look pretty."

The actress nodded toward the racetrack. "Have you a favorite?"

"Me? No bets. Anything can still happen."

"Well," said Constance Talmadge, brushing aside her dress again for a quick look down, "he's all yours."

"Thank you, dear. I promise I won't keep him."

The thin beauty went on her way with her little fanny swishing left and right, down the aisle, swish-swish, knowing all the men's eyes were on her.

"Why did you call her Dutch?"

"It was her family's pet name for her. She was evidently quite a chubby child—with an unfortunate pageboy haircut."

"It doesn't suit her any more."

"No," said Norma. "You see, Grover. I told you there were prettier sights around."

"Norma?" called a male voice. Then the secretary came from the stall and held back the flap for us.

From what I read in the movie magazines, I expected to find Thalberg dressed like a sheik and sitting cross-legged on a pillow with a hookah or something. That's how exotic he seemed from the articles of that time. He stood smiling in a dark pinstriped suit and a tie with a silver stickpin, his dark hair shiny with pomade.

If he was embarrassed any about being caught in a tryst, there was no evidence of it. He couldn't have stood more than five-foot-seven, and probably weighed less than a hundred and twenty pounds. But standing there before him in my dusty Levi's and cowboy flannels, I felt like a panhandler at a glitzy wedding.

How mortified my mother would have been to see me there with him. I could hardly recall my last visit to a barber, and here was Irving Thalberg nicely groomed and looking like a million dollars. It irked me that he was no more than a year or two older, and yet here he was entertaining beautiful ladies in a private booth with all the power of a king to decide the fate of those that crossed his path.

"Norma, did I tell you this morning how smashing you look?"

"I'll always listen to it again," she laughed. "Mr. Thalberg, this is Mr. Grover Link."

He reached for my hand and gave it a friendly shake, ignoring all my scruffy unworthingness. "Nice to meet you."

"Mr. Thalberg," said Norma. "I would never have bothered you like this, but this is a serious matter."

"Okay, let's hear it," he said.

"Grover here is taking part in the race. I know you care about animals as much as I do. I want you to listen to what he has to say."

"Of course." He motioned to the empty chair next to him. "Mr. Link, why don't you have a seat?"

I took him up on the offer because my knees were so rubbery by then I was afraid they might buckle. I settled myself next to a small table holding two half-empty glasses of ice. One had a red smudge of lipstick on the rim. Above me, I sensed Thalberg and Norma trading a silent message.

"Grover, I'll wait for you outside," she said, and I heard the canvas flap drop.

"Can I get you a drink?" asked Thalberg.

"No. I can't stay really."

"You weren't in that smash-up, were you?"

"No. I'm just one of the horse wranglers."

"Oh?" He paused before sinking in his chair to grab hold of the crease in his trousers. "I'm a kind of a wrangler here myself," he joked, crossing his leg. Then he picked up his glass. "You a vet?"

"A vet?"

"I'm sorry. A veteran. You know—the war?"

"Oh. No."

"I envy vets. I wanted to go. I admire those who help make the world a better place." He rattled the cubes around in his glass.

"What's important to me at the moment, Mr. Thalberg, is—"

"You can call me Irving."

"Thanks."

"May I call you Grover?'

"Sure."

"Tell me, Grover, do the stands look full to you?"

"They're pretty full, I think."

"Pretty full? I wanted every seat to be filled today. I wanted the place packed. It's the producer in me, I guess."

"The men and I are worried about some of the horses—"

"Norma seems to think you're a bright young man. Do you know the way one makes a change in the world? First you have to change people's hearts." Thalberg watched the cubes tumble around some more. "I don't know why others make movies. But that's why I make movies. It's why I want to see this studio succeed."

The sun must have emerged from another cloud because the wading pools on the spina cast shimmering reflections on the canopy over our heads. I could see tiny figures down on the track erecting curtain poles around the crash scene.

"Mr. Thalberg, excuse me, we're running out of time." I scooted forward in my seat, wanting to run but knowing I had to stay and try to make him see. Imagine being rude to fellow like Irving Thalberg that way. Imagine a ditch-digging nobody like me telling a man with a bad ticker how fast his time was running out!

This little king whose whole empire rested on borrowed time was being reminded of the books he would never read, the movies he wouldn't make, the lands left unexplored. A small sadness showed in his dark eyes. "Oh, of course," he mumbled in his glass.

"I'm sorry, sir, but more horses are about to be destroyed, and if you can't do nothing I've got to get back down there and—"

"Grover, please sit. Give me just a minute. You see, we have addressed the problem."

"You did?"

"It happened before, you know. In Italy, during one of the practice runs. They solved it with flags. Colored flags. They weren't properly prepared, but now they are. The drivers will be signaled of any trouble ahead. There won't be any more pile-ups, you can believe that."

"Mr. Thalberg, one of the horses down there now belongs to my friend. It may be a broken leg, but whether it is or not they're fixing to shoot her. It's all because some A.D. named Burr who's got it in head—"

"What's the name again?"

"Delmer Burr."

"No, I don't know him. Go on."

"Well, he said there's no time to wrap the leg and get Polly the care she needs. And Norma—I mean, Miss Shearer—she said you might hold up the race, at least until we can get the injuries attended to."

Whatever misgivings he had felt, Thalberg twisted in his chair and seemed about to take charge. He felt for a coin in his pocket and brought up a quarter, rotating it absently from his fingertips.

"Do you know who Mr. Mayer is, Grover? He's the president of the studio. Believe me, you don't want to see him when he gets agitated.

You don't want to be around him. And he's heard what is being said about this whole project being 'jinxed.' You know that word? It's a carryover from the Old World. Things don't go wrong, it's no one's fault, they're just jinxed. You can fix problems, but when something's jinxed, well, it's out of your hands. Understand?"

"No," I told him, "not really."

"Things went very wrong in Italy. I convinced him to try again. But if they look like they're jinxed here, if things go wrong right in front of everybody in Hollywood, that could be a disaster—for Mr. Mayer, for me, for the whole studio."

Thalberg didn't seem to be talking to me anymore. He was looking down at the coin and speaking as if passing a thought around in his mind. Suddenly he grabbed the coin to turn in his chair to face me.

"Listen, Grover, you believe in fair play, don't you? Fair play is a good thing. But only if the playing field is level. What if you're playing against a cheat, a liar? What if you've got young ones at home depending on you? What if you've got teammates to look after, and they've got families too? Is it still fair play that matters most?"

To me, that sounded like a lot of hooey. I started to tell him again about Polly's life being in danger and he went on like he didn't even hear me.

"Mr. Mayer, you know, he's a dear old soul. He can be tight with his money, but he really cares for the people who work for him. He thinks of himself as a father to us all. If he knew that a driver was hurt in that accident, or that some horses had to be destroyed, he would be devastated. I can assure you of that. He'd be just struck dumb. He wouldn't know where to turn. He might close down the set and send everyone home.

"Who knows if it would get going again? At the least there'd be a whole new crew. So all these people, think about it, out of a job through no fault of their own. And you know the sad part? If they knew it was because of you and your personal concerns, they'd hate you for it. Isn't that lousy? Here you just want to do the right thing, and other fair-minded people end up hating you—for just wanting to help a friend. Where's the 'fair play' in that?"

What Thalberg was saying didn't add up to me. Sure, I might take the heat if the production shut down. But Mr. Mayer knew about Italy, and he must have seen the wreck. And from what Eason said, Mayer even had some private money riding on the race. He wasn't likely to call it quits until he got something to show for his money.

That was what I said to Irving Thalberg then, and he listened to everything I said before nodding with an almost sheepish grin.

"Well, Norma was right. You're a bright fellow. Okay, Grover, I didn't think I'd need to explain this, but you have to hear it. You want to know the real reason I can't do what you're asking? You've got to keep this between you and me, understand? If I'm ever asked about it, I'll deny it. ... I can't stop this race because it would shake Mr. Mayer's faith in God."

I think I might have snorted in his face. "Mr. Mayer's faith?"

"His faith in God, yes."

I thanked him for his time then and started to rise.

"Now, wait. Hold on, please, I'll explain."

"I'm probably not smart enough to understand."

"Give us both a chance."

I eased back down in my seat and waited.

"It's the gambling," he said.

"The gambling? You mean his bet?"

"It goes back long before today."

Then he told me a story about all the studio heads, and how they had been getting together for their weekly game of poker. At first, the games just helped them blow off steam and hone their skills at bluffing and bidding. Poker was a safe way to match wits with business rivals and get a feel for their nerves and values. But it became a kind of therapy to some, a way to see how they were measuring up. The pots got bigger, the stakes higher. Before long, no one wanted to miss a game to go on vacation or take a business trip to New York.

Thalberg thought it might have something to do with being wealthy now, and their guilt over having so much when back in the Old Country their relatives lived in such misery. Why had they escaped? At bottom, Thalberg said, every poker hand they drew was a sort of test—a recall vote. Gambling went beyond just fate or the luck of the draw. For them it had become a measure of their worthiness in the eyes of God.

"Yes, Mr. Mayer has a little of his own money on this race. But what's important is that if he loses here, he'll know he's jinxed and that God has given up on him. The picture and the studio are done for. Might as well send everyone packing.

"You see what I'm talking about here?" said Thalberg. "I couldn't call off the race now if it meant a hundred horses' lives. Mr. Mayer wouldn't allow it—not until he finds out today if God is for him or against him."

There was a quiet scratching, and Norma Shearer peeked through the flap. "Men-talk over?"

"Norma, come in. Well, we solved part of Grover's problem. There'll be no more pile-ups on the track—right, Grover?"

"Wonderful!" said Norma, beaming at me. "And what about Polly?"

Thalberg gave a sober shake of his head. "I can't intervene. Not if it jeopardizes the shoot. For Mr. Mayer's sake. I am sorry."

"Oh, what a pity. Grover, it's so sad, isn't it? Well, we had to try."

"I've got to get down there," I told her. "Are you ready?"

Then my sweet guardian angel hesitated and seemed suddenly at a loss. In that brief opening, Thalberg sensed an opportunity.

"Why don't you stay here, Norma?" he said, pulling out my chair. "You can watch everything with me."

"You're not expecting ... *anyone?*"

"No. We'll be alone. I'd love a chance to chat. You know, Ramón is asking for you to be in his next picture."

"Yes."

"Sit down. Let's talk about what *you* want."

Norma seemed quite pleased with that. She brushed by me and took her place next to the lipstick-smudged glass. Even before I got to the canvas flap I heard them talking as if I were no longer there.

"I forgot you were such an animal lover, Norma," Thalberg told her.

"Well, of course. I was raised to respect all of God's creatures."

"Ramón is pushing this sound business," said Thalberg. "He wants audiences to hear him sing."

"I'm sure my brother would adore telling you more about it."

"Of course, Mr. Mayer's against the idea. He's afraid sound dialogue will ruin the world market."

"That shouldn't stop people like you and me from making the pictures we believe in."

"We can try," he said.

"As the poet asks, 'How high the moon?' "

I let the flap fall on Thalberg's response and Norma's lilting cascade of laughter. "Well, Norma," is what the Boy Wonder had said, "if one has to ask, he probably can't afford it."

Norma and Thalberg, it occurred to me, were like two express trains running on parallel tracks. Somehow I had thrown the switch that put them together on the same course. I couldn't blame Norma at all for the way it turned out.

But I was alone again, more alone than I had felt in my life. No one on Earth cared what became of me. I was caught doing the bidding of people like Louis B. Mayer and Irving Thalberg, left to the mercy of the Delmer Burrs of the world. All of them had their own twisted ambitions, with little or no time left to concern themselves with a heartsick little pup named Grover Cleveland Link.

CHAPTER SIXTEEN

The Race Resumes

Through my whole meeting with Irving Thalberg I tried to keep watch on the track. But at some point I had stopped paying attention, and I left so absorbed by despair that I could barely think beyond my own next step.

I kept hoping Norma would come chasing after me like Eliza on the ice, in a frenzy to escape the hounds and chains of her overseers. I prayed she would come to her senses and proclaim her love and ask me to forgive her for being so weak and forgetting the one thing in life that truly mattered.

Just like in the movies.

But no one charged down the steps behind me, and in time I remembered Buddy and Polly and the whole rotten situation. The drapery panels were hanging in place now, and I saw Delmer Burr's horse and saddle tied off nearby. People scurried past as if to avoid bearing witness to whatever would happen next.

There was a rat-tat-tat of drums, and onto the track ran a baggy pants clown chased by some midgets in a crazy bull suit. People in the stands welcomed the attempt at entertainment, and applauded the antics of the clown.

Then Delmer Burr came out from the spina, and blanched some at the brightness of the sun. I instantly picked up my pace, then took the steps two at a time until landing in the sand with both feet. "Burr!" I hollered, "Hold on a minute!" and hurried to head him off.

He shaded his eyes with a hand to see who was yelling. And just then came the crack. My first instinct was to dive for the ground, but Delmer stood stock-still, as surprised as I was. I looked at his free hand, hanging loosely at his side. Above it was an empty holster.

I took off running for the curtains and pushed my way through. There was Buddy standing quietly over the body of Polidoxus, named after the queen of all the racehorses.

He juggled the weight of a black revolver, and I saw the smoke rising from the gun barrel as he steadied it against his chest. He held it at such an angle that I feared he had it aimed at his chin. I started to scream out but there was a sudden clatter of curtain hooks behind me and we both stopped to look back.

There was Powder Keg, holding up a section of the drapes and sticking his head underneath. All I could see was the white of his eyes, but it had never been bigger. Unable to hear what the rest of us heard, he had come to see what I now knew: The deed was done. Beyond him, off in the bright sun, Delmer Burr shifted from leg to leg and gave a single approving nod.

With the barrel still leaking its smoke against his side, Buddy passed by without hoisting an eye to me. I could see no sign of mournful emotions in him at all, just the bone-tired weariness of a dirt farmer headed home after a harvest.

When he got to Delmer Burr he stopped and handed him the gun without a word and continued off down the track.

"All right, then," Burr called out after him, "get your rig ready and let's get on with it!"

From time to time that afternoon I would pass small groups of employees on a smoke break. They might take a deep draw on their tailor-mades and watch me go by, and then someone would whisper something like, *Wasn't that the fellow called "Runaway," the new kid with that old-timer who had to shoot his horse?*

As if it was me who deserved the pity.

***

Right after the pile-up, track officials got busy mapping out the new starting positions for the chariot teams. Working from diagrams and notes, they set markers in the sand based on their relative positions at the time of the crash.

Bushman's team was directed to the farthest point, a good six strides ahead of Pedro's rig. The Ben-Hur car and its four whites was placed half a length behind Pedro's rig. We found Buddy's marker another eight meters back of that. Then came MacNeil, Moore the Merrier, the Greek driver and four others I hadn't met bringing up the rear. A flag was placed for the unknown team being assembled to run in place of Garrigan's busted-up buggy.

Rusty came out walking next to Powder Keg, leading a handsome dappled mare. Buddy stepped all around her, giving her a thorough inspection and taking her measure.

"What do you think?" Rusty asked him.

"She looks like she might have some fire in her," he said. "If she's half the strider they say, she'll flare up nice when she feels the sand in her face."

We all felt better after that, and strapped her up at the inside position, making her the new team leader.

Before long I heard the approach of a car, and up rolled the Garrigan replacement outfit. It was a fancy yellow chariot decorated in licking orange flames, and it was being pulled by a team of four matched sorrels. Standing behind them at the reins was the young Irishman, Squeaks, wearing an open-chested toga. His face was now smeared with mascara and such, but even if I hadn't recognized him I couldn't have missed that white silk scarf rippling at his neck.

He waved to the spectators, then shook his crop at the team and let out with some choice Irish war whoop, clearly having the time of his life. Lagging behind his car was a crew of wranglers, among them that spooky Italian fellow the men called Santa Claus.

Squeaks steered his rig up nearby us and yanked the handbrake. He waited for Buddy to look over at him. "I have only this to say to you, Buddy Ardale," he boomed out. "I know not why you did what you did, but I'm sorry for the loss of Polly. She was a fine animal, which I needn't tell you. You raised her up, and you knew the worth of her. So I suspect you had your reasons. And now I say good luck to you. May the best man win. That's all."

Before Buddy could answer him, up cantered Delmer Burr on his dark steed. "You, there!" he shouted at Squeaks. "Get that rig back where it belongs." Then he took note of the white scarf and pointed a finger. "And take that fuckin' thing off your neck. This ain't some cattle town rodeo!"

The young Irishman rubbed the silk fabric and then heaved a sigh as he pulled the scarf free and tucked it inside his toga. We all watched Burr kick his mount and gallop away before passing around our looks of disgust.

"Squeaks!" called Buddy as the Irishman took up his reins to drive.

"Yeah, Buddy?"

"If you're throwed, get out of the way quick as lightning, hear? Don't count on 'em stepping over you."

Squeaks gave him a puzzled look.

"Good luck," ended Buddy.

Then with a grin and a flick of the reins he rolled away, warbling some jaunty Irish tune at the top of his voice.

Just as Thalberg promised, the field directors distributed bundles of red warning flags among the wranglers. Me and two others were sent to take up a station at the southern turn, so I wished Buddy good luck and hurried away toward the statue of old Mr. Atlas.

None of us could see the starter flag from where we stood, nor could we hear the announcements. So I can't report exactly what happened while we waited. But we knew the race was on when the bleachers exploded in a roar of cheers.

The thunder from those thousands of human feet as they jumped up and stomped against the floorboards drowned out even the hammering of the hooves.

Bushman's chariot was the first we saw rounding the northern turn. As it charged ahead it was pursued at a reckless gallop by Pedro's team, then Novarro's stand-in driver with his matched white stallions, and then at last Buddy. They remained apace down the track and were almost upon us when MacNeil and Freddie Moore appeared in a virtual dead heat at the bend. They skidded to the side as the horses leaned their shoulders hard into the turn. Other teams followed in a spreading swirl of dust, with Squeaks' orange-flamed car finally cutting through it from the inside.

Now the ear-punishing wall of noise doubled as the leaders went flying past the stands. A wrangler near me shouted up to a spear-holder on the wall for a report on what he saw. Some camera assistant yelled back down that Bushman was still in the lead but that "the little Mexican" was whittling away the gap.

When the drivers next appeared at the bend, Bushman was barely a length ahead of Pedro's team. Both lead cars were now being challenged on the backstretch by the furious advance of Ben-Hur's whites. Still pacing himself in fourth place was Buddy, biding his time while giving the horses just enough reins to know the force of his will.

With his wheels fully on the straight now and feeling free of the eyes of the crowd, Pedro lifted high his crop and let it down in a stinging blow to the rump of his lead runner. The horse looked startled and jerked ahead to escape its pain. The car shivered with the break in rhythm as Pedro's pacers nosed ahead of Bushman for the first time. The team charged on in a tornado of fright, and Pedro had his hands full just keeping his car steady.

As the leaders braced for the southern turn, I looked again to the next group approaching. Squeaks had somehow won a position at the wall and was pulling ahead of MacNeil, leaving Moore in a cluster with three or four others.

The Irishman hunched low across his shield and slapped the reins as he yelled out to the animals in some unknown tongue. I was so impressed by Squeaks' handling of his team that I did not see the threat from the Greek's chariot as it surged up behind.

The Greek laid a whip across the backs of his runners, and I saw Squeaks shake a fist at him and curse. Then he returned to scream at his own team in a voice I could just make out above the din: "See, my dears! See the sort of brute we're up against! Work your legs, me darlings! Throw your shoulders into it now for the love of glory!"

The two cars roared along side by side toward the turn. Then as the teams shifted in their harnesses and fought against the force of the pull, I saw Squeaks' carriage rise up off the ground, its two thin wheels spinning and whistling in midair. For one timeless eternity the young Irishman floated above the action on a cushion of God's grace that was yanked away too soon.

The chariot twisted to the left and went flopping on its side, then hurtled end over end in the sand, bouncing on its shield and sending wooden spokes and painted timber flying in all directions. I caught a glimpse of Squeaks' body as it fell with a thud upon a ragged heap of wood as his sorrels pulled their yoke loose and ran off with their chains slapping angrily behind them.

In an instant, cowboys were grabbing up the semaphore flags and running on the track. I hopped down and started to wave my arms over my head to alert the approaching drivers. Some charioteers planted a foot on the top railing as they strained mightily at the reins and the handbrakes to bring their hurtling wagons to a stop.

My heart was having a race of its own as it pounded and leapt. I was sure Squeaks must have been injured in the fall. Now he looked like a rag doll on what remained of his chariot. He had one a limp arm tucked under his back and his pelvis turned at an unnatural angle. One leg was pinned there near the orange lick of a wooden panel.

"Don't move him!" ordered a field director. "Wait for the medics."

I lifted up a chariot wheel detached from its axle and pulled it aside as Buddy came running up with his headgear in his hand. He dropped on one knee beside Squeaks and felt for some sign of life.

"Help's coming!" someone else shouted.

I stepped closer to see if the Irishman would speak.

"Irish?" called Buddy. He reached out to loosen the twisted folds of the toga around his neck.

"Yeah?" answered Squeaks. It was a haunting voice, rising out of somewhere inside him just as calm and normal as could be. He did not even open his eyes to see.

Buddy gave a gasp of relief and smiled. "The doctor's on his way."

"Better hurry," replied Squeaks. Then he lifted one eyelid to gaze at the old cavalry soldier. "Buddy? You see my scarf anywhere?"

Buddy reached up a hand and pulled on a corner of white fabric poking out of the young man's costume. He stopped when it began to turn soggy and red. "It's here," Buddy said. "Right where you put it."

"Good. I was afraid I lost it." Then he gave Buddy a weak smile and shut his eyes, and after a second he seemed to let out a long sigh. As far as I could tell, he might have died then and there.

Even before the studio's "ice truck" rumbled to a halt and a studio doctor jumped down, word was out that the chariot driver was badly hurt. I watched close as the doctor bent over and listened at his chest and peered in his eyes and such. If he detected any flicker of life there worth the fanning, he didn't betray much interest.

A couple of studio men in suits showed up to speak with the doctor in private, and attendants laid Squeaks on a stretcher and slid him in the back of the truck. Two other bosses in suits ambled over, and one of them I recognized as the same sweaty-faced man who pulled that reporter off me that morning.

The doctor climbed up into the back of the truck with Squeaks, and an attendant slammed the door and ran around to the front. There was a grinding of gears and a screech of tires as the ambulance sped its way off and out of the coliseum.

The meeting of the bosses seemed to come to an end and the oldest one of the group held up his arms for quiet. "It's up to the medical men now, fellows," he said. "The boy will get the care he needs. I'm told he should be back on his feet in just a matter of days."

There were relieved grins in the crowd, and more than a few

doubtful frowns. Mostly, though, people looked satisfied that it was done with and were ready to resume their places. Buddy just stood where he was, looking drained and hollow.

"All right, fellas!" shouted Delmer Burr. "Let's clean all this mess out of here. Get to it so we can all get back to the race!"

Over on the stadium side someone started to yell into a megaphone, telling the crowd there had been "a little accident with one of the chariots," but that "no one was seriously hurt." He said there would be a half-hour break while a new car was hitched up, and then the race would go on.

The crowd grumbled about the delay a bit, then greeted the last words with applause. It seemed like the only things anyone was thinking of anymore were the purses and the damn bets.

On our stretch of the track another impromptu studio huddle was getting started. I was curious to know what was being said there, so I dragged my broken chariot wheel over toward a spina alcove until I was within earshot of the officials.

Judging from the bits and snatches of what I heard, the managers were arguing about how to handle the reporters on hand. They agreed to some tighter security at the entry gates and to an increase of guards in the bleachers. Mostly they were determined to keep anyone on the track from mingling with onlookers in the stands. Any talk of injury needed to be snipped in the bud.

They all agreed that there was nothing to the accident, anyway, since only a few horses had been hurt and the driver was off being treated for his "cuts and scrapes." They expected the little setback would even boost interest, and ensure that their big shoot would be remembered as the most thrilling event in Hollywood history.

As the bosses grew aware of my presence, I carried the wheel off into the spina and let it drop. From there in the shadows I saw Delmer Burr approach Buddy. He leaned close and whispered something, and I might have started to think there was some glimmer of good in the man after all. Or maybe he was just feeling guilty for putting an untrained driver like Squeaks in charge of a team.

Then Burr looked around to make sure no one was watching, and he reached in his vest and pulled out a brown pint bottle and slipped it into Buddy's toga. The old horseman nodded once and Burr went on his way. After a few seconds, Buddy rose, waved off a few offers of consolation, and walked off on his own.

I hurried off to find the others and came upon Rusty speaking privately with Freddie Moore.

"The bastard!" cursed Rusty when I told them what I saw. "And you know why he done it, don't you?"

"He didn't do it out of pity for Buddy," said Moore. "He's just concerned with keepin' the race on track."

Rusty wagged his head. "No. What he knows is Buddy can't drink no more. My bookie pals tell me Burr's got a shitload of his own money on one of the other rigs. He'll stand a heck of a better chance winning with Buddy out of the running."

Moore overflowed with outrage. "That son of a bitch! We got to go warn Buddy!"

Rusty grabbed him by the arm. "No. Let it be. He's going to do what he wants to. He's not looking for reason not to."

Moore nodded with a determined set to his jaw. "This is the last straw," said Moore. "The bastards knew the cars were nothing but deathtraps. There's no reason Squeaks should've flipped like that. If he turns up badly hurt, it'll be the straw that breaks the studio's back."

"Squeaks is dead," I said flat out, and both men stopped to look at me. "I was standing right there. I watched him breathe his last."

"If that's so," said Moore, "we'll own these bastards!" He looked from Rusty to me and back, then jumped to his feet and hurried off.

Rusty looked at him disappear in the crowd. "What do you think?" he asked me.

"Fool's likely to get himself thrown off the picture."

"Of get us all shut down. ... You think Squeaks really bought it?"

I told him how the doctor acted after examining the Irishman's body. After a moment I asked, "Anyone know about his next of kin?"

"Don't believe he's got none. Not in this country, anyway. ... You see who gave him that silk scarf?"

"No."

"Someone should look for her. She'd probably want to know."

"You don't think we should go and stop Buddy?"

"Naw. A drink might be just what he needs now. Could do us all some good," he added with a wink. He hiked open his vest so I could see the silver top of a flask sticking up out of his belt. "Come on. It'll be an hour at least before they're set to roll. Let's go find us some privacy."

CHAPTER SEVENTEEN

The Dark Trail of Moonshine

Rusty Bigelow seemed as eager as me to get away from all the noise and the reminder of Squeaks lying in the rubble of his chariot. We headed out the south gate past the livery and the stables back up toward the food trucks.

We found things already packed up there for another day's shoot. The tin awnings were lowered and padlocked; the tables collapsed and stacked one against the other in a line. Rusty found a patch of shade out around a wagon and settled back against a wheel. I eased myself down on a dirt mound near him, and we were pretty much alone except for the occasional worker who happened by, double-stepping his way toward the outhouses.

It was a surprise to realize how bone-tired I felt. It wasn't much past one o'clock, yet I had had my fill of this day. How would I feel at two-thirty? at four o'clock? Where would I be tonight at eight, and how many more whippings would I have been handed out by then?

Rusty unscrewed the cap of his flask and wiped its spout with his sleeve. "To Squeaks," he said, raising the tin a bit, and took a big swallow before passing it to me.

It tasted like real whiskey, all right, not that nasty, chemical-smelling stuff you got in the *speaks*. It was strong but smooth and the first swallow should have gone down easy. But I hadn't eaten much all day other than a slice of apple at Mrs. Addison's. The liquor sent my windpipe in a tailspin, and I coughed and gasped for air.

Rusty's sourness gave way to a smile. "You all right?"

I passed the flask back and as my voice returned, I asked how he wound up in this line of work.

"You couldn't prob'ly tell it now," he said, "but I was a hell of an athlete in high school. Shot put. High jump. Javelin. ... I could run the hundred yards in ten-two, by God. I could've gone to the Olympics—least, that's what the coach said. But the family needed support, you know, and I had to leave school. Everyone was sayin' there was jobs in California. So I came out and went to work for a mean old buzzard who rented out construction equipment.

"One day I had to deliver a cement mixer to the old Metro lot. I stopped to watch 'em film this guy leap onto a moving car to wrestle the driver. I thought, hell, I can do as good as that guy. After that, I made sure I got all the studio deliveries, and I got to know who was doing the hiring. I was a cocky son of a bitch back then."

He tipped his head and took another mouthful, then handed the tin to me. "Guess I'm still cocky ... when there's a new guy on the lot," he said with just a quick glance my way.

I knew it was his stab at an apology, and I wanted to return the favor. "You did right by Molly, too. You been a good brother."

He pursed his lips and nodded. "I tried."

Then I knew I had to level with him or he would never trust a thing I said. "Rusty, I was the one that punched Squeaks. This morning. That was me in the spina with ... your sister. I thought I should tell you."

"Hell," he said, "I knew that. Anyone could see that from the guilty look on your face. If Squeaks was all right with it, what did I care? It's the guys with power, those dudes stuck up there in the special boxes, them's the ones that keep a brother awake nights."

We drank a bit more in silence.

"You know something?" he said after thinking some. "You ought to put in for Squeaks' job now."

"No, I don't think so."

"You should. Buddy'd vouch for you."

"Work for some little shit like that Delmer Burr?" I said. "It takes one cold S.O.B. to do a thing like that, give a bottle to a fellow he knows can't drink."

"He was just playing an angle."

"Yeah. Pushing a live horse off a cliff—that's an angle too."

"You ain't taken much of a fancy to him."

"Fellows back in Missouri—we had some like that. Delmer *Burr*," I repeated. Then I must have cackled or something, because Rusty gave me an odd look.

In truth, that moonshine was rushing to my head. I said his name over and over again, getting louder each time and pretending to shiver from the cold. "Delmer *Brrrrrrr*," I said, "Delmer *Brrrrrrrr*." I was like some kid breaking into an empty house and poking his head in each room, letting out a holler just to hear the echo.

Rusty gave a twisted grin. "Hey, you suppose that's how he got that name? Maybe when he was born he sent a shudder up his mama's spine."

"Guys like him don't have mothers."

Then we traded a few crude guesses back and forth about Burr's possible origin, and shared some laughs, the way guys do. But it all came to an end in a while, and I remembered how Buddy pulled out that bloody piece of Squeaks' scarf.

"You know, when Squeaks volunteered to drive the chariot..."

"Yeah?"

"I was just wondering. ... Why wasn't it you? You been at this longer than Irish."

Rusty took another swig. "I couldn't walk out on Buddy like that. Besides," he said, and tapped a knuckle against his fake leg, "I can't do what I used to."

"You lose it in the war?"

"Naw. We were shooting this western picture, and I had to squeeze out of this runaway stagecoach and climb up to the driver's bench and grab the reins. It was kind of my specialty, 'cause I got lots of upper body strength. I did the same stunt in a half-dozen pictures. This time, though, we were by this railroad track, and the gag was I was supposed to climb out and grab hold of the reins and drive the coach across the track just before the train comes by."

"What happened?"

"The coach wheel jumped a rail and bucked me off. Broke my leg in three places. The studio docs fixed me up, but it never set right, and it bothered me more'n I let on. After a time I went to see a specialist and he said the leg had to come off."

"Did the studio pay?"

"Never asked 'em. Figured they wouldn't use me no more if they knew. I told 'em I was signing with a Wild West show on a tour back East. When I could get around again all right, Buddy made 'em take me in—thirty bucks a week, no questions asked." Rusty eased back against the wheel and took a long drink.

"Buddy sees I earn my wage, tending horses and setting up the gags. He knows I can't do anything fancy no more. I'd lay down my life for that man."

"What do you think made him do it, Rusty?" I asked. "Shooting Polly like that, just to stay in the race?"

"There's more you don't know. Neither did Squeaks, not all of it. I wish I'd told him. Might've made a difference."

"Told him what?"

"About Buddy. And his accident."

"Buddy had an accident?"

"Car accident. It was—let's see—almost six years ago now—1920. January sixteenth, to be exact."

"Prohibition?"

"Yeah, the day before old bushy-eyed Volstead took to spying on us, and Congress decreed it a criminal matter 'to manufacture, sell or transport alcoholic beverages, punishable by five hundred dollars in fines or thirty days in jail, or both.'"

"I know what the Eighteenth Amendment says."

"Well, there's more you don't know."

"Did Buddy go to prison, is that it?"

"No. Let me tell it, will you? You know what a patriotic old horse soldier does when he gets caught between a weakness for hooch and his oath to honor the laws of his country?"

"No, what?"

"He makes up his mind that on January sixteen he ain't doing nothing but spending the last day before Prohibition getting his rightful fill of legal spirits. Because after that he knows he'll be spending the rest of his days as dry as Kansas in July—the most pitifully sober son of a bitch anyone ever saw."

"Oh."

"So he and Caroline go out for a last big bender."

"Who's Caroline?"

"That's Buddy's wife—are you listening?"

"You didn't say a thing about any Caroline."

"Well I'm coming to her. ... She's Buddy's wife, okay?"

"Oh. Go on."

"Carol, now, she never was the drinker Buddy was. But this was a special occasion. Everyone in the country was going out that night."

"Salooning?"

"Sure. What'd you think?" Rusty took another gulp. "They was on their way from one stop to another, and they cracked up. That's all."

"How'd they crack up?"

"I wasn't there. How do I know? Their car swerved or something and it run off the road and hit a tree."

"Was Buddy hurt?"

"Not a scratch. And Caroline, she was fine, too. That's what amazed everybody. Just a bit of a wrenched back."

"You might've been a good stuntman, Rusty, but you're a piss-poor storyteller."

"What're you saying?"

"That's what you should've told Squeaks?"

Rusty looked offended. "Squeaks knew all about it. You're the only one sitting here in total ignorance."

"There must be something you aren't saying."

"Caroline's back got worse over time, okay? Pretty soon she couldn't hardly walk at all. That's when they found out she had some crushed bone in her spine, or some such thing, crimping her nerve. Buddy said it was all his fault."

"So he starts drinking again?"

"No. He just throws hisself into his work. Signs up with the studio full-time, trying to provide for their kids. You met Lacey."

"Yeah. They got others?"

"Two more, both still livin' at home. Tommy and Teddy, still in grade school."

"So, how's his wife now?"

"She's walking again. Docs say some operation might fix her up, so Buddy's been saving up for it, little by little. That's the bad part."

"What happened?"

"Lately, went and found out Buddy's got a stomach cancer. That's what Lacey came to talk to me about. Buddy figures he ain't got that much time left, and he's scared of leaving Caroline and the kids with nothing."

"That's tough."

"So, that's why the race means so much to him, more even than poor Polly. Lacey come cryin' to me. 'Keep an eye on him,' she says. 'Make sure he don't take any dumb chances out there, do somethin' foolish.' ... It's going to break her up about Polly."

"What happened ... it wasn't your fault."

"No. But maybe if I'd took Irish aside, told him about what this race means for Buddy, maybe he wouldn't have turned like he did and gone off to risk his neck on that untried team."

"I don't know. I saw the way that car flipped. I'm not so sure it had a thing to do with the horses."

"Don't get ya."

"His car took a bad bounce, just like Fisher. Mighty convenient for someone, don't you think, to have Fisher, Squeaks and now Buddy all out of the way."

"What are you saying, goddamn it?"

"I wouldn't put it past a guy like Delmer Burr to have had a hand in things, that's all."

Rusty stared at me open-mouthed, and glanced around before responding. "What you're talking about," he said, lowering his voice, "is murder."

"Yeah. I guess so."

Rusty mulled it over a second before pushing it away. "Best not even think about that."

"Why not?"

"A murder's got to be investigated. That means police, detectives. The race is over, done with. And so's Buddy and everybody's money."

"Oh."

"I been puttin' dough aside all year just in case there was a race."

"I put up all I had." I took another drink. "But if we don't tell no one, it's like letting 'em get away with it. Murder, I mean."

"Aw, you're just flapping your trap. It was an accident. And even if it wasn't, why are you so sure it was Burr? The union men have something to gain if things go wrong today. ... Or more likely, it's mobsters."

"What mobsters?"

"Who d'you think runs the bookies? If the race is stopped, they're the ones who walk away with the cash."

"No," I said after thinking about it. "Bookies make their money no matter how it goes. I say it's Burr. He's new here, and he give Buddy that bottle."

Rusty looked away and shook his head. "This used to be a damn good business, full of great people. Like Breezy. Fisher. Dozens of 'em. Prohibition fucked it all up."

"How so?"

"Making movies ain't like making buggies. Each time out, you got to close big deals, get those names on the dotted line. It takes business lunches, and negotiations over drinks. They couldn't let

Prohibition put a stop to all that, so in come the rumrunners and the ass-kissers and the jailbirds—people looking for a toehold in the business. Creeps like Delmer Burr. They made it a different place. I'll take their money, sure. But risk my neck for their sake? Never again."

I wondered where that flask had gotten to, and then I saw I was holding it in my own numb fingers and the damn thing was light as air. Just to make sure, I tipped it up above my tongue and felt a final drop spread its friendly sting.

"She done for?" asked Rusty.

"Yeah."

"Too bad."

Then I had my brainstorm. "I know where we can get more."

"Oh?"

"Lots more."

"Where's that?"

"A hidden stash belonging to—guess who?"

"Who?"

I took hold of my arms and exaggerated an icy shiver.

"No! Little Delmer?"

I nodded again.

"How you know about Little Delmer's private stash?"

"A little birdie told me. No, it was a hummingbird!" And I started to chuckle to myself.

"Where is it?"

"Safely locked away in the trunk of an old gray Nash convertible. I can show you."

Rusty gave me a long, serious stare. "Missouri, I'm thinking Mr. Burr owes us a round."

"Hell, after all that's happened, he owes us two rounds!"

"Three!" corrected Rusty, climbing unsteadily to his feet. "Come on."

Suddenly we were an invincible team. It was Rusty and me taking on all challengers. We would start by invading the enemy homeland, attacking the very stronghold of the evil prince's power. And then ... who knew? We might just go on to solve Squeaks' murder and finish the day by helping Buddy win the race!

***

Despite a mysterious onset of double vision, it was no problem for me locating Burr's gray Nash. Popping its trunk proved a snap as well, especially after Rusty borrowed a horseshoe bar from a passing blacksmith.

"Holy be-jesus!" gasped Rusty when he opened the wooden crate and pushed aside a matting of straw. Four dozen quart bottles stuck up just high enough for us to see that each was filled to the top with golden nectar. We gazed at the cargo and never questioned our right to claim it just like salvage out at sea.

Rusty uncorked a bottle to satisfy himself it was genuine. Then he went off to slip it to the smithy for the loan of his tool. Passing laborers gave me suspicious glances next to the open trunk, so when Rusty returned I told him we should probably just grab what we could carry and go.

"We can't leave all this," he objected. "This here's the center of Delmer's power! This is what got him where he is. If we leave her here, it's like saying to him 'it's just fine what you done, Delmer, lad, you just keep on doing it.' "

"What can we do?"

"Give me a hand," he said, reaching down for a thick rope handle on the side. He nodded for me to do the same, and together we hoisted the crate up and Rusty slammed the trunk, and we went waddling off across the parking lot lugging our pirate's bounty.

At first we seemed to be drifting back to the food trucks, but when we got past the parked cars, Rusty headed toward the coliseum.

"Where we taking it?"

"I figure Delmer meant to share this with others. Seems to me there's lots of thirsty folks in those stands, and plenty of dry throats on the track. It must've just slipped his mind."

"You're right," I said. "Poor guy's had his hands full lately, shovelin' the shit the way he does."

The coliseum was still a hundred yards off and the rope handle was cutting through my fingers. I looked around for a way to tote it, and that's when I spotted one of the two-mule teams used to drag off the carcasses.

"Hey, Rusty," I said, nodding toward the team. The animals were tied at a post, still wearing their harnesses of chains and hooks.

Rusty fastened an iron hook around the rope handle, and I got the mules roused from their trance. We were feeling pretty pleased with ourselves as we started the crate of bottles clanking over the dirt and gravel, sounding like dairy day at the old orphanage.

We headed for a gate under the stadium stands. An old-timer in a doughboy hat sat slumped on a stool at the wall. He was still half-asleep when he heard the ruckus and jumped up to swing back the gate for us. Rusty gave him a tip of the head as we passed through.

The scaffolding of metal pipes and boards went on quite a ways, and there was a wedge of sunlight at the end opening on the expanse sand. Someone in the seats above us must have heard the clatter, and when he tried to have a look through the floorboards he sent a bottle rolling toward a gap by the bench.

Down the bottle fell, landing hard on the rump of one of our mules. The beast let out a yelp and spooked his partner and all at once they had bolted for the shaft of daylight. Rusty yelled "Whoa!" and grabbed at the chains, but the mules were fully awake now and determined to escape.

The crate went bouncing and whipping across the ground as I ran after it. I heard glass breaking into shards and just as the mules emerged into the sun, the crate sprang open and straw began to fly everywhere.

The racket attracted the attention of those at the front of the stands, and they accepted it as another circus act for their amusement. A chorus of laughs rang out followed by delighted claps for the *Amazing Running Mules and Their Mysterious Leaking Crate.*

The noise of the spectators scared the animals all over again, and they beat their hooves up the track, pulling the broken crate and braying as they spread a dark trail of moonshine in the sand.

It was useless for me to run any more and I felt foolish all at once. So I played along like a performer and took my bow. The crowd cheered louder and I had just straightened up when I heard racing hooves.

Through a haze I made out Delmer Burr galloping out to head off the mules. He swooped down a hand and caught hold of a nose strap and walked the team to a stop. Then he saw what they were dragging and his eyes seemed to comically bulge. They followed the trail back through the sand to me.

Wranglers ran out to take the mules, and Delmer Burr gave his horse a jab with his heels and came charging down the track. I knew Rusty was watching from the shadows, but I did not want to lead

Delmer to him, so I stayed where I was and continued to wave to the crowd.

"Link! Where'd you get that crate?" hollered Delmer as he pulled his mount to a halt.

"What crate, sir?"

"The crate they was dragging."

"You must mean the box I pulled out of a rat hole."

"You're drunk!" he said, scooting up in his saddle. "Follow me," he commanded, starting his mount off toward the grandstand. I blew the audience a farewell kiss and turned to follow.

Off in the shadows Burr must have tossed his reins to a wrangler and slid off his saddle, because he was waiting there as I stepped out of the sun.

"How'd you know about that stock?" he asked again.

"The thing about rat holes, everyone knows where they are. Even rats," I said, still feeling amused with myself. "Whatever's in a rat hole is up for grabs. Particularly when it's against the federal laws. Jail's no fit place for a rat. Jail's too good for 'em."

"Who helped you?" he said.

He seemed to split in two then, and I didn't know which of them to answer.

"I know you didn't lift that crate by yourself. Who helped you? Might as well say. Who else knows?"

"Somebody. Somebody knows plenty! Somebody also knows about that cliff and the poor dumb horse that was pushed off it."

"What the hell you talking about?"

"Somebody knows why you made Buddy shoot Polly and gave him a bottle, to boot."

Delmer stood and let me go on with not even a hint of worry. In fact, both Delmer's now had a sick little grin on their faces. It was the same grin he was wearing back at the curtains when he heard that gunshot. It put me in mind of something in my past, but I couldn't think where it might have been. It was a challenging sort of smile that said *I'm on top and you're going down, and all the talk in the world won't save you.*

All at once I wanted to hit him with the biggest weapon I had, to club him good just once and knock that smile off his face. "I bet the newspapers would be interested in what happened to Squeaks. I bet they'd like to know what really went on here. A few good stories about dead horses and dead stuntmen—that might sell a few papers, don't you think?"

I must have known I could go too far, but there was no holding myself back. All the giddiness from my endless gulps of moonshine had turned to fire in my blood. Before he could raise a hand I cocked a fist and sent it whizzing into the center of the blur that was Delmer Burr's face. I must have connected with his jaw, because he flipped around fast and went tumbling down with no time even to cushion his fall.

He lay stunned on the ground for a second maybe. Then he turned and looked up at me, his disbelief at what just happened changing instantly to fury in his eyes.

I felt I should run but I'd seen animals in the wild trying to outrun a predator. They squandered their strength and ended up bowing to their fate. Better to stand my ground, I figured, and put up a fight before I got too tuckered to lift an arm in my own defense.

In a split-second Delmer was up and on me. I felt a blow to my stomach and some glancing strikes to my head. I got off a few punches of my own but it was too late and I was too dizzy. I folded into a ball of drunken surrender and covered my head.

It was Rusty and some of the others who pulled Burr off of me. As he struggled and spit to get loose and take another swing, he screamed out that I was washed up in Hollywood. He was having me thrown off the lot and he would leave instructions to the guards never to allow me to set foot inside his gates again.

He promised to wipe my name from the studio's employment file so I could never claim my pay. "It'll be like you was never here," he shouted, "and then it won't matter what you tell the papers because no one will believe you or any of your goddamn lies!" Burr turned to his helpers. "Get him out of here!" he hollered.

I was vaguely aware of being hoisted by the arms and carted off. I felt my toes scraping through the dirt and fought to keep from passing out. I slid along a tunnel toward some growing patch of light. I was being birthed all over, pushed from my dark place of comfort and thrown into a blinding circle of lights. So I shut my eyes and welcomed the velvet folds of oblivion.

CHAPTER EIGHTEEN

The Mind Races

Line, please! Oh, what is my line? Why is it always that when all my most important scenes appear, I must stand around waiting for the next page?

Norma struggled to appear calm. It wouldn't do to come off flustered or to stammer like a novice.

Here Irving had just delivered a heartfelt speech, a very important speech, the one beginning, "I must tell you, Norma, I very much appreciate the kindness you've shown my mother."

Lord, what to reply? This was not business as usual. He wasn't giving dictation to a secretary. In this speech he was acknowledging the importance to him of his mother and of her feelings. He was telling her how much it has meant to him that she *has shown his mother kindness.* That's not too hard to comprehend. This is a *huge* speech. It takes their relationship to a whole new level.

"You know I think the world of Henrietta. She is a darling."

Oh, God, rewrite!!

That sounded so disingenuous. A line like that might get past the Hollywood press, but not the New York papers. They would see it as self-serving and calculating. Louella might laud it to the skies as a sweet sentiment from a generous spirit. But Louella was owned by the studios, and frankly, when did her opinion matter to anyone?

How about this:

"Mothers have a very difficult job. And Henrietta has done wonderfully well at hers, if you ask me. It couldn't have been easy raising Irving Thalberg."

Yes! I've gotten him to smile! He loves it when I bring everything back to him.

"No, it wasn't easy. I caused her a lot of concern."

"And given her much pride, too. Don't forget that."

Is there a long pause here? We are meant to go back to watching the track? Perhaps there will be a cutaway. Close-ups on the horses or something.

"You're a sensitive woman, Norma. You did right, bringing that young man in to see me. I hope I calmed his worries a bit."

Here was a speech coming from a man fully involved in his role. Yes, he is owning this moment. Perhaps he is waiting for her to deliver his next cue.

"I know you did."

"And I'm sure you know as well as I do the damage—well, what could be done if he took his concerns to the wrong people."

Perhaps I should appear pensive here, as if some thoughts are going through my brain. Cut away to a title card, Mr. Fleming. Let the scenarist come up with something witty and delightful for me to be thinking.

"If nothing else goes wrong, we should be all right, don't you think?"

"Are you asking me?" she said.

"Frankly, yes."

This is immense! He's concerned about the studio's image again—and he's sharing his concerns with me. Oh, this is much better than "Should I send in a wind machine?"

"I am touched. It makes me feel good to know you value my opinion."

"Well, I do. I always have."

"We should be able to keep those reports tamped down, don't you think?"

"Absolutely."

Wait. What sort of reports does he mean?"

"If there aren't any more accidents, you know … injured horses and all. Our people should be able to handle it."

He's trying to persuade himself. Or is he asking for advice here? That's it, I think. He's asking me to about the running of his studio. This is immense. He would never go to Dutch for help with on such a matter.

"Half the prosecutors in Los Angeles are here today as guests of Mr. Mayer," she said. "If it were Thursday night, they'd be down at Melrose Avenue betting on the cockfights. Next weekend they'll be off to Tijuana to watch the dogs. I can't imagine any of these officials jumping up and down over animal welfare issues."

"You're right. Dutch always says I'm worrying about nothing."

"Oh, I don't believe that's so, Irving. You have to make so many important decisions. Don't let anyone brush aside your concerns."

No matter how beautiful she may be.

He nodded and smiled at her then. "It's just that we're so vulnerable. This picture has to be a hit. It wouldn't do to have a scandal. The union people will latch onto any issue that might give them leverage."

"When I first got to New York, mother thought I could earn some money playing piano in a movie theater. It turned out the musicians had their union. It was very powerful. It prevented even people like me from performing for money."

"It could happen here. After seeing the havoc they caused in Italy—"

"But that was there. This is Hollywood. Besides, I don't believe unions are the issue here. It's handling any malicious gossip or news account that happens to slip out. Isn't that so?"

"Yes."

"Well, then inoculate yourself."

"What do you mean?"

"Plant a bigger lie. Start the rumor that a hundred horses had to be destroyed. Dozens of stuntmen rushed to hospitals. Dare anyone to repeat it and earn the wrath of Mr. Mayer. The columnists will pooh-pooh it. They were here, writing their fabulous reports for their Aunt Minnies. A maverick reporter might go looking for facts, and all he'll learn is that it was all outrageous lies. The rumors will be discredited, and no one will look any further into the stories. It will all appear some exercise in anti-studio gossip. Blame it on anarchists or whatever. When your picture comes out and it is the hit we all know it shall be, and everyone is making loads of money with it, that will end the tongue-wagging."

"Norma, you are amazing. I knew any girl who was such a shrewd contract negotiator must also have a good head for business."

"Don't sell yourself short, darling. You knew exactly how to handle that young man. I wonder where he is? Have you seen him down there?"

"No. They all look alike from here." He stopped to search her eyes and appeared suddenly serious. "As soon as the race is done, what say you and I get away? Have ourselves a drive up the coast, maybe stop for cocktails by the sea?"

"That sounds enchanting, darling. Are you sure you dare leave?"

"Niblo and his people seem to have things under control."

Oh, what a charming smile. Such deep, dark eyes. I just want to mother him myself.

So it was a special invitation after all, sent to her in that poor, typewritten envelope. Who would have suspected it held such possibilities? All her nasty impatience and fretting had been for nothing. Needless, truly.

The Cyclops Queen would be no more. She could clearly see before her a glorious new role: *Mrs. Irving Thalberg.* It sounded so natural, almost made to order. It would make a perfect fit for her talents.

She must begin planning her approach. There was a pamphlet she heard her about: "Making the Conversion to Judaism," or something like that. Who was it had told her about that? Where could she pick up a copy? There would doubtless be many lines to learn—but she was used to that. It would be no different from any other script, working out the proper emphasis, learning her motivations. There would be new costumes and fittings before she went into rehearsals.

When the time came she would know what was expected. She would exude pure confidence. What was there to doubt? It was the role of a lifetime.

And when her performance was over, instead of walking away with reviews or nominations she would have her handsome leading man. He would be hers and hers alone to hold and to cherish forever and ever.

PART THREE

CHAPTER NINETEEN

Evicted

No one alive now is likely to know me. That's why I never set out to make this account too much about myself. But I see that certain things need to be explained in order to understand how it all turned out the way it did.

So bear with me as I go deeper into some personal matters than I ever meant to.

Somehow at the center of it is that cruel little smile on Delmer Burr's face. Now I look back and I think it was the sight of that smile that touched off my temper and ended up getting me thrown off the set.

Certainly I was not thinking about it then, lying in the warm dirt outside the coliseum. My senses were numb, my mind still groggy from the liquor. Putting aside my pain and humiliation, I tested my legs and then stumbled off to the paddocks.

There was a bucket set aside for watering the horses, and it was half filled, so I splashed a little in my face and ended up dumping it over my head, hoping to wash away the blood and clear my brain.

I took a seat on a stool near a rough-hewn hitching post, and for the second time that afternoon I thought of my mother and what she would have said if she were there.

"Grover, look at yourself," I could hear her voice gently scolding. "When was the last time you had your hair cut, boy? Remember what I told you about your grooming? You see where it's gotten Mr. Thalberg? And look at your clothes, son. Don't you have a clean shirt to put on? Land o' Goshen. You take those dirty things off while I get a wash kettle going."

That was Mother. You would think that with four kids and a house full of men she wouldn't have taken on one more worry. But she always found time to care for each and every one of us.

She and Father and my uncles and grandparents—they all wore glasses, and their lenses were always getting smudged and soiled working on a farm. So after the dinner dishes were done, Mother would go around and collect everyone's eyeglasses and dip them one lens at a time into her suds and carefully wipe them with her apron.

Everyone's spirits improved along with their vision, and it just seemed like one of the most loving things she could do after all of us were fed. When I got older, I was always looking for things I could do that would make her happy.

Dad was a hard worker, too, though he never had a thing to show for it until he married and started a family. First came Daps, then a girl named Icy Dora, who was bitten by a copperhead rattlesnake and died. I had come along by then, along with my little sister Margaret. Then Dad pulled up the family and moved us all from Cape Girardeau to the territory around Everton.

We slept in the open at first, curling up under our wagons when the air got chilly.

One time—I don't know whether it was while we were still on the move or later—Mother had to sit with the dead body of a woman whose family we met on the trail. She promised to keep watch over the body while her husband went off to notify authorities. The wolves came sniffing around in the thick of night, and they started howling and she peeked out the tent and all she could see was their eyes catching little flashes of moonlight. That was life on the prairie not so many years ago.

Dad was offered work by a certain cattle rancher named Roby. Mr. Roby offered us a shelter on his property that was set aside for horses, if we cared to fix it up. Mother and Father and Daps set about doing just that, and even though I was hardly more than a toddler wearing hand-me-down dresses, I can remember how happy Margaret and I were to once again have a roof over our heads.

After a while Mr. Roby made Father his foreman and we all got to move into a real log house. It had a huge dining room, so Father built an extra long table right in the middle of it, with plenty of chairs for guests. The ranch included a nice orchard of fruit trees and several different kinds of nut trees.

Pretty soon I had another young sister, Rose, and my father's brothers Sam and Chester came to live with us. Then my Grandfather John and Grandmother Jane moved in there, too, and right away Grandma started a garden. Grandpa took charge of the orchard and tended the bees and set up a honey farm to help with the table.

Mother often went down to the valley to take food and home remedies to any folks who needed them there. She also boarded the hired help if they needed a place to stay, and did their washing on the washboard and tub.

I'd try to help when I could. I remember carrying the water in from one of the rain barrels in the yard so she could heat it in the boiler on the stove. She also used to fix lunches for crews of railroad workmen and telegraph wiremen and such. In spite of all that, Mother always took time to clean up and put on a fresh dress each afternoon to sit on the porch doing hand work of some kind.

The road was just a little way from our house, and campers would sometimes stop there under the big trees. By this time Father had bought the whole ranch from Mr. Roby, because he was going off to Colorado Springs to live. Daps was working in the fields with the men, so I passed my time out of school with a friend from across the river named Zachary.

Zach was a year older than I was, but most people couldn't tell it because he was sort of short and frail—"a runt," is how my father referred to him. And he was always trying to prove something, maybe because his house was hardly more than a shed—"so small," joked Daps, "that you couldn't cuss out the cat without getting fur in your teeth." But that didn't bother me, and we were pretty tight in those years.

Always after the campers cleared out, Zach and I would scout around to see if we could find anything they left behind. One day I did find a gold band ring there, and Zach fought me for it but I won, and I ran with it in a hurry and gave it to Mother. She wore that ring all the rest of her life. It was the only one she ever had and it made me real happy for her. But things were never the same between Zach and me again.

Once some men came to see Father on business from St. Louis, and as Margaret and I had always sat at first table for our meals, this time we had to wait and we didn't like it. So we kept opening and rattling the latch on the door. Father would shake his head at us, but we kept it up. He came and told us to behave and leave the door closed, and that if we didn't obey him he would whip us when his business was through.

We didn't believe him, as he never had punished us before, but he kept his promise. He came after us and we ran but he caught us and whipped us. It nearly broke our hearts, and it hurt the rest of the family, too. So my Uncle Sam came out where Margaret and I were hiding behind the house, and he petted us and got us to stop crying. That was the only time Father ever touched us in anger. He was always so good and patient with us.

It was at the same time that war broke out in Europe, and nothing could have seemed less real or important to us out on our that ranch. Daps would talk about it at dinner and say it just might make a difference in the world. Grandpa had seen his own father ride off to join General Jo Shelby in the War Between the States, and he liked to quote President Wilson that "there is such a thing as a man being too proud to fight."

Many a night after dinner, Grandpa and Father and Daps all sat around arguing about the uselessness of wars and whether or not it was possible to stay neutral when allies were being killed. Daps always seemed to head off to bed after concluding that it was every good citizen's duty to listen to the President.

And so my brother was all but packed to go when Mr. Wilson changed his tune and declared this war a crusade to make the world "safe for democracy." Daps didn't wait to be called to duty. He signed up, and the day he went off to start his training Zach was so green with envy you could hardly see him coming through the trees.

All Zach's brothers were younger than him, and he sure wasn't old enough to go to war, so that meant my family had a soldier in it and his did not.

Things were quieter at home after Daps left. He was the natural musician in the family, for one thing. He played the fiddle and on Saturday nights all the neighbors would come over to dance and party. A neighbor lady played our piano, and a couple of the men played guitar, and everyone pitched in and helped keep the beat by stomping and clapping or beating on tubs.

But with the fiddle missing it wasn't the same. It was hard to find the beat and things got more raucous than musical. Grandpa and Father no longer held after-dinner arguments about world politics, and their discussions of grains and seed cycles and such must have bored even them.

I kept up with the war news as much as anyone could in those days. You just knew that a lot of the odd names of those French war towns and rivers even puzzled the local newspaper folks. Months went by and we never got a letter from Daps, and it appeared like the fighting was never going to end, which seems funny to me now because our part in it only stretched from April 1917 to November of the very next year.

We heard reports about Missouri sons being killed, but they were mostly from the big cities and no one seemed to know any of them. When we heard peace was declared, Mother and Father started to get jumpy, because we still hadn't had a letter from Daps saying he was coming home. I remember praying that nothing had happened to his fiddling fingers and that that wasn't the reason he hadn't been writing.

So I was relieved when Daps showed up one day, just walking down the road. As I shook his hand I counted his fingers and was happy. Mother cried to see him, and even Father never scolded him about scaring him half to death.

Zach's dad was a kind of peddler. He would find things in one part of the state and peddle them to folks in another part of the state. Somehow he had made a lot of cash during the war years and was using the money to buy up local land. He made my dad an offer for our farm, more because of its fruit orchards and nut trees than for its crop fields, but a handsome offer just the same.

Little Zach started making cracks about allowing us to stay on and live in our house even after his father bought us out. He said his dad might even give us a salary to keep doing what we were already doing. I didn't like the sound of that, so I was glad when Father turned him down.

About the first thing Daps did that summer was marry a city girl named Martha Caylor. She was slim and pretty but kind of frail, and no sooner did she become pregnant than she started having female troubles. Right in the middle of harvest season, Daps had to rent a place for them in Everton so Martha would be close to her doctor.

They came back to the ranch after the baby was born, but Martha was having chills and fever, and she passed them on to another, and then another came down with them—so every few days there was somebody in the house having chills and fever. That's when a doctor came out and told us there were others in town with the same nasty flu. It had been brought from St. Louis and other places where the soldiers had come back from Europe. People were dying in those cities because there was nothing the hospitals could do for them but make them comfortable while the influenza ran its course.

Martha and the baby died within a few days, and Daps was so weak he couldn't even attend their funeral. Mother sat with him in his room night after night, putting towels on his head, and I could see her getting worn out herself. I think I started to hope Daps would just go on and die so that Mother could return to us. Daps did die within the week, but Mother kept getting weaker and took to her bed.

Uncle Samuel decided he better get Grandma and Grandpa Link out of there before they caught it too, and so they all moved in with my crazy Uncle Ches in his log cabin out past the walnut grove. But I guess they didn't move in time because it wasn't long before all three of them were shivering and quaking with the sweats, and soon I was out there with Father, digging more prairie graves.

One night my father went in to say goodbye to Mother. He told her, "Don't worry. You're going to a better world." And she replied, "I can't imagine a better world." That was my mom.

When Mother was gone, Father took Margaret and Rose and me back to Cape Girardeau. He agreed to let Zach's dad buy our ranch, but he had him put it in the contract that they would always honor the patch of prairie graves just beyond the trees. And then we packed up what we could get in our wagon and went to live with my father's relatives.

It was as we were pulling away from our front porch that little Zach hopped up to wave good-bye. He said he was sorry to see me go, but in that moment when he was waving to me I saw on his face that cocky little smile for the first time. It was hardly a grin at all, but it did suggest a sort of happiness to see me sad. His family had won out, and he got what he wanted. He didn't care if I was hurting. In fact, it seemed aimed to hurt.

I couldn't wave it aside like some unkind thought that pops through in an unguarded moment. It was more like some holdover from our animal past, an echo of a howl that said to the pack, "I survived," whatever the cost of another creature's life. It was part of the natural order in lower animals, but there on a human face it was mingled with self-awareness and intelligence. It was enough to make any young boy sad, a testament to some ugly part of man that was no more than raw selfishness. To people like me in their moment of defeat, it appeared as pure evil.

That was the smile I saw that day on Delmer Burr's face.

How long I sat there by the hitching post I can't say—less than half an hour, I suspect. But the more my mind cleared, the more restless I got, and itched to be on the move.

Burr had bet his own money on the race. So two prospects gnawed at me, and I don't know which was worse: Either Buddy would finish up the race half-drunk and maybe lose because I wasn't there to help, or he would win it and I wouldn't be there to see him wipe that damn smirk off Delmer Burr's face. I decided that one way or another I would have to get back inside that coliseum.

The guards at the gate would be on the lookout, but if I could get past them somehow, I might get up to explain things to Irving Thalberg. He might reverse Delmer's orders and put me back with my team. So I started to scout the walls, moving stealthily between cars and wagons and counting up the sentries at each entry gate.

At one point I heard a side gate creak and out came the sleepy old-timer in the doughboy's hat, the same man that had let Rusty and me through earlier. He held the gate back as a couple of wranglers came out leading our old mule team. The animals dragged one hoof up after the other as if still spent from their run.

Even the gatekeeper grew bored waiting, and when he went back inside and left the gate open I seized my chance. In an instant I was at the wall, wedged tight behind the iron hinge. Through the crack I saw the old-timer with his back turned, gulping loudly from a brown jug. I slipped around and hurried off beneath the bleachers.

"Hey, you!" he yelled, and I lit out at full speed then.

Someone blew a whistle, and as the wind whistled in my ears the bands of sunlight from above flickered on me, and I felt like the hero of some slapstick comedy. I laughed to myself when I took a look behind and there in full pursuit were three Keystone Cops, waving nightsticks and shouting out, "Stop! Stop!"

I toppled sawhorses and barrels in their path but they leapt around them, their coattails flapping and mustaches nipping at their ears. It just made everything more comical.

The bleachers were coming to an end at solid plywood wall. My only escape was through an archway out to the track. From there I might spot a way up to the stands where I could lose myself in the crowd.

In the bright sun I saw a low section of wall and hoisted myself up and over, landing at the feet of some startled Arab chieftains. A pair of Roman centurions standing up on the next landing stopped to look, and when they heard my pursuers calling out, they started down the steps. I sprang over another divider and fell in the laps of more costumed extras.

Now with the Keystone Cops coming from below and the two

centurions on their way down, there was nowhere to go but back over the wall and onto the track. A hand ripped at my shoulder as I ducked through a curtained passage under the next section of seats.

In the darkness I was bearing down on a group of men working around a horseless chariot car. I charged between them, scampering up the wagon tongue and over the front shield. I landed on the rear so hard it tipped the whole car backward, and I glanced around in time to see the tongue rise up fast into the crotch of a pursuer. He howled out and fell to his side in the dirt, as two other Keystone Cops reared back and raised their sticks at me in outrage. Behind them came the Roman centurions and a handful of vigilantes, and off I went again as fast as my legs would carry me.

My options seemed all played out. I couldn't double back against such odds. My only hope for avoiding another beating was to storm the guards posted at an outside gate. They weren't looking for anyone trying to get *out* of the coliseum, and I had no trouble flying through them. I didn't stop running until I was sure no one was coming, and finally stopped by one of the parked trucks to let my breathing catch up.

All that effort had left me back where I started. At least I tried, I told myself, and there was nothing left to do but call it a day. I got to the edge of the lot and stepped over a chain and on the other side of the street was a quiet neighborhood. I walked back into the old world I knew of bankers and traffic cops and foremen. If I got lucky, I might find someone willing to trust me with a shovel.

***

By the time I came to the next corner, my situation grew clearer. Gloom had descended and I knew I had been not just fired but forsaken. Ever since I saw my mother and family buried and we lost our farm to Zach's dad, I hadn't seen much use for God. Now it looked like the feeling was mutual. I started to wonder if going on with the struggle was even worth the effort.

Up ahead was a bus stop. An old woman sat at one end of a bench and there was a dusty bum down at the opposite end. The old woman was throwing popcorn to a small gathering of seagulls. I took a seat there at the middle and tried to remember how long it had been since I had eaten anything at all.

After a while the old lady saw how I was watching her toss those kernels to the birds.

"You hungry, son?"

Maybe it was how she said it with just a hint of care, or the fact she called me "son," but all at once I was knocked for a loop by welled-up feelings. Tears must have flowed down my cheeks, but I couldn't say if they were for me or for Buddy or Squeaks. All I know is I could hardly muster the strength to answer.

The old lady probably thought I was some kind of foreigner who didn't understand her language.

"Here, take it," she said, holding out what was left in her popcorn bag. She bounced it under my nose to show, I guess, there weren't any strings attached.

I had just taken her offering when a city bus came rolling up and let out a big sigh of relief. It was going in the wrong direction for me, so I watched the lady gather her sacks and climb up inside. She took a seat by the window above me and gave a half-smile as the bus pulled off in a whoosh of fumes.

The smell of that diesel gas put me in mind of my months back in Cape Girardeau, living on a noisy downtown block that always had the same stink of bus fuel and gasoline. That's where my father and little sister and I lived in a crowded walkup apartment together after Father announced he couldn't stand another day living on the charity of his big-city relatives. Truth was, he didn't get along well with either of my uncles or their families, tracing back to bitter feelings they had all nursed since childhood.

I wasn't all that sad about moving into a smaller place, even if it was in the stinky heart of downtown. I only had one more year of high school before me by then, but I didn't care about it one way or the other. I couldn't see much point in studying up for a life that was getting set to peddle my hide on the open market.

So I packed up my bags one night and went back to Everton on my own, getting a job helping a man with a stable. I tried to take up again with a girl I knew there named Alice Jane. Alice Jane was a sweet girl, even if she was the daughter of a Baptist preacher. She was also sort of a wild thing, and liked to go with the boys skinny-dipping outside of town.

One summer on our old farm, Uncle Ches was off cutting trees and Alice Jane and I snuck inside his cabin and started kissing on his bed. One thing led to another and pretty soon I had given Alice Jane my virginity. She was ready to take it, too, because later I found out she took away Zach's virginity the very day before. When I learned about the two of them I put my foot down and told her she had to be faithful to me, and she pretty much withheld her affections altogether and gave them to Zach, who didn't really care if she was true to him or not.

Zach was not happy to see me move back. I found a place near Alice Jane, and when I had some money to spend I took her to movies and bought us treats at the soda parlor. Zach came storming into the stables one day and all but ordered me to leave town. Well, he didn't have the power to make me do that. We both knew I could beat him if it came to a fight.

It wasn't long until the sheriff came looking for me. He said Alice Jane claimed I had overpowered her and forced my will on her, and it was Zach out spreading that lie around town because Alice Jane herself had told him it to get him to stop beating on her. It was my word against the preacher's daughter's now, and then a couple of other town girls came forward to make similar charges, and the next thing I knew I was cooling my heels in jail and wishing I'd never left Cape Girardeau.

When it was time to air her claims in court, Alice Jane withdrew her charges, and then so did the other girls. I was let out of jail but the judge said I'd still have to face a charge of resisting arrest, and he told me not to leave town. But late that night the old bastard sheriff came looking for me again, and he said I better get out of Everton fast and never come back or he'd set a local pair of redneck hunters on my ass.

And so Zach won again and no doubt was smirking all over Everton for the next month or two. I left to find a new life for myself, first in Indiana, and when that didn't pan out, a couple years in Kansas, and finally all the way out to Southern California, where it was way too sunny for the miserable old prairie God of any brimstone Baptist minister.

That popcorn settled my stomach, and the old lady's kindness gave me back a glimmer of faith in the goodness of people. I looked over to the bum at the end of the bench, and for the first time I saw he had a book out and was thumbing through its pages. It looked familiar, and in an instant I knew I recognized it.

"Where'd you get that?"

"What?"

"That book. Where'd you get it?"

"What's it to you?"

"It's mine. It belongs to my landlady." I reached out to grab it.

"Hey, watch it!"

We tugged back and forth on it for a second, and all at once he let it go.

"Ah, take it," said the bum. "Nothin' in it but names anyway."

"It's an autograph book. Someone took it off me."

"Looks like you took a thrashing, too."

"Where'd you find it, anyway?"

"A couple fellas give it to me."

I must have had a suspicion. "One tall guy and one short one?"

"Maybe."

"Wait a second. Who are you?"

"Name's Walt."

"Not *Walt Altskellar.*"

He reeled back, not believing his own ears. "Do I know you?"

"No. But I heard what happened. At the food trucks."

"You there?" he asked, and gave a mostly toothless grin.

"You came on the lot, looking for a handout. That's what I heard."

He shook his head. "Nah. It weren't that way at all. Fellow paid me to show up and cause a ruckus. He didn't say I was goin' to get socked, though. But that's okay. I done worse for money."

"I don't understand. Who paid you?"

"Oh, what's the difference? A fella."

"What's his name?"

"Moore, if you have to know. A fella name of Freddie Moore."

"Moore the Merrier?"

"That's him."

"He paid you?"

"Said he'd give me a fiver—ten, if I made it look convincing. I did, too. Just like I used to in the movies. He was pleased. Gave me the ten spot. And *that book.* Didn't tell me it was just a bunch of names."

Pieces were starting to fall into place, but I didn't know what picture they were forming. Just then a long shiny limousine came cruising up to the curb with its window rolled down.

The driver wasn't wearing any uniform, and wasn't dressed like any chauffeur I'd ever seen. He slammed the limo in park and scooted across the seat to poke his face out at us. "Hey, you two guys, how'd you like to make a fast fiver for just planting your butts in some bleachers and watching them shoot a real Hollywood movie?"

CHAPTER TWENTY

A Far Cry from Heaven

Never in her life had Ada Redburn watched a picture being made, and she could hardly control her excitement. Her neighbor and lady friend Enola Hutchins was more reserved. Enola didn't care a hoot about movie stars or Hollywood as long as she got paid and it didn't take up the whole rest of her afternoon. Both ladies had families to cook for, and both had been on their way to the market when Russell's studio car swooped them up just before stopping for me.

So now it was the three of us in the back seat, and smelly Walt Altskellar up front with Russell. The big sedan made a turn in a vacant lot and headed back to where we were told "the big shoot" was already going on.

As far as I was concerned, this was just another sign that fate had designs on me. For reasons I might never understand I was meant to be there to the end of that race. It wasn't up to me, so I might as well get used to the idea.

Russell let the four of us out at the wardrobe trailers and pointed Walt and me toward the men's section. Old Walt wanted no part of any costume, he said, and headed off for the stadium. But I figured a good disguise suited me fine and might get me where I was going.

The two ladies behind the table never batted an eye at my bloodied cheeks and swollen lip. They probably thought it was makeup for the part I was playing. In a way, they were right about that.

They sized up my height and handed me a burlap shift and a yellow sash. When I came out of the changing room they showed me how to tie the sash and gave me a studio bag so I could carry my street clothes along with me. But I still looked too much like myself, so I asked if they had any more wigs and maybe some fake facial hair to go with it.

The ladies couldn't have been more pleased. They must have been trying to get the male extras to wear those silly things all day long because there were boxes full of them back on the shelves. I picked out a curly brown wig several shades darker than my own hair, and they stuck matching spit-curl whiskers on my cheeks and chin with a smelly rubber glue.

When I got out of there I looked like an acrobat from some flea-bitten circus troupe. The burlap dress fell only to my knees, and the breeze made it feel like the whole world had gotten down on all fours to blow air up by backside.

With that hair and my puffy eyes, my own father would have walked right by me on the street. To be safe, though, I mixed in with a fresh group of recruits lined up at a flight of steps, and had no trouble getting through the checkpoint and inside the first section of seats.

The rows had filled up some since lunch, and the crowd was running even more short of patience. Here and there people openly passed around hip flasks, or jumped up to rudely call back and forth across several rows. A group rose as one and came brushing past me on their way toward an exit before being turned back by the guards.

Until that minute I still had it in mind to somehow get to Thalberg's box. But being dressed up like no one would know me gave me a different idea. Thalberg wouldn't likely help me anyway. What I had to do was get down on the track and find Rusty and the others.

Working my way casually along the aisle, I found an unguarded flight of steps down, slipped onto the track and then doubled back under the bleachers.

People all over the track now were moving at a slower pace. Some of the horses were feeding, and others were getting a little warm up before being strapped back in their harnesses. Most of the waiting chariot cars had their wheels wedged in place by concrete blocks. I spotted Buddy's rig near its old starting position, being tended by a stranger holding tight to a bridle.

"You seen Buddy or Rusty?" I asked him.

"Rusty," drawled the handler, pointing with his chin toward the paddocks.

"Thanks."

Outside the south gate I saw orange locks off in a corral and as I got closer I could tell it was Rusty. He tried to shoo me off at first, but his attitude changed when he saw it was me under the fake hair.

"Runaway! Goddamn, how'd you get back on the lot?"

"They offered me five bucks. Couldn't say no."

"No shit?"

"Where's Buddy?"

"Damned if I can say. We been looking. Can't find Powder Keg neither. And they're getting' set to start again."

The men had all been on edge since the crackup, Rusty told me, and Francis X. Bushman dropped out of the race over what he called the "reckless amateurishness" of the drivers. Another driver would also be standing in for Squeaks, so all twelve cars would be ready for the race—provided we find Buddy.

Rusty said Freddie Moore was whipping up support for a strike. Most of the others now thought Squeaks was hurt worse than the studio let on. Some were saying he was killed outright. Now there was a rumor going around that it might not have been an accident at all.

Knowing what I did about Moore the Merrier, it irked me to think that people were still listening to him. But I didn't have time to tell Rusty about that now. In any case, Rusty was telling me the revolt was already over.

"When the bosses got wind of what was going on," he said, "they raised the winner's purse to fifteen hundred dollars. That put an end to any talk of a strike. You can't blame them. They're used to risking their necks for a paycheck, and fifteen hundred's more'n most of 'em will make all year."

"Buddy could sure use that money," I said.

"Not if he's gone and wandered off the lot."

"He wouldn't do that, would he? Not after ... what he did to stay in the race?"

"Depends on how much drinkin' he's done."

"You say you looked everywhere?"

"Sure did. Me and the boys."

"Anyone check in the spina?"

"Why there?"

"That's where they took Polly, right?"

Rusty didn't need a second to think. "Let's go see," he said.

***

In the dark interior of the spina, my own brooding thoughts were a universe away. All that worried me was finding Buddy—and the shape he might be in when we did.

An odd swishing stab echoed under the low ceiling, sounding like someone warning us "*shush.*" It turned out to be a steel blade plunging into the wet dirt.

We found Buddy sitting with his legs spread, absently playing mumblety-peg with his knife. The bottle Delmer Burr had slipped him was lying opened on its side.

"Hey, captain, we been searchin' for you," said Rusty.

It took a second for him to recognize Rusty, and he showed no interest at all in me. His dark eye grease was smeared down his cheeks, and he looked like some specter out of a story by Edgar Allan Poe.

"How'd you know where I was?" he asked.

"We didn't," said Rusty. "That's why we were searching."

"You all right, Buddy?" I asked.

He looked at me long and hard before he lit with recognition. "Runaway, that you? What they got you dressed up for?"

"That's a long story. Why're you sitting in here?"

Rusty picked up the bottle and turned it upside down to show me it was empty. "You been drinking, huh, Buddy?" he said. "You a little tipsy?"

"Rusty, ol' pal," he answered, "you could take my leg off right now and I wouldn't fight you for the boot." He chuckled, and his head dropped back as he fell against the fold of a black tarp. The canvas lifted just enough to see a length of golden fur and a couple of hooves. It was the body of Polly.

"He's passed out," said Rusty. "Give me a hand."

"What do you suppose he meant by that?"

"What? About the boot? Something from his army days, I suspect."

Together we got Buddy upright again and Rusty gave him two quick slaps on the cheeks. "Wake up, Buddy, talk to us. You been drinking here? You been sitting in here drinking all by yourself?"

"No, no. Polly's with me," he mumbled. "A good ol' horse, Polly is."

"She is that, Buddy," said Rusty. "But they're getting ready to start the race."

"Shit," he scowled, and his face became a grotesque mask. "Hell with it. Ask Squeaks. He'll tell you. It's all over."

"No, it's not, Buddy. There's four laps left to run, and we're gonna win. We're gonna win it all for Caroline, remember?"

Buddy kind of wobbled and bobbed there uncertainly as he groped around in the dirt for a stretch of brown fabric. He was half sitting on it, and he almost fell over again when he gave it a violent tug.

"What's that?" asked Rusty.

"That's a *soo-veneer.*"

"Where'd it come from?"

"Squeaks' chariot," he said, twisting around to see behind him. "It's back there—what's left of it."

"Lemme see that," said Rusty and took the cloth from him. "Why, it's just an old canvas sack."

Buddy shook his head and frowned. "That's good material—good, strong stuff. Tight knit. You can't rip it open with both hands."

I was starting to think that Buddy was beyond the point of making any sense, but Rusty turned the bag over and studied it closer.

"He's right. Look here. It's one of the sandbags, I bet. And it's not ripped, it's been slit with a knife, one end to the other." He held it out so I could see the clean gash down the side.

"You do that with your knife, Buddy?" I asked him.

"I told you. It's a *soo-veneer.* From Squeaks' chariot."

"You found it in Irish's rig?" Rusty echoed, taking a closer look at the material. "Missouri, you know what this means? This fits in with what you were saying. Someone saw to it that Squeaks lost his sand."

"Then it *was* murder!"

Rusty weighed the limp canvas sack in his hand. "Sure looks like it."

"That little bastard Burr. He was against the whole idea of using sandbags. You heard how he threatened Buddy."

"Makes sense to me," he said in a whisper.

"And then he got me thrown off the lot when I asked about it."

Rusty let out a long silent whistle and took a seat in the dirt next to Buddy. "I gotta think," he announced. "This is serious. We gotta tell someone about this."

"But, won't they—like you said, stop the race? Shut it all down?"

"Sure. But don't kid yourself. Look at him," he said, and we both stopped to look at the old horse soldier. He was awake again now, though he was paying no attention to us. He reached out for his knife and returned to his game of mumblety-peg.

"He ain't in any shape to run a race," said Rusty.

"You could do it."

Rusty barely looked up. He just raised a side of his lip into a sneer and gave a little snort.

"You could," I repeated.

"Lay off it, okay?"

"You were the best. That's what you said."

"Cut the crap!" he blurted out angrily, and his words ricocheted off the ceiling like a gunshot. "Besides, the race ain't even the half of it."

"What do you mean?"

"If we bring the cops in on this, it'll be the biggest scandal in the history of movies. Bigger than Fatty Arbuckle. Bigger than Bill Taylor's murder, maybe. A killer on the payroll of a million-dollar religious picture? Bookies and bootleggers running wild? Even if the studio survives, we'll be washed up in Hollywood. No one will ever hire any of us again—you, me, Buddy. ... Not even Molly."

"But, we didn't do anything wrong," I muttered and went over to sit on a nail keg.

"We ratted on our studio, that's what they'll say about it. That's the way people here are going to take it."

"But *we* didn't murder anyone."

Then Rusty's face clouded over and his brow wrinkled up in the most pitiful way. "I did. I killed Squeaks as sure as we're sitting here."

"You still going on about that?"

"I should have told him. I shouldn't have let him run off like he did."

Suddenly Buddy called out something about taking the hill and watching our flank and keeping our heads low, and a jumble of other such battlefield cries. Then he closed his eyes and started to tilt to his right, passed out again. Rusty got up to wedge an empty bucket under his side to keep him from toppling.

"Where do you think Squeaks is now?" I asked Rusty after a pause.

"Probably waiting in a morgue somewhere."

"No. I mean ... his soul?"

"Oh. *That.*"

"Don't you think about where folks go when they die?"

"There's either something better waiting or there ain't," said Rusty. "That's how I see it. Some folks say that life on Earth is heaven. Now that bothers me. You mean, this is it? This is our reward for floating around for eternity like a bunch of dumb space rocks?"

I had to chuckle, and Rusty settled himself on a paint barrel. "There was a fellow back in Raleigh named Tommy Lelandorf. We used to call him 'Tommy the dolt,' because he couldn't do nothing right. He was clumsy, you know. Always spilling things over folks, hitting his head on doorways. Of course, he was real tall, so that didn't help.

"One day we heard he was moving this metal ladder around outside his mother's house, and he touched an overhead electrical wire and poof! That was the end of Tommy. After his funeral people started talking about him with respect, like he was really somebody after all. It seemed to me that death gives us more dignity than we ever get from life. Hell, little 'Tommy the dolt' was no different than Alexander the Great or Shakespeare or Abe Lincoln. They was all equals then. That's what dying did for old Tommy Lelandorf. So it can't all be bad."

Just then all hell broke loose. A tall figure with long naked legs came barreling through the entry, and behind him flew a big dark form holding tight to the first one. The two bodies sprawled in the dirt and lay there thrashing around as Rusty and I ran over to pull them apart.

When the dust cleared I saw that the dark one was the missing Powder Keg, and the other that creepy Italian fellow known as Santa Claus. He wasn't dressed in a black duster anymore. He was wearing a dirty blond wig and a long tunic the color of oatmeal.

Rusty pinned the Italian's arms behind him while I helped Brady to his feet. "Powder—what the shit? What're you doin'?" demanded Rusty.

Old Santa Claus jerked one arm free and took a wild swing at Rusty, but he managed to duck it and they wrestled a bit. The foreigner was wiry, and he kicked around and flopped like a decked marlin until finally Powder Keg pulled Rusty off and plopped down mightily on the Italian's back. I heard the air go swooshing from his lungs like a blacksmith's bellows. After that we didn't look for him to put up more struggle.

The colored man sat there breathing hard as he wiped his brow and spoke out for the first time ever in short, jagged bursts.

"Been watchin' … Mr. Bigelow. … Been seein' what … he's up to. Hangin' 'round … the wagons."

"Powder, you numskull," said Rusty. "That's just the Italian fella they brought back from Rome. They got him made up to drive for Squeaks!" He stared hard at the black man to get his attention, then pantomimed holding reins and bouncing along as if he was driving a chariot, finally pointing down again at the winded Italian.

"No, *suh*," said the man. "I watched. He was alone."

"That's right," I said. "I saw him too, after lunch. He was walking around the teams. Someone was humming. ... Hey, was that you humming?"

Powder Keg didn't know what I was saying. He just went on, forcing his words out between breaths. "He was doing somethin'. Don't know what. But ... he got a knife."

At the mention of a knife, Rusty pulled back and frowned, then dropped down on a knee at the Italian's side and started feeling around in his tunic. Soon enough he pulled out a white pearl handle and snapped open a five-inch serrated blade. "There she is," said Rusty. "Fishin' knife. A beauty."

"Just now I saw him," our teammate continued. "He made sure no one was lookin' ... he was gettin' set ... to do something ... to Mr. Buddy's rig."

Rusty shot a look at me. "Missouri, go check it."

I ran off with my heart beating a mile a minute. I remembered how the Italian had been there with Squeaks' chariot before the race. He had lots of chances to put a gash in that sandbag. If we could prove it was him, everything might still turn out all right. We could hand him over to the studio cops and finish up the race as scheduled.

Buddy's chariot was tied to a post several yards up the track. I didn't even need to bend close to see some telltale grains of sand at one edge of the bag. When I lifted the corner slightly, a whole stream of sand poured out in a pile. The slice in the canvas was shorter than the one in the sack Buddy found, but it was the same sort of clean cut. I dropped the corner and hurried back to tell Rusty.

"That settles it, fellas," said Rusty with a relieved smile. "We've caught ourselves the killer."

As soon as he said it, though, his grin faded and a darker realization came over him. He stepped up close to where the Italian was lying and pulled back a leg. He gave the man a hard kick to the ribs with the toe of his boot. The Italian grunted and laid still.

Powder was still sitting on top of him, and hollered out at Rusty to stop. I grabbed him so he wouldn't do it again.

"That *was* for Squeaks, you son of a bitch!" shouted Rusty. He then grudgingly straightened up and wandered away.

I leaned down to look in the stricken face of Santa Claus. "What's wrong with you, mister? ... Don't you like Americans?"

The foreigner stared back at me blankly.

"He don't know English, *suh*," said Powder Keg.

I spoke slower. "You got something against America? Huh? *Comprende?* Bolsheviki?"

At that the foreigner started to wriggle and squirm to get free. He was hot with anger and squeezed out a few choice Italian words at me before grimacing in pain.

"What'd he say?" asked Rusty.

"Can't say. Sounded like *'vengenza'* or something … You think that's dago talk for vengeance?"

Rusty shrugged.

"Wot's going on?" asked Buddy, sitting up again by Polly's carcass.

"Powder Keg's caught our killer. He saw the Italian slashing up a sandbag. Here, see," said Rusty, waving the pearl handle under Buddy's blurry eyes. "I took this off of him."

I was still thinking about the word the foreigner had used. "Sounded like he said vengeance," I repeated. "Maybe someone he knew over there in Rome got hurt or something. Maybe he was in the race, or knew one of those that got drowned or something."

I looked directly in his dirty face, as if I might be able to read the truth in his eyes. "Is that it? You lose a friend or someone makin' that movie in Italy?"

He rattled off some more dago lingo as Rusty got up and wandered closer to hear.

"You understand any of that?" I asked him.

"Not a word," he answered. "But look, whether he's got a beef or he's just some loon, the cops can sort that out."

"What if the cops don't take Powder Keg's word for it? What if they don't care about what some Negro says he saw?"

"I got his *knife*," said Rusty, shaking it at me. "That's proof, ain't it?" He went closer to the black man and shook his head up and down. "Go ahead. Let him up."

Powder Keg wasn't more than a foot off of him when the prisoner sprang shoved him aside and made a headlong lunge passed Rusty. We were all caught by surprise, and before Rusty could grab him he had jumped a barrel and was heading toward the open archway.

There was no way to stop him, and once he was out of the spina he'd be free. But as he reached the exit there was a flash of movement in the dark and suddenly there was Buddy Ardale, on his feet and stepping into the Italian's path. Buddy startled him, too, because the Italian gasped just before they collided, and tucked his arms against his sides.

Buddy caught him by both shoulders and slipped a leg around behind, dropping him back to the ground. Then the old horse soldier lifted the foreigner's head and in one quick jerk gave it a hard twist that made a loud snap. The Italian tumbled forward, limp and sightless, onto the cold gravel.

CHAPTER TWENTY-ONE

Cave of the Dead

Someone was coming our way. Rusty heard the crunching same time as me and we both froze where we stood. Was it Delmer Burr, looking to find out what the commotion was? I took a gulp of air and hung on, waiting to see what sort of bird would poke its head in the door and find Buddy there kneeling on the dead dago.

But the footsteps didn't stop, and then they grew softer, and when it was safe to breathe again I let go a "*whewww.*"

"Hey, Missouri," said Rusty Bigelow in a suddenly normal tone. It confused me. It made me wonder if things were as bad as they seemed.

"Yeah?"

"Let's get this dead cocksucker out of the doorway."

That answered that.

Buddy grunted as he pushed himself to his feet, then stepped aside so we could get to the body. Rusty took one arm and nodded for me to take the other. The wrist I caught felt warm and heavy, with nary a twitch of life left to it.

"Where we goin' with him?" I asked.

"Over there, by Polly," said Rusty.

"Hold on," called out Powder Keg.

Rusty stopped, clearly annoyed. "What is it?"

"You move him … they gonna know."

"So?"

Instantly I saw that Powder Keg had a point. "He's right. If we hide the body, it's going to make us look guilty."

"Look, he didn't just walk in here and die of some dago disease," said Rusty. "His neck's busted. Now pull."

We dragged him off toward Polly and scooted him around behind the horse's hind legs before letting him drop. The Italian's head plopped down just under Polly's tail, so Rusty reached out a toe of his boot to shove his face nose-first into the animal's anus. It made a moist, squishy sound. Then he yanked the tarp down over both the bodies.

Buddy Ardale shuffled over and settled back in his old spot like he was set for a nap. I was in misery, quaking to my marrow, and it was all I could do to lower myself back on the nail keg before my knees gave out.

I don't know how long we waited like that in silence, trying to figure out our next move. There was no ducking the fact that we were all mixed up in a murder now—accessories, or maybe even accomplices. I was looking at hard jail time, that was certain, and I would be lucky to ever draw a breath as a free man again.

Then I looked at Powder Keg. He was standing still as a steeple, his eyes glossy and the edges of his mouth taking on a pale green cast. Jesus, I thought, whatever they'd do to me, there was no telling what they would do to him. Los Angeles was nothing like the Deep South, but it might as well have been when it came to a Negro involved in the murder of a white man.

"You okay?" I asked him.

"Yes, *suh*," he said. "Jes' as fine as a dead man can be." He righted an empty nail keg and eased himself down on it.

Rusty was pacing back and forth like a batter facing a ninth-inning tie. He stopped to snack his lips. "Sure wish I could had another bottle of that moonshine now."

Then there was a sound like snoring, and Rusty heard it too because he stopped to listen and went over to bend close to Buddy's chest. "Dead out," he said, standing up and shaking his head with amazement. "Like he ain't got a care in this world."

"Wake him up," I said.

"What for?"

"He got us into this."

"You can't say the dago didn't have it coming."

"We'll never know for sure now, will we?"

"The only question for us is what are *we* gonna do?"

"What do you mean?" I said.

"We can't just leave it—him—here. They'll find his body."

"So?" I said.

"He's got a broke neck. It can't hardly be called suicide."

"Won't they just think he's a poor foreigner, got himself in a fight and ended up dead?"

"No. There'll be an investigation."

"There will?" I said. "He don't have any relatives here. As far as we know, he never even got papers to be in this country. Won't the studio hush it up—like nothing happened?"

"I'm not so sure," said Buddy. "The cops might try to find out who done it. They'll go around asking folks who saw him last and who was with him."

I looked over at the colored man until he raised his eyes to mine. "Anyone see you with the dago? See … you … together?" I sort of signaled with my hands and ended with a shrug.

Powder Keg shook his head but I saw lines of doubt forming on his face.

"What'd he say?" said Rusty.

"I don't know. Maybe we should just go to the police," I said.

"Oh, now you want to bring in the cops!"

"Well, we don't know what folks saw. Besides, if we don't tell 'em what we know, they won't know a thing about the fishing knife or the sandbags or none of it."

"You want Buddy to go to prison?" said Rusty. "You want him to leave his wife in a pickle and lose every penny he ever made—after all those years serving his country with honor?"

"It was an accident! The Italian was trying to get away and Buddy grabbed him and his neck broke. That's the truth."

"Okay," said Rusty. "You be Buddy. I'm the judge. 'Uh, Mr. Ardale, would you step up here and show the jury just how the dago's neck got broke?'"

"I'm not saying I got all the answers. But a smart lawyer might."

"You gonna help pay for that smart lawyer? Because the studio sure won't. By the time those eastern attorneys get done with this, they'll make it look like it all happened miles off company property and Buddy was never officially on the payroll at all. You haven't been around long enough to know, Missouri, but I have, and I tell you that's how it'll be."

"Rusty, why do you think he did it, anyway? You know, slit those sandbags?"

"Who the crap cares? For fuck's sake! That's the last thing I need to know right this minute."

Powder Keg was sitting there sort of rocking himself, and suddenly he started to hum.

"That was you humming!" I said. "After lunch. It was you."

He gave a weak grin and sang softly in a deep, rich voice. *"I looked over Jordan, and what did I see, comin' fo' to carry me home ..."*

"I never knew deaf folks could sing," I said. "You got a fine voice."

Powder Keg continued on. " *... A band of angels just coming after me, comin' fo' to carry me home."*

It gave me solace to hear it, and I asked him if he knew any more gospel songs.

"Je-sus!" said Rusty. "This ain't time for no tent meeting! We got to think what we're going to do now!" Then he went back to his pacing.

"*Ah* used to sing, Mr. Grover," said Powder Keg. "In vaudeville— even before. Back in the minstrels."

"No kidding? Minstrels? I thought those were just white folks pretending to be colored."

"We had our minstrels, too. Played all over the South, goin' into churches and revivals. Fat ladies bring us warm food. Fried chicken by the bucket. ... Glorious days. ... I was with Bert Williams fo' a time. *'Camptown racetrack five miles long, oh de-do-long-day,'"* he chanted out in a sing-song voice, smiling all the time.

"How'd you learn songs if you can't hear?"

"Tappin', tappin' and singin' too. But pictures paid more, and they used colored folks in the early days. The bigger jobs—the servants and house slaves and family folk—they was mainly white ladies and gentlemen, made up to look colored. But the studios used us, too. Pullman porters, African slaves, sharecroppers—we got lots of work. I was in that first long picture, too. 'Birth of a Nation.' I was a soldier in that one. Friend of mine played a senator. Some colored folks pick-eted theaters that showed it. They said it wasn't good to show my people like that. All I know is, we was workin' then."

Rusty was pacing slower now, and it occurred to me that he was listening to Powder Keg talk. He was probably amazed to learn after all these years that the black man had a voice, much less a story to tell.

"There was lots of places—theaters in the South, but other ones up north, too—they wouldn't show pictures if there was coloreds in 'em. So studios stopped using us then. Me, I was married, a father, with two young 'uns. So I took me any job I could get. Runnin' into burnin' houses, jumpin' in icy rivers, gettin' bit by dogs—I'd do it if it paid."

"How'd you lose your hearing?" I asked, pointing to my ears.

"We was making a picture about a mine. There was s'pose to be a cave-in. Too much dynamite, some folks said. ... BAM! Prac'ly right next to me. Busted my 'drums." He grinned wide. "But my kids still had their pa."

"So that's why they called you —?" I started, but couldn't force myself to finish the sentence. I looked to Rusty for help.

"Sorry," he muttered.

"You know, Mr. Rusty," he said, trying to hold back a laugh. "I's the perfect hero for pictures," he said. "*Ax* me 'how come'."

"How come?"

"Dey can't talk and I can't hear, dat's how come!" Then he roared with a chesty chuckle, his shoulders pumping up and down until the sight of it made me laugh too. So there we were, two fools chortling away in our mirth, surrounded by unburied bodies and the weight of destiny about to crush us.

Rusty was growing more disgusted by the second. "I'm sure glad you're such pleasant fellows to be around," he scolded. "It sure will be good to have you with me there in our cell. You can just tell jokes and sing all the day through."

That focused my thoughts again on the dead Italian and the jam with the law. Powder Keg must have gotten the gist of what Rusty said, too, for his face suddenly grew serious and his eyes seemed to fill with visions of torches and ropes.

"Why'd dat dago have to go and die?" he blurted suddenly. "Why couldn't he have jes' waited and got hisself busted up in the race and let it be all you white folks' worry?"

The blast of Powder Keg's sorrow re-ignited my own fears, and I was about to argue again for throwing ourselves on the mercy of the court. But when I looked at Rusty all I could see was that his expression had changed. His frown was gone and he was lit up like a new dad on Father's Day.

"Fellas," he announced as if he could almost do a jig, "say hello to freedom and prosperity. Our troubles are over!"

***

Rusty laid out his new plan, and as scary as it sounded to me at first, it seemed like the only way to save Buddy and keep us all out of jail.

We would send Powder Keg out to bring the Italian's chariot up close to the spina. Then we would wrap the dago's body in a blanket or something and stash it up against the front shield. One of us would put on his wig and tunic and drive the last leg of the race, making sure to flip it at some point. Officials would find the body with its broken neck on the field, and the whole incident would disappear, just like the drownings in Italy.

There was only one hitch to Rusty's plan that I could see. Doing it and actually having it come out right seemed like a real long shot, and I told them as much.

"Lookee," answered Rusty, "I may be one sorry excuse for a cowboy with my bum leg and all. But I got a wife now, and a sister to look after, and if I can just come out of this with a little stake, we might still make a life for ourselves."

"But look at Buddy," I said. "Cracking up a chariot and walking away from it? He's not in any shape to do a thing like that."

"That's why I'm gonna do this little stunt myself," said Rusty. He instantly began to strip off his vest and unbutton his shirt.

"You?"

"Who else? Powder Keg can't pass for an Italian, and you wouldn't live long enough to collect on your bet."

"And what's to say you can do it?"

Rusty turned that one over in his mind a second. "I used to do tougher stunts than this."

"If you don't move away from the wreck pronto, they'll find you with the body. You could face some tough questions," I pointed out.

Rusty looked from me to the black man, who was just sitting there watching our lips and trying to follow what we were saying. "Powder Keg'll be standing by, ready to pull me clear before the dust settles. ... You'll do that, won't you?"

"You te' me where to be, Mr. Rusty. I be *dere*."

Rusty gave him a smile and sat down to tug off his boots. "Bring me the Italian's duds," he said.

I stepped across Buddy's legs and bent down to pull up the tarp, then stopped and stood up again. "Aren't we forgettin' something?" I asked.

"What's that?"

"Buddy."

All three of us looked down then at the sleeping horse soldier. Not even if we had a whole kettle of java to give him would Buddy be in any condition to finish the race.

"Well, hell, Runaway, ain't you figured that one out yet?" cackled Rusty with a grin.

"You don't expect me—?"

"We all seen how you handled your reins this morning. We were proud of you, son, weren't we, Powder Keg?"

"You'll do just fine, Mr. Grover."

I stammered and spit about how taking a buggy for a ride was a whole different proposition from driving in a race. But they could see I was just throwing up dust to hide the fact that I was shaking in my boots.

"You got to do it, Missouri. I'll have my hands full just taking care of my end. But it'll all be for nothin' if we don't settle this race and grab that purse. It's got to be you in old number three, hear? There's no runnin' away from it this time. We both gotta see this through. *For Buddy.*"

CHAPTER TWENTY-TWO

Ben-Hur and Me

Just as I got the tunic stripped off the Italian's skinny limbs and pulled it over his head we heard a call of bugles. Production chiefs from all around began screaming through megaphones for drivers to return to their rigs. Rusty stopped in his skivvies to listen, then turned to get Powder Keg's attention. "Hey, Powder, you go fetch the dago's rig. Pull it up close as you can," he mouthed. "Got me?"

The colored man gave a nod and hurried away. When I handed Rusty the dead man's costume, he looked at it like it was the most confounding garment he ever saw. He turned the embroidered edges this way and that until he found the neck hole and managed to stick his head through it. Then the sound of seams giving way filled the dark as he forced the fabric down over his bulky chest.

He tied up the sash and waited for my approval. "How do I look?"

"Now I know why men don't wear skirts. Better rub some dirt on that leg."

"Which one?" he asked.

"The pretty one."

"Oh."

The Italian's naked body looked pale and lifeless in the dark earth. "What about Santa Claus?"

"Put your outfit on him. I'll go find something to wrap him in."

"But—what'll I wear?"

"You got to put on Buddy's costume, remember? You gotta pass for Buddy if you're driving his team."

"Oh. Right."

"Here," he said, reaching down to fling his own pile of clothes at me. "Put this stuff on Buddy."

"Sure, Rusty."

Buddy didn't even wake up to grunt as I slipped his legs into Rusty's jeans and yanked them up over his hips. Then I peeled off his costume and threaded his thin arms into Rusty's flannel shirt. By the time I was finished dressing everybody, Rusty had returned with a wide, paint-spattered roll of canvas.

"Couldn't find a blanket," he said. "This'll be better, anyhow. They find it on the track after, they'll think it just blowed there."

We rolled the body up inside it, making sure to cover its head. Its feet stuck out a ways, so Rusty grabbed the empty sandbag and fed the toes through the gash and wrapped a cord around the ankles.

It made for one long, awkward package. Luckily, the foreigner was skinny enough that he wasn't hard to tote. We dropped him near the entry and I saw Powder Keg coming down the track, leading the Italian's horses and rig.

My queasiness returned to take up residence in my gut. But it was too late for further discussions. We were all into this way too far to change direction.

Powder Keg overshot the entrance by a yard or two, then gently coaxed the team back until the chariot was close enough to touch.

Rusty looked up and down the track, taking a quick peek into the bed of the wagon. "All right," he told me, ducking back inside. "First we gotta pull the good sandbag out of the back. You'll need to swap it for the cut one inside Buddy's rig. Okay?"

I nodded, but my mind must have been on other things. I was waiting for the next move, and after a second Rusty clicked open the Italian's knife, took a deep breath and darted outside. He kept his head low as he set to work, and I heard a couple of grunts as he ripped through the leather straps. Then the blade snapped shut and I heard the sandbag dragged to the edge.

That's when a new series of footsteps came running up. I gasped and tucked myself close to the inner wall.

"Hey, boy, what d'you think you're doing?" said a stern but familiar voice.

"Leave him be, Moore."

It was Moore the Merrier, challenging Powder Keg's right to be there. "Rusty? I didn't see you back there. I saw the darkie here walking away with the team."

"I asked him to fetch it," Moore. "Where you supposed to be?"

"I'm still looking for Buddy. You ever spot him?"

"You look in his rig?"

"Yeah. It's up yonder. But no one's in it."

"He was having a problem with his costume. He's probably off attending to it."

"I wanted to tell him we called an emergency meeting. Tonight. Eight o'clock at the Water Hole."

"What's it about?"

"Everyone's fired up about these accidents. We want action taken."

"Yeah, that's fine."

"You're welcome to come, too, of course."

"Thanks."

"You'll tell Buddy about it?"

"Sure will."

"Don't forget now."

"Damn it, Moore. I said I'd tell him."

"Oh, I saw Molly."

"Where is she?"

"Up in the stands. Wally Emerson invited her to sit with him."

"Who?"

"Casting director, or so he says."

"Don't know him."

"Well, if she was my sister I'd be worried. You know, a union would help protect our women from scum like him."

Powder Keg must have been biting his tongue because he knew time was almost up. From my angle, I could see him standing there with the lead horse, the sunlight glinting off the beads of moisture above his lip. "Mr. Rusty," he blurted, "we *gots* ta get this team goin'."

"All right—" began Rusty, but Moore cut him off.

"You hold on, boy! We're talking here. We'll tell you when we're through!"

I could make out just enough of Rusty to see him bristling over Moore's disrespect. "No cause for being rude, Moore. Powder's just another workin' stiff."

Moore gave a faint snort. "Anyway, when you see Buddy, wish him luck for me. Too bad we can't all be winners."

"Well, that's what makes it a race, don't it?" muttered Rusty.

I peaked out to see Moore walking off. He had on his own driver's get-up now, with a leather headband and belt around a burlap toga.

Rusty hoisted the sandbag out of the chariot and heaved it at my feet. He saw I had been watching him and Moore. "Buddy crushed the wrong windpipe," he said.

When he came back inside I told him I'd found out something about Mr. Moore the Merrier. I gave him the whole story of my meeting at the bus stop with Walt Altskellar, and about how Moore was behind a lot of the bad things going on all day.

"Well, I always knew that Moore was a weasel," said Rusty when I was done. "I didn't know he was a snake too."

"I thought you ought to know."

"That business about Molly and a casting guy." Rusty shook his head and wiped his hands up and down his tunic. "I think Mr. Moore and me may have to have a private meeting when all this is over."

Momentum was picking up everywhere now. Around the track the drivers jockeyed their chariots toward the markers while wranglers tugged on harness straps to keep the animals in line.

In the confusion it wasn't hard to swing the Italian's body up inside the rig and get it positioned around the curve of the shield. Rusty came out wearing the dago's blond wig, which he had pulled down to his ears until just a few reddish locks stuck out here and there. He gripped the chariot rail and pulled himself up into the bed, then wiggled his toes beneath the canvas.

As he wound the reins around his palms, Rusty looked down at Powder Keg so there would be no misunderstanding. "You know the spot where Squeaks cracked up? You wait for me there. Second lap around, she's gonna flip. You pull me out of there fast. Okay?"

"Second lap," repeated Powder Keg. "Yes, *suh*. I be there."

Rusty turned and gave me a forced smile. "Good-bye, Missouri. Good luck."

I was moved by his words all at once, and I found myself saying something I would never have dreamed that morning that I would say. "It's been a pleasure gettin' to know you, Rusty."

He smiled shyly and sort of scowled, the way men will. But it was clear he was touched. "Just do what Buddy said. Hang tight, and don't let go. I'll meet up with you at the other end—one way or the other."

Then he nodded and was ready, and he gave the reins a snap. Powder Keg tugged the leader's bridle forward and the outfit started up the track.

I took a long, deep breath and adjusted my wig. All at once my knees were made of rubber again.

Powder Keg must have seen my doubts. "Mr. Grover, you know what you doin'?" asked the black man.

"For such a fine singer," I said, "you got a damn poor sense of timing."

And so we started off, both of us so resigned to our fate that neither of us remembered to pick up the new sandbag back in the spina. It grew farther from our reach with every step.

The crowd in the stands was all worked up again, and there was a general jostling for the best vantage points at the rail. Groups of men shouted out wishes of "Good luck!" and "God speed!" when they saw me drive by in car number three. Even a lady here and there could be heard shouting out some blessings.

Everyone had had lots of time to fret over the bets they placed, and I suspect that the fear of losing their money alternated with the dream of a making a killing. I waved back at them and smiled as I marched on, trying to keep my knees loose and my legs from buckling beneath me.

Powder Keg ran ahead to unwrap the bridle of the dappled gray and steady the wagon for me. The floor bucked to and fro, and suddenly I was in the old school yard again, just a kid playing on Uncle Ches's pitchin' board, ready to take on all challengers.

As my confidence built I shifted a foot and heard a crunching. There on the floor lay a coating of sand and above it the sliced sandbag. The sandbag! I walked off and left the good one in the spina! I was about to shout for Powder Keg to run and get it but at that instant the clamor ended with a blast of bugles. The bleachers seemed to clench with anticipation and everything fell very still and quiet.

Wranglers with colored flags scurried into position, and I knew it was too late now. This bag had lost some sand, but there might still be enough to keep me on the track. I would have to take extra care, that's all, and leave one foot anchored above the slash.

A prayer now seemed the right thing to do. I prayed for God to watch over Rusty as he flipped his chariot, and to bless Buddy Ardale who deserved every favor. I made a vow then and there that if He saw fit to let me come through this alive I would turn over all my race money to Buddy's wife. I sealed this silent vow with a half-spoken "Amen," and gripped tight to my reins.

A man hollered into a megaphone somewhere, and his hoarse voice came ricocheting back from every direction. I was far enough around the bend, though, that I couldn't hear him well, nor make out just what he was saying at first. He wanted the crowd to know that the question of the drivers' safety was taken care of, and that they would proceed with the race now straight through to the finish. Then he asked everyone to look excited and interested in the race because the cameras would be cranking away.

As a sort of afterthought he warned the onlookers not to jump up and down too much on the boards because there were a lot more people there since lunch, placing a lot more weight on the stands. That gave the crowd a moment's pause, and there came a rustle of murmurs as confusion spread.

After a second the man with the megaphone returned to say he had just been assured by studio engineers that there was no cause for concern because they were all "a hundred percent confident" that the bleachers were solid.

Then someone with a much smaller voice took to the megaphone and said a few garbled words I couldn't make out at all. After that there was another bugle fanfare, and the drivers around me started to crouch low and brace themselves for the shock of the starting signal.

I was looking all over for flag men, I guess, when the next thing I knew there was a loud crack and before I was sure what happened the crowd erupted in the stands. Wranglers dropped the bridles and jumped clear of the wheels as drivers screamed to their teams and slapped leather on their flanks.

Pushing my tongue to my front teeth, I gave out with a shrill whistle and snapped my straps, and the chariot pitched forward and threw me hard against the side as off we charged.

Right away I could see this was going to be something other than a brisk buggy ride. All my senses were under assault as I struggled for breath and balance in a violent hail of rock and gravel. The pelting of sand stung my forearms and cheeks like a storm of needles.

There was no way to be prepared for the sudden speed of the team or the fury of their hooves as they pummeled the earth. *Ka-THUD-i-ty, ka-THUD-it-y, ka-THUD-it-y.* The creaking of wood and squealing of the metal axles tore at my ears like the retching of a food-poisoned child as I pumped the reins and tried to herd the dapple gray toward an inner position at the spina.

I turned my face from the punishing sand to see the ground whirling past like a grindstone. Mere inches from my heels bounced the precipitous edge of my universe. I watched with longing the civilized world shrink away, and in its place moved another team, its hooves a frothy blur of action and its driver bent fast to his reins.

My team must have sidled over the track by instinct, for all at once I felt the cool shade of the spina spread its balm on my wind-stung cheeks. Crooking an arm against the sandstorm I made out other chariots moving swiftly now beside the inner wall. The spokes of their wheels dived backwards, one after another, and yet the cars sped forward as if in contradiction to God's own laws.

Due mainly to my advantage at the start, I was only three lengths behind the matched white stallions of the Ben-Hur rig. Two other cars ran ahead of them, and already they were easing into the first turn. The other chariots were behind me, though the next closest team was working up speed. I could see the noses of the runners flare as their driver whipped them hard to leave the safety of the wall and make their bid to pass on my right.

The bend in the track now approached, and I remembered to make sure my foot was pressed firmly on the sandbag. I could feel my body pulling to the right and I shifted my weight to offset the drift. The horses, too, struggled to keep their footing against the resistance of the tongue.

Sunshine exploded on my face and I squinted into a fireball that quickly waned and gave way to ordinary daylight. I was bearing down on the virgin length of the backstretch. The sight of the beauty of the horses and the color of the chariots combined to overwhelm the senses as we galloped in the sun.

As soon as we cleared the turn I popped my reins to let the team know our job was not done. I called out to them the way I had seen Squeaks do: "Come on, my beauties! Move you, dappled gray!" I felt that if I bent forward and strained I might reach out and pat the rump of the leader, but just as I thought it we hit a bump and the outfit quaked and I was reminded not to tempt disaster.

The team worked well together now, each horse pumping in perfect adjustment to the others, their rhythmic gait becoming at once our billowing sail on the wind. The dappled gray was wisely chosen and set a good pace. It was clear to me that we were closing the gap on the matched whites of Ben-Hur's car at the lead.

Now as we came to the spot where Squeaks had crashed, I remembered Rusty and looked back for his chariot. All I could see was another team coming up at my rear, straying to the side and getting into position to move around on my right. The sun fell full in the driver's face and I saw a leather headband and then caught a glimpse of my pursuer. It was Freddie Moore. Moore the Merrier grimaced with determination as he raised his crop aloft, ready to take full advantage of the backstretch. I heard his leader whinny as it felt the leather sting on its rump, and the other animals snorted as if in reply and strained harder to pick up their hooves.

Moore's rig inched forward and his team edged up until it was almost even with my own. I gave my horses more play of the reins, as if the duty of winning was theirs as well, and when next I glanced over, Moore was studying me and trying to see below my flapping beard to make out who I was. He started to shout out but the wind snatched the breath from behind his words, and he gulped and shook his head and then looked back and shouted again over the roar: "Where's Buddy?" he called. Then his car swerved into mine and our wheels clanked raw iron and my whole buggy pitched and quivered again.

A panic rose in my breast and for a fleeting instant I wondered if I could jump clear of the wagon at this speed and survive a fall to the ground. Then I remembered all that was at stake for Buddy and I shook off the thought. I would hang tough and see what came next.

As we approached the south end, Moore began to drop back and prepare himself for the turn. I braced myself as well and looked down to check my footing and it was then I saw that I was no longer standing on the sandbag. The sack stretched out flat at my toes like a starving porch hound melted into its own folds.

A cheer rose from the crowd as we came out of the turn and thundered up the track before the stands. From their roar you could tell they were no longer just pretending their interest. Those of us charged with the chariots and the horses weren't the only ones invested in the outcome.

I felt a surge of pride at being among the front-runners, even as I poked my sandbag and tried to figure out where I could stand to stop the flow of sand. I cursed my luck. Wasn't that always the way? Just when I had things under control, fate had given me a split sandbag!

Before I knew it we were heading into the north turn again, leaving the shade of the spina and hurling into the sun. I struggled to hold my team back as Moore came racing up on my right, ready to use the backstretch to overtake me.

He hadn't dared use his crop in front of the spectators, fearing that the crowd would turn against him. But here safely out of view of the bleachers, he could do as he pleased. Up went the crop and down it lashed again and again, the flogging no longer restricted just to the leaders. His horses moved ever faster as they struggled to escape that punishment, until the team pulled past me and I began to feel the faint spray of sweat rising off their coats.

Once again Moore swerved his car toward mine like a battering ram. This time the wheels clashed with such force that I feared my chariot would fly to pieces. I looked down and saw a million tiny grains of sand dancing toward the back ledge. Each grain seemed precious to me. Watching them dive off the bed was like watching the last seconds of my life tick away.

Again Moore's axle hub bumped into mine, and the hooves beat insistently in what seemed like a different rhythm. Then I caught sight of a new team approaching from the center of the track, pulling an unfamiliar chariot. My heart leapt up as I recognized the driver. It was Rusty Bigelow, charging into action and aiming his team straight at the heart of Freddie Moore.

CHAPTER TWENTY-THREE

The Photo Finish

We were quickly coming to the spot where Squeaks took his spill. Up behind a pillar waited Powder Keg, peering from the shadows with glowing eyes. No doubt his heart was thumping as wildly as my own as he watched for the decisive move.

We all knew the roughing-up that a body would take in the gravel at this speed. I wanted to stop it. I wanted to leap down from my chariot and go to Rusty, running with my arms waving over my head and shouting, "No, wait! Save your neck! No sack of gold is worth this risk!"

But even as I thought it, I must have known it was a lie. It was a fairy tale given credence by the rattle of the chains. Rusty simply had to go through with the plan we set in motion, and it was up to him alone now to make the ending right.

A hard jolt brought a new pummeling of sand in my face. I covered my eyes with an arm, and when I looked again the land and sky had joined together. There was no more up or down, only a painful, twirling tornado of impressions. Fleeting images of a dead Italian, of Buddy straddling his back for that fatal twist, of Polly and Molly and the hairy knuckles in a prison window, of Daps and my mother, and a child's view of pine coffins lowered in the mud.

A grinding mesh of metal snapped me back to the moment. Freddie Moore's chariot had drifted too close and its left wheel was wedged behind mine. The two rims clashed in a shower of sparks as his wheel clawed against my axle and the driver whipped his team to set the tangle free.

I saw the eye of my dappled gray rotate backward in its socket as it tried to account for the jerking of its load. Then Moore raised his whip high and brought it down across the side of my outside runner.

Panic swept from horse to horse. The rhythm of the team's gait fell into disarray as the animals struggled to regain control. My chariot shook and began to drop back and then Moore's wheel all at once broke free and he lunged again at me with greater speed.

Freddie Moore was so determined to get past me and do damage to my team as he went that he did not see Rusty's team bearing down on his right. I will never know how his horses found the extra drive, or how he timed the blow to come when it did. But it was in the very next second that his lead runner rammed into the ribs of Moore's outside mare.

Their harnesses smashed mightily together, sending both wagon tongues skittering like branches in a flood, yanking the teams along across the speeding patch of ground. Rusty's horses moved with the force of the load behind them and had nowhere to go but straight on, driving ever harder against the side of Moore's rig.

For a second or two they hung suspended together, both fours joined as one team in a flying wedge. Moore's features distorted with rage as he cast a vengeful eye on Rusty Bigelow, and Rusty's gaze returned a cold defiance.

"Eat sand, you bastard!" hollered Rusty.

Then Moore yanked his reins violently toward Rusty's wagon and the two of them pulled farther to the right. Now the lane was clear ahead and the animals knew what to do. Lowering their necks as one, they pointed their noses for one headlong dive through the widening gap.

It wasn't until I was through the opening that I dared a quick glance back. Rusty was driving his leader in a final dash at Moore. Both teams seemed to willfully rebel at the prospect of one more collision. The closest horses raised back and tried to halt the onward rush of the wagons. But the tongues continued forward and pulled tight the harnesses until the beasts could do nothing but fold up and drop. The cars screamed as if alive and vaulted into the midst of a rising mound of bodies and dust.

My own team was coming to the bearded statue of old Atlas as we headed into the southern turn. I could tell we were hewing too close to the inner wall, and I braced myself for the force of the curve. My sandbag was no more than two flapping covers now. I kicked it with my boot and a loose corner flew back and caught the wind and the whole canvas casing went whisking away.

The horses pulled to their left and I felt the chariot begin to tilt as its wheel lifted from the track. Leaning into the rising wall, I grabbed fast to its railing and pulled myself tightly to it, ready to ride it like a sled down a wintry slope.

In my dreams sometime even now I am there again clinging to that wall, the floor no longer under my feet, the sky tilting. I feel suffocated like a fly in a honeyed ooze of amber. In truth, it lasted probably only seconds before the team pulled us through the trough and straightened into the homestretch. The wheel made its return to earth, and I shifted my weight to the front, settling at the center just as the side came slamming down with a spine-crunching thud.

All sound was swallowed by the sudden pandemonium in the stands. The shouts of the bettors reminded me that I was still in a race and the outcome would be determined by what happened next.

There was no time to worry about Rusty. What was done was over, and there was nothing behind or ahead but open track for me. I thought of the lap markers atop the spina, and raised my eyes there just as an official turned the final dolphin's nose downward.

And so we entered the last lap of the course. Some three lengths ahead of me ran the Ben-Hur chariot with its four white Arabian stallions, and ahead of them was Pedro's rig. Out in front of all but barely maintaining its lead was Bushman's team, pulling the villain Messala's lavender car. Pedro seemed to be overtaking it, and I set my sights on doing the same to the car before me.

Without the added weight of the sand, my chariot felt leaner and swifter on the hoof. The Ben-Hur matched whites loped along as if growing bored with the run. Their stand-in driver had no keen interest in doing more than turning in a good showing.

Lacking fire in his belly, he lit none under his team, and my dappled gray quickly whittled down the gap between us. The driver looked over and smiled as I passed, and I returned his smile while I plotted my strategy for the coming turn.

I could afford to let my team go wide on this one, I figured. That way I would maintain my pace without opening us up to grave danger. Then I would close in on the leaders in the backstretch and do whatever necessary to win an edge for the final dash to home.

I gently urged the lead runner away from the wall and into a wide, smooth arc around the curve. Both my wheels stayed grounded this time, and when we straightened up I gave a series of snaps on the reins to build our speed.

Pedro's team was almost even with the Messala rig now. Each driver was so busy worrying the other that neither noticed me speeding up from behind. I was starting to feel like a battle-proven charioteer. I took each jarring bump and unexpected tilt in stride, keeping my focus on the track ahead and my mind free to seize any opportunity that arose.

"Run, you beauties!" I shouted to my team. "Run for Squeaks, and for Buddy! Your stables will be filled tonight with apples and oats soaked with egg!"

My spirits fell soon enough, though. I was coming again to the spot where Rusty staged his attack. Some wood chips and a few deep gouges in the sand were all that marked the place, but off inside the spina I could see the broken shields and axles of two chariot cars. I looked quickly around inside as I passed, searching for any clues of what had become of Rusty or Freddie Moore, but my speed was too great and I saw nothing.

All the best stations were abandoned now. Even the wranglers had moved along to the other side to catch the final sprint for the finish line.

Then I got the idea to make a straight dash across the track ahead of the curve and to cut in there at an angle. I would have to cover more ground that way, but it would be less dangerous for me in the bend. And at my lighter speed, I figured, I might make up for any lost time by getting to the other side first.

Messala's horses slid into the turn just ahead of Pedro's, and both wagons were still pitched and skidding to the right when my team bore down and charged for the inside position. By the time the others righted themselves and opened into the homestretch, I was already there at full gallop and headed for the flags.

Pedro's rig was suddenly cut off behind me. Only Messala's horses on my right threatened to nose ahead. I looked over half-expecting to see old Francis X. Bushman at the helm, stately and forceful in full mastery of his team. But the familiar winged helmet seemed to float lower behind the steeds, and then I remembered what Rusty had said about Bushman bowing out after Squeaks' accident. In his place and wearing his outfit was a much smaller driver. A striking sight then! I was staring into the cruel eyes of Delmer Burr!

Suddenly it all made a kind of mad sense to me. This was what fate had intended from the beginning. It all came down to a final match between us two. From the very first instant that I heard his name from the other men, or maybe even before that, I was meant to deliver his final comeuppance, or he mine.

That's why I was here, why even getting thrown off the set couldn't stop it. It was why Delmer Burr and I had each schemed and clawed our way to this moment, to these chariots: I was to have a face-to-face showdown with the man who took a hard, quick jab at my belly without a word of warning. The man who placed that gun in Buddy's hand and willed him to fire. The one who tempted him with whiskey in the hope he would fall, and had left countless broken lives and bloodied bodies in his wake—all just so he could be in this final race!

There he stood, hunched over the reins of his team with a primed and hungry glare, like a winter cougar with his eyes fixed on a colt, no less dead-set on prevailing than was I.

It seemed only now to dawn on him that Pedro was no longer pressing up from behind, and that instead he had a new contender on his right. He looked over quickly and then back to his team, stealing away for a longer look to understand what he had seen.

I grinned at him and nodded, but he still couldn't make out my features. So I reached up and pulled some whiskers from my chin and let his eyes focus on me again. His lips pulled tight in an unheard curse, and he turned away like a maddened demon to bring down his whip on the haunches of his runners.

His car inched ahead of my own and I was pelted with a new flurry of gravel and sand. My outside mare must have felt the sting as well, for she whinnied and snorted and my whole team threw itself forward to protest the downpour.

Burr was not about to let lose his grip on victory now. He laid his whip across my team, and then snapped it back and sent it full against my side. The blow caught me unprepared and I lost my balance and had to catch myself on the rail. I was suddenly staring down at the onrushing track, and the fear of falling off and being trampled under Pedro's chargers overtook me and made me think of backing off and letting the devil go.

But it was in that instant that Delmer Burr made his grave mistake. He must have seen my eyes flash fear and surrender, and as his chariot surged ahead he looked back at me. There upon his features rose an old familiar smirk, the strutting mask of evil at its moment of victory.

I felt my veins harden with righteous resolve. Damn my measly neck! I would not give up or run away—not this time, not ever again! Burr would not win this one. I would hold my ground against the beast to the last breath of my being!

To this day still when the house is quiet and I am surrendering to sleep, I hear the crowd's roar turn to a chugging cadence as we approach those final flags. Burr's horses are massive and strong, and my own ponies seem exhausted and panting. But my rig flies on.

Twenty yards! On past the stands we run, first Burr's team nosing ahead of mine, then mine nosing up on his. Faster and faster. Burr knows I am there. We are fighting it out with every breath of our team.

Fifteen!

The crowd is on its feet. The flagman draws his white banner up above his head.

Ten yards! My team is magnificent. It seems to group for a final effort. The animals stretch out their necks. Then Burr plays his last ace, bringing out his crop to give his leader a hard swipe across the haunch. At this insult the animal pulls back its head and seems to bristle. The others follow suit, and in the instant that we all come to the finish line my horses hold their necks rigid and their noses low and proud while Burr's team draws back its heads in protest.

The difference is there for all to see as over the line we fly.

We have won!

The other chariots, one after another, charge in front of the officials. Wranglers leap down and come running to catch us, while excited young men dive over the bleacher rails and hurry toward the finish line. Most rigs swing around to double back for their applause.

There will be more parading now, I know, and actors preening for the cameras. But I no longer care about the envy and acclaim of men. Nor do my horses seem to want to stop and be swallowed by the crowd.

So I give the team some rein and let them lead us back around the northern turn and the freedom of the open backstretch. My job is done, and it won't do for anyone right now to get too close a look at me. All that's left is to find Buddy and put things back the way they need to be—that and, I should add, learn Rusty's fate.

***

The whole sunny length of track seemed peaceful again now. A few banners snapped and billowed in the breeze, with barely a whiff of dust waiting to be settled. I drove on toward the section where I saw the wreckage, and old Powder Keg stepped out of the shadows ahead.

He had one arm around the waist of Buddy Ardale, who stood with an arm slung across the black man's shoulders, standing none too certainly on his feet.

From his direct gaze I could tell the old horse soldier had sobered up some. He was wearing Rusty's dirty tunic now, and he wiped the back of his hand against it absently as he watched me bring up the team. When it stopped he grabbed a bridle strap and calmed the leader with a reassuring rub.

"That'a girl," he said.

Powder Keg stood grinning at me.

"You see it?" I asked. "You see the end?"

"Yes, *suh*," nodded the black man, "we sure did, Mr. Grover."

"We won."

"Didn't I say you was up to it?" said Buddy.

"How'd Rusty make out?"

Powder Keg gave a sad shake of his head. "He in bad shape," he said. "He lost his leg."

"Where is he?"

"Inside."

Solid ground felt odd to me. It sloshed and rolled under my feet like the race was still going. As I handed the reins to Buddy I had to take hold of a railing until a spell of wooziness passed.

"Gimme a hand here, will ya," said Buddy with one foot up in the bed.

"Don't forget this," I told him, and ripped off the whiskers from my chin to stick them onto his. Then we managed to boost Buddy up into the chariot bed.

He checked the leaders and sorting his reins, but I could tell he was really searching for words. "I don't guess I can thank you," he said uncertainly at last, "for what you did."

"Vaya con Dios," I answered. That's all that was said about the matter, which sounds odd, but that's how men are. Later I thought what I wished I'd said was, "I'll never forget you, Captain Ardale," and maybe even offered him a salute. I think it would have made him feel good, and it might have made me feel better, too. Just saying out loud that I would remember him would have been the right thing to say to any old horse soldier whose glory days were done. So there it is, for what it's worth. I've finally got it out. And maybe that will end my regrets on the matter.

Powder Keg and I watched the chariot roll away and we went to find Rusty.

The redhead was sitting up inside the spina in his underwear holding a canvas tarp across his loins, waiting for someone to bring him his lost leg. "Did you find it?" he called out to Powder Keg when he saw us coming.

"No, *suh*. I'm fixin' to look some more now. It gots to be on the track somewhere." We both watched the man lope off into the sun before trying to speak.

"That was some stunt," I told Rusty. "One for the history books."

"Probably my best stunt ever. And I can't even brag about it down at the Water Hole!"

"You saved my hide."

"Enough to make a grown man bawl."

"Did they find ... the dago?"

"Yeah. Poor bastard. They rushed him off to the hospital, but I'm afraid his neck got broke." He chuckled to himself.

"What happened ... to Moore?"

"He won't be at the meeting tonight. Busted four or five ribs, at least. He can say whatever he wants when he's ready, the little shit. No one's gonna believe him now, not after I tell everyone what he pulled today."

"What about Burr? He knows it was me driving Buddy's car. You think he'll cause any trouble?"

"Old Delmer won't welcome anyone looking into Squeaks' accident, that's for sure. Way I see it, we've all lassoed the same angry bull. No one dares let go of his rope for fear the whole damn thing'll bust free."

"I hope you're right."

"You just start worryin' about what you're goin' to do with your share of the purse."

"Well, I already know. I made a promise that if I won, I'd give it to Buddy's family."

"That's a fine idea. And you still got your wager money coming."

I didn't feel like telling Rusty that I had vowed to give that up as well. "Let me go get on my own clothes and see what's going on outside."

"Missouri, if you run into Molly, you can tell her she's always got a home. Tell her Rusty said that."

"Will do. You just goin' to sit here and wait?"

"I sure ain't goin' nowhere without my damn leg."

I turned to leave and Rusty called me by my true name for the first and only time.

"Grover?"

"Yeah?"

He said I had done fine out there. Since Rusty wasn't real big on compliments it seemed like a big deal to me and caught me off guard. Finally I pulled myself together enough to answer that I was as surprised as anyone. "I might've gone my whole life not knowing I was a born charioteer," I joked. I hoped he didn't see that my eyes were pooling up.

It felt good to strip off that scratchy burlap costume and slip into my old Levi's again. That was my blood on its front from that beating I took under the bleachers. And the fanny was caked with dirt from when I was thrown out of the stadium on my ass. There might even have been a whiskey stain near the crotch, now that I think of it.

The point is, they were my jeans. It might sound funny, but I felt I earned the right to wear them again. My history was mixed in there with its fibers. Those old blue jeans were like an ancient shroud, testifying to the validity of my existence. I wondered if Irving Thalberg owned a pair anything like them, something marked with the stuff of his life's adventures.

I doubted it.

The day was done for me, I remember thinking, and I felt more happy than sad about it. But I was mistaken again. Fate still had one more surprise in store.

CHAPTER TWENTY-FOUR

God's Blanket

The racetrack was crowded with bodies and the sounds of popping corks and blaring horns. The loudest laughter was down at the finish line, where stone-faced Buster Keaton was clowning around on one of the chariots. He was pretending that he had dropped his reins over the shield and couldn't quite reach them no matter how low he stooped.

He stopped to encourage a handsome, black-haired young onlooker to step up and join him, and the man jumped on the back and clung there as if frightened to death. No one seemed to know who he was until he pulled out a pair of dark-framed glasses, then waited for the screams as he slipped them on and magically turned into screen comic Harold Lloyd.

Beautiful actresses wandered this way and that across the track, heading nowhere but looking peeved when they were forced to hoist up their beaded hems to keep them out of the sand. High in the stands, the rows sat mostly deserted now. I searched for Thalberg's stall again, just to satisfy myself that it was empty too.

A few of the chariots continued circling for photographers, and farther up the track came Messala's lavender carriage, rolling slowly through the parting crowd. I expected to see the unhappy scowl of the defeated Delmer Burr. But back at the reins instead was my old friend Francis X. Bushman. He had returned to take charge of his team to pose for his fans like any former sculptor's model.

To see his confident and steady grin was to feel that his triumph and the success of the movie "Ben-Hur" were all but guaranteed. Perhaps he was thinking that from that point on he would have only to live up to his legend. If that is so, he couldn't have been more wrong.

Bushman's remaining career would consist of just eighteen forgettable movies and the matinee serial "Dick Tracy." In the 1940s he made a short comeback in radio drama, while grabbing any stray movie role that happened along. He passed away in 1966 after doing a small speaking part in the "beach blanket" comedy "Ghost in the Invisible Bikini."

Studio publicity men and reporters were out in full force now, encouraging the stars to preen alongside new starlets and badgering them for interviews. At the center of one group stood Ramón Novarro, appearing dark and dashing amid a giggling pack of female admirers. I more than half-expected to spot Molly there, but she was nowhere to be seen.

I had just started back toward the spina when I heard someone shouting, "There he is! That's him! Didn't I tell you he was on the lot!" Delmer Burr was on foot and leading a small posse of studio cops and race officials.

"I told you he was driving that chariot. It wasn't Buddy Ardale at all. He must have gotten back on the lot somehow. His name's Link. I want you to arrest him for trespassing, and I want Buddy Ardale's chariot disqualified!"

"What do you have to say about this, Mr. Link?" asked one official.

"Me?" I replied, wearing my most innocent expression. "I just came down to congratulate the winners."

"You were in the race. Don't you try to deny it. You were supposed to be a wrangler, but you overstepped your bounds. You caused a delay in shooting and I had you thrown off the set, isn't that so?"

"You booted me off, all right."

"So how is it you're here?"

I told him the truth—that a man in a studio limousine offered me five bucks to sit in the stands with the extras.

"He's lying!" shouted Burr. "He snuck back on the lot and stole Ardale's chariot and drove it himself. I want him arrested!"

The largest of the cops looked like he decided it was wisest to do what Burr was asking, and he reached out to take me by the arm. But at that moment came a commanding voice, calling to me gaily from off to the right.

"Grover! My boy, congratulations to you!" Gracefully bounding across the track now was Douglas Fairbanks, looking most dapper in his dark blue sports jacket and light brown trousers. His wide, tanned face beamed with joy as he sprinted up to shake my hand. "Thanks for all your help, my boy. You were absolutely right about the race. What a beauty!" Then he noted the sour expressions of the officials. "Anything wrong here?"

"Well, Mr. Fairbanks, Mr. Burr claims this man raced illegally. He wants us to disqualify the winning chariot."

"Nonsense! Grover was up in the stands with me through the entire race—eh, Grover? He was helping me and my friends handicap the cars, if you want to know. You just tell Mr. Mayer he was with Douglas. Or if you'd like, I can go talk to Louis B. myself."

"No, Mr. Fairbanks," said the official, suddenly alarmed. "Your word's gold with me."

At that, Delmer Burr realized he had to speak out. "Look, Mr. Fairbanks, I know you're respected in this town, and you have powerful friends. We should be able to get together on this. I have friends myself, and they appreciate what I can do for them. I could do the same for you, if you know what I mean."

Douglas Fairbanks gazed in steely earnest at him a moment. I am sure he knew what Burr was offering—a handy new supply of bootleg hooch, with no risks attached.

What Delmer Burr did not realize was that Douglas Fairbanks was a strict teetotaler. He had signed a temperance pledge at age twelve, and as an athlete he pursued the fruits of training and self-discipline. He saw how alcohol undermined the human will and destroyed lives.

No dinner wine or cocktails were served at Pickfair, the famous estate he owned with Mary Pickford. What liquor was there came in through the Pickford clan. Mary's mother and brother were both alcoholics, and "America's Sweetheart" herself was at the mercy of the disease. I did not know it then, but Mary Pickford passed most her evenings alone, privately drinking away from the prying eyes of Douglas's famous houseguests. She had been America's first movie queen and the supreme love of Fairbanks' life, and yet alcohol had driven a wedge between them.

What none of us could have known was that the world-famous Fairbanks-Pickford marriage would not survive the decade. They would divorce and each would remarry. Fairbanks would end up dying alone of a heart attack at age fifty-six, ending forever his dream of reconciling with his one true love.

All at once I saw a sharp, cold blade of loathing flash from Fairbanks' eyes. When he spoke, it was as if he was shoving daggers deep and hard into Delmer Burr's chest. "Mr. Burr, the truth is I have no use for you or for your friends. You should be ashamed of yourself, the way you flogged that horse. There were a lot of cruel things going on with those teams today. I think someone needs to look into that. I'm going to speak to Mr. Thalberg personally. I'm going to tell him you should be prevented from ever working at this or any other studio again. I wouldn't be at all surprised if you end up facing criminal charges."

Delmer Burr knew he was licked. He shot resentful looks at each of us in turn, then yanked his shoulder around and stomped off to nurse his wounds. The studio officials gave us meek nods all around and excused themselves as well. Suddenly I found myself standing alone with "the son of Zorro."

"Thank you," I told him.

"Grover, you know, you made me and my friends a lot of money here today."

"I'm glad it turned out that way."

"That tip of yours was golden. We wanted to express our gratitude. So we all chipped in some of our winnings and it would make us very happy if you would take it." He pulled out a wad of bills and held it out to me. "There should be eight hundred dollars or so there. Take it with our good wishes."

Then with a flash of his legendary teeth, Fairbanks spun around and gracefully pranced off into a clamoring female throng.

I stood where I was for what must have been five or six minutes, not truly comprehending what this meant. Eight hundred dollars was more than enough to get me back to Missouri to straighten out my legal situation. I might even be able to swing a loan on a forty-acre farm and send for my dad. It would mean a lot to him to be living on a place of his own again.

But I couldn't help feeling sad at what I would be giving up. My eyes idly scanned the bleachers, settling for a time on the small private stall where I had kissed Norma Shearer.

I'll never know for certain if it was me who brought Norma and Thalberg together, but I like to think so. All the books now note that there was a sudden change in their relationship at that time. Some say it was because he had a serious heart attack the next month, due to the pressure he was under getting "Ben-Hur" on the screen. There's no doubt in my mind, though, that it was on that day of the race that Thalberg stopped viewing Norma Shearer as a studio asset and began to look on her as a wife and mother.

Thalberg and Norma Shearer announced their engagement in August 1927 and were married in September 1928. Some say he rededicated M-G-M to the task of immortalizing his wife in a whole series of major productions. Ultimately he approved her playing the sixteen-year-old Juliet in "Romeo and Juliet" when she was nearer in age to Juliet's mother.

Thalberg authorized endless retakes and ever-more-lavish sets and costumes, doing for Norma exactly what he had fired Erich von Stroheim for doing some fifteen years earlier. He even ordered the musical score rewritten a dozen times. Still, a preview audience found the Shakespeare adaptation a bore, and with its official premiere on hold, Thalberg worked himself up a case of pneumonia and died at age thirty-seven.

"Don't let the children forget me," were reportedly Irving's final words to Norma. But I don't know about that because I wasn't there.

Though Norma Shearer never reigned again as a top-rank star after "Romeo and Juliet," she continued working in films through the 1940s. Most people remember her for her last screen roles in "The Women" and "Idiot's Delight." But in my opinion she was no longer the beauty she was when we shared our kiss.

Most female stars of the silent era had no real future in the movies. Constance Talmadge's lighthearted charms and screen success were seen as artifacts of the Jazz Age. "Dutch" left Hollywood in 1929 and married a Wall Street broker named Walter Giblin. An old screen-writing friend of hers named Anita Loos wrote of their accidental meeting in the early 1950s in New York.

"I happened to be crossing the street in front of the Drake Hotel," wrote Loos, "when I noticed that a smartly dressed young woman just ahead of me was unsteady on her feet. Suddenly she fell smack onto the asphalt. As I stopped in shock, a traffic cop hurried to pick her up. The lady was not too tight to thank him graciously, at which the officer remarked, 'Don't mention it, Mrs. Giblin.'

" 'I won't if you don't,' said she, and they joined in a friendly laugh over her drinking problem."

In later years, the prettiest of the Talmadge sisters grew fat and became a Beverly Hills recluse, not even allowing friends to drop by for a visit.

Dutch's sister Natalie divorced Buster Keaton in 1932, largely over his drinking problems. And Norma Talmadge, the first and most serious of the three actress-sisters, left movies altogether and saw her marriage to studio mogul Joseph Schenck dissolve by the mid-1930s. In later years she famously cut short a pesky autograph-seeker with a haughty, "Get away, dear. I don't need you anymore."

The saddest case involved the actress that Squeaks had been so taken with, Barbara LaMarr. She didn't even live long enough to see "Ben-Hur" break box office records. The former Reatha Dale Watson had come from Yakima, Washington at age thirteen and was arrested straight-away for "under-aged dancing." M-G-M talent scouts gave her a new name and a made-up identity as the daughter of an Italian count. She was married so many times she lost track of the number, and binged on cocaine she kept in a gold, piano-shaped case.

Despite her success in movies, she was more interested in drugs than in a career, and in November 1925 she was arrested for the last time carrying forty cubes of morphine out of a drug house. M-G-M lawyers got the trial postponed, but before her day in court she died of an overdose in January of 1926.

I'm not sure how long I stood there looking up at those stands and all their ghosts. I didn't hear the waves of laughter around me any more. I must have seemed a pretty forlorn figure, because after a time I was roused by a distant voice calling out by name. I looked up to see Ramón Novarro headed toward me.

"Grover, my friend. What is this I hear about your Mr. Burr? I hear he is spreading tales about the driver of the winning chariot."

"All lies," I scoffed.

"Of course. Any man who mistreats horses must be a liar. He thinks the whole world is full of dumb animals that will stand for his abuse. No one believes what such a barbarian says. Of course, sometimes a man with binoculars can see beyond the lies." He tapped a small pair of opera glasses hanging near his vest pocket and smiled at me.

"I like to watch very closely when one of my students performs. You learned very quickly. I could not have done it better myself. But why are you looking so unhappy? You should be light and carefree at this minute."

"It's strange," I told him. "The better things turn out for me, the more I regret the bad things. A few minutes ago I was broke, but it was okay, because I knew I could survive. Now it seems I am not broke after all, and I can have what I want. But that left me feeling sort of blue. Why is that?"

"It's called being human, my friend. Let me tell you something my father used to say to us children when we were feeling low." Then Ramón spouted something in a fine and lilting Spanish. I could only make out a few words here and there, like "God" and "Earth" and "skin." When he finished he saw I did not understand. "In English, it would be something like 'God covers the Earth with a blanket of flesh ... then sticks His head up through it and laughs.' "

Ramón smiled and gripped my shoulder like an older brother. "It's true, there's enough sadness for everyone here below. But life is a sweet gift, my friend. Never lose sight of that."

Novarro meant to cheer me up, but I didn't know how to take his father's words. As the handsome Mexican bid me goodbye and disappeared again into the crowd, I remember thinking what a kind and caring person he was.

Ramón Novarro did indeed become a worldwide star after the release of "Ben-Hur." He continued to play leading roles well into the sound era, when he finally got to sing in early musicals. He even went on concert tours in Europe and South America, where he was always mobbed by his fans. But this was more because of his role as Judah Ben-Hur than to the quality of his singing.

To escape his own celebrity, Ramón took to traveling incognito, dressed in a fake mustache and beard. I don't think that Ramón took easily to living such lies. By the end of the 1920s, after playing a string of Arabs, South Pacific Islanders, Greeks and various Continental types, he grew obsessed with finding his true identity. He rejected the efforts of studio publicists to present him as a suave Continental playboy, and used his own money to pay for glamour portraits by George Hurrell of him dressed to the hilt in native Mexican garb.

Louis B. Mayer knew of Novarro's homosexuality even before the male bordello incident, but he tried to protect his star by arranging a cover marriage for him. Ramón refused, though he did have a short fling with a female pilot named Florence "Pancho" Barnes. She was not Mexican herself, but in her youth she had flown guns to revolutionaries in Mexico. He once gave her a blue suede flying suit with powder-blue boots that he had had made especially for her in Brazil.

In the end, Ramón's "secrets" were his downfall. In late 1969, a poor street hustler he befriended and brought back to his Laurel

Canyon home, snuck down late at night and opened a back door to an accomplice. Together the two robbers beat Ramón Novarro to death. He was the final victim of the "Ben-Hur" murders.

"Ben-Hur" opened on schedule for Christmas, 1925, at Grauman's Egyptian Theater, and soon thereafter in New York. The chariot race had opening night ticket-buyers standing on their seats and cheering at the screen. The movie went on to become the phenomenon everyone predicted.

Due to its ultimate cost of six million dollars, however, it was decades before it made back its investment. Of course, that's only what the accountants told the tax collectors. I notice that M-G-M managed to thrive quite nicely through another two generations at least.

After "Ben-Hur," Louis B. Mayer added horse racing to his list of gambling addictions. He was instrumental in getting California to legalize pari-mutuel wagering, and in 1934 he and his financial partners helped open Santa Anita Park, the first modern racetrack in the state. Mayer bought up stables full of champion racehorses and pursued the life of a wealthy sportsman until the late 1940s when the M-G-M board of directors voted him out of power in favor of more "socially conscious" leadership under Dore Schary.

B. Reeves Eason also got a comeuppance in time for his "breezy" disregard for the safety of the men and animals on his sets. He was increasingly criticized for the practice of "trip-wiring" the legs of horses to make them take spectacular dives for the camera. So many horses were injured and destroyed in 1936 while he was shooting the battle footage for "The Charge of the Light Brigade" that Eason found himself at the center of a Congressional investigation.

"Ben-Hur" ushered in a new era of animal welfare activists. The American Humane Society became a fixture on every movie set in Hollywood. Eason continued to be one of M-G-M's favorite action directors, though, and won great acclaim for his handling of the "burning of Atlanta" sequence in "Gone With the Wind."

It is still a mystery to me why Eason singled me out from all the others at the casting call that day. If he hadn't, things would have gone differently for me, and maybe for everyone else as well. Who can say?

How can any of us know the truth about the things that shape our lives—from the full bladders we cannot control and the guardian angels we cannot forget, to the silly autograph books we carry along just to please our landlady? We seem perfectly free to forge our own paths, but the farther in time we get from our decisions, the more it seems that life is the true master director calling the shots.

My ending up in Culver City for that race appears to me at times to be part of some grand scheme. Wasn't I the young, exiled prince in General Lew Wallace's novel? Hadn't I been falsely arrested and driven from my family by unintended events? Didn't I exist as a sort of galley slave until my chains were broken and I seized the chance for salvation?

Over the years I've thought back often on Ramón's father's words to his children: "God covers the Earth with a blanket of flesh, then sticks His head up through it and laughs." Now as I prepare to surrender to the hands of my own fate, I think about those words more and more.

When I was a fugitive, I accepted that life was much like Uncle Chester's pitchin' board—a mindless contraption more or less rigged to test our endurance. It would jostle us around and provide some great thrills, but in the end no matter how skilled we became it set our poor heads spinning and sent us flying off the sides.

Like I said, that's just how I used to look at things. Now I've come to think that Ramón's father was probably closer to the mark.

THE END

About the Author

Born and raised in Los Angeles, John W. Harding grew up amid all the magic and drama of movie-making in the 20th century. For 20 years he covered the film industry as a writer and award-winning editor with the Tribune Company, leaving journalism in 2012 to dramatize the lost era of cinema via a series of historical novels.

"As a storyteller, two things in particular interest me about the early movie-makers," he says. "The first is their innocence, and the second is their corruption."

"The Ben-Hur Murders: Inside the 1925 'Hollywood Games'" grew out of research by the author into primary letters and documents stored at the *USC Film and Television Library in Los Angeles*, and from archival material held at the *Academy of Motion Picture Arts and Sciences*.

His novel "The Designated Virgin" is also based on research, and is set in 1909 at the time of America's first battle over motion picture censorship. It is also available from Pulp Hero Press.

He currently lives in Maryland with his wife.